FICTION NO MORE

A Vincent Malone Novel
TED CLIFTON

Fiction No More (A Vincent Malone Novel)
Ted Clifton
ISBN 978-1-77342-083-7

Produced by IndieBookLauncher.com
www.IndieBookLauncher.com
Editing: Nassau Hedron
Cover Design: Saul Bottcher
Interior Design and Typesetting: Saul Bottcher

The body text of this book is set in Adobe Caslon.

Also Available
E-book edition, ISBN 978-1-77342-084-4

CONTENTS

Prologue

1988. *Ronald Reagan is president of the United States, serving his final year in office. The candidates in the upcoming presidential election are Vice President George H.W. Bush and Democratic nominee Michael Dukakis. Bush will win a decisive victory. Maverick millionaire Ted Turner starts Turner Network Television. NASA scientist James Hansen warns Congress of the dangers of global warming. Roy Orbison dies, and the record of the year is* Graceland *by Paul Simon.*

San Mateo, New Mexico

A large man with an ugly scar on the side of his face walked up to the pumps.

"Hey, asshole—you work for the goddamn electric company?"

Vic Miller didn't need ESP to see this was trouble. He was in the middle of nowhere, at a small, no-name gas station and convenience store, surrounded by eight thuggish-looking Hispanics—or maybe a couple were Indians—who all looked furious about something. He could see their hog motorcycles parked by the side of the station. He continued to pump gas and tried to keep his cool.

"Yep. I'm an employee of Electric Public Service Company, just like it says on the side of the truck. If you're upset about your service or your bill, you'll have to call Albuquerque, I'm just a workin' man, doin' a survey."

"What the hell you surveyin' out here?"

Vic had been in Nam, and he could smell danger. He calculated how quickly he could get his gun out of the glove box, but figured he would probably be dead before he could make it. Then he noticed the main biker was carrying a tire iron, and realized there was no time to calculate jack shit. He pulled the nozzle out and sprayed the big bastard with gasoline.

The goon panicked. "The motherfucker sprayed me with gasoline! Get his ass!" he bellowed as he ran, just in case the electric man had a match.

The distraction gave Vic time to get into the cab and grab his Beretta. *Now what? Run or fight? There's no way I can outrun those bikes. I hope to hell someone in the gas station calls the cops.*

He could see the leader at the end of the building splashing water from a rain barrel all over himself, even dunking his head in. Gasoline does not smell good. Vic rolled down his window and pointed his gun at two other bikers who looked the most aggressive.

"I sure as hell don't want to kill anybody, but I will. What the fuck is wrong with you guys? It's just the electric company. Don't you want electricity out here?"

One of the bikers hesitated a little, but spoke up. "They want to put through power lines, and we don't want them to. This is our land, but they gave the damn Public Service company a right-of-way just so the assholes in Albuquerque can have cheap electricity. What about our lands? We've got burial sites out there that'll be destroyed. You just work for the wrong people, asshole."

"Look, I'm a nobody. You kill me, they'll send someone else just like me. They won't even give a shit I'm dead. It won't help you at all."

"Maybe, but it'll get someone's attention. You're in the wrong place at the wrong time."

"Nobody's going to do anything." Standing on the front porch of the gas station was a man who looked to be ninety years old, holding a double-barrel, 12-gauge shotgun—the backwoods equivalent of a cannon. "I'm not going to let you boys kill this man. I let you do most anything you want around here, just because it's easier than fightin' you—*but not murder.* You better just get back on those bikes and get the hell out of here before I get so nervous I start to unload this blunderbuss."

The leader came back, dripping water.

"This is not a good idea, Jake. We live here, you live here. You should just go back into your little hut and shut the fuck up."

Jake pulled back the hammers and pointed the massive weapon at the stunned leader. "Too damn old to care much what happens to me, but you're not goin' kill this man unless you kill me first."

The leader stared at Jake for some time. "Let's get the hell out of here. I need a drink." They all got on their bikes and roared out of the parking lot, spewing dirt and rocks. Soon they were gone, and all was quiet.

"Thanks, mister," Vic said. "But I think you just made some badass enemies. Maybe you should leave with me."

"Nah. This is where I live. They might kill me, but the leader—his name is Santiago— knows that if they do, then this store and this station will close, and that'll piss off everybody within a hundred miles of here. Plus, this is where he buys his beer and whisky. I'll be okay. But *you're* in trouble. They headed north, toward where they live, so you need to head back south and get on I-25. You don't want to see those guys again today. And you tell your company what happened. Those boys are not completely wrong. The electric company bosses have been all high and mighty, wouldn't work at all with these people about the route of that power line. Last time they had a county meeting, the electric guys showed up and treated these people like shit. That don't give them no right to kill you, but your bosses are not very smart."

Vic wasn't about to argue. This was his last month with EPSCO. He'd been offered a job in Kansas, and he and his family were moving. Both of his kids wanted to stay, but his wife was ready to leave, and the decision had been made. New Mexico had been a good place to live until he began to hate his bosses.

"Well, thanks, old man. If you hadn't been here, I think somebody would have died today."

Vic paid Jake for the gas, thanked him again, and let out a deep breath. Been a long time since he'd had that kind of adrenaline rush. He smiled. He had about a fifteen-minute drive north to finish his readings—or he could head back south as Jake had suggested, and piss off his supervisor. Maybe he'd overreacted. Those guys had seen a company truck and had wanted to scare him a little, maybe knock him around some. But, kill someone? That was pretty far-fetched. He headed north. The old man didn't see his decision, he had already gone back inside.

Vic had taken sightings in the area before, so he knew where he was headed. Only a few more miles. The road was lightly traveled, and he hadn't seen any other vehicles. He entered more mountainous terrain with switchbacks and steep drop-offs. The scenery was magnificent. It was strange that people traveled to crowded national parks to see nature that was available for free, with almost no tourists, if you just looked. He was pretty sure Kansas wouldn't have this kind of postcard scenery. He was approaching his turnoff when he heard the sound.

Motorcycles. He looked in his rearview mirror and saw his tormentors, immediately regretting his decision not to take the old man's advice. He reached down and pulled his gun closer. At the first opportunity he was going to make a quick U-turn and head back south, but at this point the road was too narrow.

The entire group was behind him, and he could see the leader's face. Santiago was furious, and looking for revenge. This was not going to end well. Vic sped up as much as he could on the twisting road, then slammed on the brakes, causing panic behind him. At least two of the riders went down, and it looked like one might have gone over the side. He was able to get the truck turned around enough that he could go back south. He pressed the accelerator to the floor, his heart pounding.

He looked in the mirror and saw three bikes closing in.

He couldn't go any faster and still keep the truck on the highway. He reached for his gun, just as he heard a glass-shattering blast. A bullet entered through the back window, grazing his head and exploding out the front windshield. The last of his frayed nerves snapped. With the windshield now a spider web of cracks and breaks, he could no longer see the road ahead. The truck glanced off a guard rail and went airborne. He crashed with a thunderous, violent crushing of metal, tumbling down the side of a ravine.

After a minute or so there was mostly silence.

"Take that, you son-of-a-bitch!" Santiago was angry and terrified at the same time. What the hell had he done? He stared down into the ravine as the dust and debris settled onto the crumpled truck, steam escaping from its engine compartment.

One of his scrawny companions looked on, wide-eyed. "What the fuck do we do?"

"Give me that whisky." Santiago grabbed the bottle and slid down the side of the ravine. He could see the electric company man hanging out of the driver door, his head smashed. There was no doubt he was dead. He got closer and poured whisky on the body and inside the cab. When he saw that the guy's left foot had been severed, he shivered and felt like he might puke. He clawed his way back up.

"Let's get the fuck out of here."

Lights from a group of five emergency vehicles flashed onto the ravine from above the crash site. It was a large number for Cibola County. One was an ambulance from Grants, and the rest were from the Sheriff's Department. As the emergency personnel were huddled together discussing their next move, a state police vehicle pulled up and stopped, though it didn't add its lights to the show.

"Hey, Sheriff, what's goin' on?"

"EPSCO truck ran off of the road down that ravine. Sent a deputy down, and he said the guy's most definitely dead. Smashed his head on something and busted it open. Said it smells like whisky in the cab, and he spotted a gun in there, too. Haven't moved the guy yet, but at this point it looks like a bored electric company employee was drinking on the job, missed his turn, and went sailing off the road to the happy hereafter." The sheriff arced a hand through the air, mimicking the truck's trajectory off the road and into the ravine.

"Yeah. Most likely. But you know, several of your citizens have made some stupid threats to EPSCO. You need to make damn sure this is an accident."

"What the fuck does that mean, Larry? Do my damned job, or the state patrol will have my ass? Look, I know about the threats, and I know some muckety-muck high up in the government will want to know if the out-of-control natives of Cibola County killed some poor bastard because he worked for EPSCO. That's why we're all still standing around here. I've sent word to the state police to send a crime scene crew to do forensics. Chances are ninety percent this guy missed his turn because he was drunk, but I know how to cover my ass. So, don't be tellin' me what to do."

"Okay calm down. I'm not your enemy. But look, you guys have already screwed up the scene here on top with all of your vehicles and people walking around. You need to get those vehicles out of the area around where the truck went off, and secure it as a crime scene. You and I both know EPSCO has a lot of clout in this state, and they're not going to be happy having a dead employee, so you *better* cover your backside."

The sheriff nodded and directed his people to move their vehicles and tape off the area above the crash site. It was too late to make much difference, but it would look better this way.

Year 1599
Spanish Settlement of San Juan de los Caballeros

After the Spanish had exploited the Native Americans in the area for cheap labor, turning many of them into slaves, the Natives revolted, but were brutally suppressed, with hundreds killed. Juan de Oñate, the Spanish leader, lost just eleven soldiers and two servants, but took exorbitant revenge, anyway. Every Native man over twenty-five years old had his left foot amputated.[1]

---

1 Florence Hawley Ellis, "An Outline of Laguna Pueblo History and Social Organization" *Southwestern Journal of Anthropology* Vol. 15, No. 4 (Winter, 1959), pp. 325–347

1

Home Sweet Home

It was late summer in Santa Fe, New Mexico, bringing cool mornings and mild afternoons to the high-altitude, bustling tourist town. There was a promise of snow in the morning air, but that would come in the future. Today, it was glorious.

Vincent Malone had become a resident of this capital city with its unique international charm, more or less by accident. He'd wanted to escape the high housing costs of Denver, and had been looking for a place to hide on a more reasonable budget as he crawled toward Social Security, retirement, and old age. He'd been confronted with declining health, and an inability to meet the needs of the small client base he had as a private investigator, due to lack of mobility after several bouts of painful gout. After his last client unceremoniously fired him, he'd decided to head south for the warmth, and maybe take a low-key job that would provide a meager living until those Social Security checks started rolling in.

Then serendipity intervened. He'd taken a job as a van driver for a new bed-and-breakfast in the foothills of Santa Fe, The Blue Door Inn. The owners, Jerry and Cindy Oliver, were just about the nicest people he'd ever met, and they'd become friends while Vincent helped them deal with some challenges that had come up when the Inn took in its first guests, including two murders—not quite the usual new-business snags.

Vincent had spent over thirty years as a PI after a life-changing fall from grace precipitated by too much booze and too little good judgment. He'd lost a promising career as a Dallas lawyer, the most gorgeous blonde wife Texas had to offer, his reputation, all his assets, and his law license. While he climbed up out of a pile of shit of his own making, he'd sought a new beginning in Denver, helping attorneys by finding facts or dirt as needed so they could better serve their clients. He proved to be a natural at this kind of sleazy work, and he'd prospered until his poor health took him down.

Now, at what he'd thought would be the point when his life would begin to wind down, he'd found new adventures, friends, employment, and romance, proving that even the most cynical person can sometimes make a new beginning.

"Appreciate you helping us out today." Jerry was smiling.

"Sure, not a problem. Where's Rick?"

Rick was the son of Hector and Mary Flores, the Inn's first employees. Hector took care of maintenance and gardening, while Mary was the resident chef and housekeeper, although she also mentored Jerry in the culinary arts. More recently, Rick had taken over Vincent's previous role as the Inn's van driver while he and his new wife explored other employment options, mostly in Albuquerque.

"He had an interview this morning. Sounded like a good opportunity, so I didn't want him to miss out on it just to drive some guests around."

Vincent nodded. "Yup, got to keep your priorities straight. I'm sure he'll find something soon. Who are the guests?"

"We've got five, all coming in on the same Southwest flight out of Chicago. Decided to offer them the van service instead of the shuttle, since all are arriving at the same time. They're part of two writers' conferences that are going on at the convention center. They're being put on by an independent publishers' group. One is for mystery writers and one's for romance novel writers. Cindy says they're going to have almost a thousand authors and publishers attending, which is a lot for Santa Fe. The group putting it on called all over town looking for available rooms. Seems the response was more than they expected. So, we'll be full for almost a whole week, with romance and mystery authors."

"That's great, Jerry. You guys are really starting to make a success of this place."

"Yeah, it's getting better. Mostly trial and error, but we're getting there. Cindy is really excited about the authors. She said it'll be much better to have people who make up stories about murders than having real people killing one another." Jerry chuckled, but looked thoughtful.

"Yeah, make-believe is way better than reality when it comes to dead bodies."

Vincent got the list of guests from Jerry and then inspected the van, confirming it was ready to travel to the Albuquerque airport. It was a trip Vincent had made many times before he'd decided to take on private investigation clients, and turned most of his duties at the Inn over to Rick. When Vincent had started at the Inn, he'd stayed in a tiny extra room that wasn't really suitable for guests, and had found a great deal of solace in those first weeks while helping prepare the Inn to open, almost as if Jerry and Cindy had adopted him as part of the family. Now he was staying with Nancy McAllen, his very recent fiancé.

My, how the world had changed in only a short time. Vincent grinned at the thought. He secured his cardboard Blue Door Inn sign, and headed out.

By the time the passengers were deplaning, he was in the arrival area holding the sign, which read "Blue Door Inn Guests." Soon he had four, all women who seemed to have known each other or made friends on the plane. It seemed they might also have enjoyed a few drinks on the flight. They were in a very cheerful mood, compared to other passengers.

"Wow, you're the van driver? You're quite a hunk." The comment brought a wake of giggles and some admiring stares from the writers, and since it had been said in a loud voice, also a few chuckles from other passengers.

Vincent couldn't help himself, he blushed, although he hated that he did. "Well, thank you. Now, let me see that I have everyone. Dorothy Evans?"

"Right here." It was the woman who'd made the remark, still looking smug. She was large, with short, no-nonsense gray hair and eyes of an amazing deep blue. She had the manner of someone in charge.

"Lucy Martin?" Another woman raised her hand. Petite

and blonde, she resembled a child's doll.

"Elsa Chambers?" Another hand. Elsa was medium height, with short auburn hair. She seemed withdrawn. Even raising her hand appeared to be an effort.

"Marsha Adams?"

"Here." More giggles, for no apparent reason, this time. Marsha was tall and lean, with an athletic body, and was smiling at no one in particular.

"And Stella Stratton?"

"She just went to the restroom. Does the Blue Door Inn have a bar, handsome?" Dorothy was looking at Vincent like she was a big-game hunter, and he was her prey.

"Yes, but even better, Ms. Evans, the Inn has a free happy hour every evening, which should be starting just about the time we arrive." Vincent had been on the wagon for some months, but at this moment felt like he might just fall off.

"Wonderful! Oh, here she is. Stella, our man needs to know you've arrived."

Stella approached, but she didn't look well. "I need you to help me. A man is following me. He has been since Chicago. What should I do?"

Stella was a very attractive woman in her early thirties, with flowing dark hair and a fashion model's body. Vincent would not be surprised if men of all ages didn't take notice of Stella Stratton. "Following you? Didn't you just go into the restroom? Was he in there?"

"No. No, I was with the group when I decided to find a restroom. I turned around and that's when I saw him—again.

He was looking right at me. It scared me, so I disappeared into the restroom. I'm sure it was the same guy following me in Chicago."

"Ms. Stratton, right?"

She nodded.

"You are a very attractive woman, and I'm sure a lot of men have stared at you."

"I know the difference between an ogler and a threat, and this guy was a threat. It wasn't sexual. I could see in his eyes that he hated me." Stella shivered. Dorothy stepped up and gave her a hug.

"Well what are you going to do?" Dorothy asked Vincent. She was clearly used to commanding people, and she'd shed her playful manner.

"Do you still see the man?" Vincent was developing a headache.

Stella looked around the terminal. "No."

Vincent had the whole group's attention now. "We can contact the police. I can tell you, though, they won't do any-thing—except maybe tell you that you're imagining things. They'll suggest that you go to your hotel and rest some, and that afterward, everything will be better. I'm more than willing to make the call, and I can be pretty damned insistent that they do something, but that might mean they'll want you to go to the police station and fill out a complaint and give them a description. It's virtually guaranteed not to get results, but I have no problem helping you with it, if it's what you want."

"No. No. I'm sorry. Maybe it *was* just my imagination."

"You do know she writes murder mysteries, don't you?" This was said by a smiling Lucy Martin. "I, on the other hand, write romance novels." She gave what she must have thought was her most alluring look.

Vincent was beginning to feel like he was under siege. He suggested they gather their luggage and start the trip to Santa Fe.

Vincent finished unloading and delivering the luggage. "I swear some of those bags must have weighed a hundred pounds. Felt like they'd packed bricks."

Jerry grinned.

"I hear you were a hit. Two of the ladies asked me if you would be at happy hour. Want to stay and be bartender?"

"I don't think so, Jer. I wouldn't want to admit it to my admirers, but loading and unloading a couple of tons of luggage has just about done me in. I think I'll head home and rest. That okay?"

"Sure, we can handle happy hour. How about tomorrow? Their conference starts at nine—could you drive them? If you can do that, I can pick them up."

"Deal. See you in the morning."

"All female authors. I wonder if most of the conference attendees are women. Have any idea?" Nancy was curious, but also teasing Vincent a little.

"Have no idea, but it wouldn't surprise me." They were sitting outside, on Nancy's tiny patio, enjoying a glass of wine. Vincent hadn't admitted it to her, but it was obvious he was tired.

"You know; it could be one day that women will just take over everything. You think the male ego could deal with that?"

Vincent gave Nancy one of his "all knowing" smiles. "Some will, some won't—but it won't matter. Men have been running things since there were things to run, and look where we are. So, unless you're some backward knucklehead, most guys will say, 'Have at it. Can't be much worse.' Do you have plans to take over some big chunk of the world?"

"Yep. I'm developing plans right now with my sisters to take over everything, except maybe trash collection and plumbing."

"It's good to have a plan."

An old habit of making notes before bed had started back in his attorney days and extended for all these years. Back then, he'd written everything down—now it was mostly a mental review of events and possibilities. Originally, it had mostly been work-related, while lately it was more likely to involve personal circumstances—hopes, and dreams, and fears. Even with all the changes, this old habit stuck with him.

Never believed in premonition. No human can know the future, good or bad. But suddenly today, when that author thought someone was following her, I had a cold feeling of dread. Maybe an omen, maybe just a draft, but it wasn't a good feeling. I'm alive today because I've trusted my instincts, especially in dangerous situations. I have no idea if there's actually danger ahead, but I'm still going to proceed with caution. Something is in the air.

2

The Past's Long Reach

Vincent's phone was vibrating, an amazingly annoying sound early in the morning.

"Yeah."

"Good morning, sunshine."

"Tucker, if you're looking for sunshine, you've got the wrong number."

"It's always good to talk to you Vincent. Makes me feel so superior. Look, I really didn't call to irritate you. Hill called me this morning, wants to see us in his office. I know you haven't warmed up to Jack, but I still think it's not wise to piss the guy off. So, how about it? Can you make a meeting about mid-morning in his office?"

"What the hell does he want?"

"Don't know. For the last month or so, I think he's been spending time on politics. He's some kind of big shot in the Democratic Party. Which surprises me in a way, because when I knew him before, he was a hotshot Republican. I think the guy just drifts with the current winds rather than being really ideological. He goes where the best deal is—the most money. But I'd guess this has something to do with politics."

"Can't imagine I can be any use in politics, especially New Mexico politics."

"I'm sure we're not talking about drafting policy papers. Most likely he's got some kind of problem that needs fixing—human-failings kind of stuff."

"Ah, sex and money. Now that *is* my area of expertise."

Tucker chuckled. "That's why you get the big bucks. Can you make it?"

"Got a quick run for Jerry, but I should be able to be in Albuquerque by eleven. Will that work?"

"I'll set it up," Tucker said. "See ya then."

Peter Tucker was a high-profile lawyer who'd been a Mafia fixer for years until his no-holds-barred tactics caused even his unholy mob clients to shy away. That had led to years of isolation and reflection. Eventually he'd crawled out of his self-imposed retirement after his nephew had been accused of murder in Santa Fe, and ultimately teamed up with Vincent to find the real killer. That process had allowed the two aging warriors to recognize a kinship of spirits that had since grown into a friendship. Tucker decided after his re-awakening in Santa Fe to move to Albuquerque, where he took on special projects for the largest law firm in the state—a firm headed by his old nemesis, Jack Hill. Hill had asked Vincent to come work for the firm, but Vincent had skillfully avoided making any commitment due to his concern that Jack wasn't trustworthy, or, as he put it privately, "He's a dick." But Hill was a very important power broker in New Mexico, and as long as Vincent was in the state, he had no desire to be at odds with the man.

Rolling over in Vincent's direction, Nancy barely opened her eyes.

"Little early for your buddy to be calling. Something wrong?"

"Nah. Jack Hill wants to meet. Tucker thinks it has something to do with politics. Not sure how I fit in, but that's no reason to ignore paid work. I'm not crazy about Hill, but I don't have to love the guy to work for him."

"I don't know the man, but I do know Butch thinks he's dangerous. Not sure about the details, but he told me once that Hill was the kind of man that made life evil."

Vincent paused. Butch Collins was Nancy's uncle—known affectionately as Santa Claus on account of his long white beard—and he'd raised her after her parents had died. He managed a small homeless shelter with a free clinic, and in Vincent's opinion was one of the good guys. "Well, if Santa thinks he's evil, I'll be doubly careful."

Vincent's first stop that morning was the Inn so he could take the gaggle of writers to the convention center.

"Mary, those muffins smell wonderful." Vincent was a great admirer of delicacies created by the cook and housekeeper at the Blue Door Inn.

"Hello, Mister Vincent. Please, help yourself." Mary gave Vincent a broad smile.

Cindy came into the kitchen to join them. "Vincent, the ladies are just about ready. Little slow this morning—they had quite a bit to drink last night. Your name came up several times." She gave Vincent a look that he couldn't quite read.

"Cindy, I'm very happily engaged, and haven't encouraged these women in any way."

She looked at him with a grin that seemed to be half playful and half a warning that he'd better be as good as his word. Cindy and Nancy had become great friends, and any bad behavior from Vincent would put Cindy on the warpath.

"I've got a meeting in Albuquerque this morning after I take the women. Do you need me to get anything for you while I'm there?" He would come back and switch the van for his beloved '94 Mustang for the trip if Cindy didn't need anything picked up.

"Oh, Vincent that would be great. I have an order at the restaurant supply store and they charge an arm and a leg to deliver that stuff. Could you go by and pick it up? You'll need to take the van, though. It's a big order."

"Sure, no problem. I should be back here by three or so."

"Perfect. We don't pick up the authors until five-thirty."

Driving the van wasn't as much fun as the Mustang, but it sure was a lot cheaper.

"Good morning, ladies. Everyone ready?" Vincent had entered the dining room and greeted the guests.

"Hey, you missed happy hour. Where were you?" The ever-demanding Dorothy wanted answers.

"Maybe I can be the bartender tomorrow night. How would that be?"

Dorothy didn't look satisfied, but said, "Okay." It was a short drive to the convention center. There were large crowds milling around in front and a line of vehicles for the drop-off spot, but Vincent was soon able to help everyone disembark. Stella Stratton was the last to leave, and grabbed Vincent's arm, gently pulling him away from the others.

"I want to apologize again for yesterday. Maybe it was just nerves. But I know I have seen that guy before, and it still feels very weird to me. I guess it could be something as simple as him being on the same plane when I flew from Chicago to Albuquerque, but the more I think about it, the more convinced I am that he was watching me."

"May I call you Stella?" Vincent wasn't always sure of his manners with women. He was a tough guy, but also old school. He felt most comfortable calling all women apart from Nancy, "ma'am."

"Oh, sure. Stella's fine."

"Thanks. Look, Stella, you're right. That could have been just a coincidence, but it could be something else. I'll give you my cell number. We don't officially have security at the Inn, but that's my background. So, if anything more happens, or if you see something that makes you uncomfortable, give me a call. You can always call the cops, of course, but unless they have an actual crime, they're pretty reluctant to start questioning folks who might just be people-watching. If you see this guy again, give me a call, and maybe we can find out what's going on. Okay?"

Stella chuckled in a way that suited her well. "Oh, thanks. I'm sure it's nothing, but for whatever reason, I can't shake this bad feeling. I appreciate your offer to help. If I see the guy again, I'll definitely call. Thanks so much." She gave Vincent a smile he was pretty sure was genuine, and turned to join the crowd entering the center.

He maneuvered the van around the crowded entrance and headed out to the interstate and his appointment in Albuquerque. He thought about Stella and her stalker. He didn't know why, but he was sure she was holding something back—maybe even the identity of the man. It was in Vincent's nature not to trust people, an instinct that had kept him out of harm's way, over and over again. Unfortunately, it had also limited his personal life to a narrow zone hemmed in by suspicion and mistrust—not the healthiest way to view your fellow humans.

"Vincent, good to see you again. Seems like we're having trouble getting you on board, but we'll just keep tryin'." Jack Hill was a politician, or in more direct language, a bullshitter. Vincent still wasn't sure if there was any substance to the man.

Hill shook his hand as he nodded to Tucker, and took a seat at the massive conference table. The whole office screamed money, success, and power. It made Vincent nervous.

"I've spent my whole life dabblin' in politics," Hill began. "I was a Republican for a while, and now I'm a Democrat. I know some people say I just go to where the money is, but it's more than that. I'm not going to give you some phony populist message, but in my old age I've decided that too much of what goes on in this country is controlled by the filthy rich and not enough is done to help the everyday guy. So, here I am, in my fancy, big-buck's office, advocating for better income equality and health care for all. I understand the hypocrisy, but I don't give a fuck. Together with a few of my well-heeled friends, we've created an advocacy group that's going to back candidates in the state who will advance a more populist agenda. We've got a lot of money to give to people who will agree with our point of view, and I need someone who can look at these people and give me a no-bullshit assessment of their character, and whether we can trust them. I've talked to Tucker, and I'd like for you to join us and do some investigative work on these people before we open our checkbooks. What do you think?"

What Vincent thought, but did not say, was: *Where is the angle? How are you going to benefit from this gambit?* "Well, Jack, I'm not very political. Republicans, Democrats, they're all assholes in my book. So, I'm not sure I'm your man."

"I wasn't asking you to evaluate their politics. Mostly I want to know if they have some kind of problem in their background that might jump out and bite us in the ass later on. Money, sex—the usual kind of stuff."

Vincent paused before he responded. His bullshit meter was about to blow up. Jack Hill was lying, but Vincent decided he didn't care—at least not for now. "I can sure do background checks for you, plus cover ground that wouldn't show up on those internet-based searches. We agreed on an hourly rate a while back, just hadn't had anything come up. So, I guess I'm ready to start when you are."

"That's great, Vincent. You'll work through Tucker. I'll get a list to him in a few days, and you can get started. Really appreciate you helping us out." Hill gave Vincent a politician's smile and handshake, and left the conference room.

"What the fuck is that about?" Vincent gave Tucker a hard look.

Tucker shrugged. "Don't know any more than you do. But there's obviously something else going on."

"You know I hate to do anything for such an obvious bullshitter. Makes me worry he might get me involved in somethin' I don't want to be involved in." Vincent spoke in a softer tone to his old friend, more a confession than a statement.

"I won't steer you into anything that I see, but I don't know what he's up to, either. So, he could fool us both."

They looked at one another and laughed.

"Not for long. We'd figure it out." Vincent smiled. "But I could use a little extra money right now—so, unless you tell me to run, I'm in."

Tucker shrugged again. "Yeah, I'm still sitting here, too. You watch my back, and I'll watch yours."

"Deal."

Vincent's phone vibrated. "Malone." He listened. "It'll take me an hour to get there. Is there a bar or someplace public where you can wait?" More listening. "Okay, I'll see you in a little bit." He disconnected. "One of the guests at the Inn thinks someone followed her from Chicago to Santa Fe, and of course, Mister White Knight Malone needs to butt in to help rescue the damsel."

Tucker looked at his friend a little too long. "And you accuse Hill of being a bullshitter."

Vincent was halfway back to Santa Fe when he remembered he was supposed to go by the restaurant supply house. He called Cindy and got her voice mail.

"Cindy, I'm sorry. I got a call from Stella, one of the guests, and she thinks she saw a man who was watching her in the airport at the writer's conference. I was headed back to the convention center to meet her and see if I could find the guy and talk to him when I remembered the restaurant supply order. I'll come back tomorrow to get it. Sorry about that—I hope it doesn't cause a problem."

The morning hubbub at the convention center had passed, so Vincent was able to park right in front. He entered and immediately saw a pop-up bar, with a bartender handling a large group of customers. The patrons sat at several dozen tables scattered around. He spotted Stella.

"Sorry I wasn't closer. Tell me what happened."

"I came out here to make some calls, and looked up, and he was sitting right over there on that bench." She pointed to a bench occupied by a lady reading a book, about fifty feet away.

"Were you right here?"

"Yes."

"What did he do?"

"He just looked at me for a while, got up and headed towards me. I don't know why he scares me so much, but I got up and went back into the session meeting room. He didn't follow me in there. That's where I was when I called you. After I talked to you, I came back out here, and he was gone. I've just been sitting here, waiting."

Vincent gave Stella his best disarming confidante's smile. "There's something you're not telling me. What is it?"

Stella's eyes shifted to the table. After a moment, she looked up again. "I might know who it is. My first book was *Warrior Ghosts*. I was a graduate student at New Mexico State, and I was going through old newspaper archives at the library. I wanted to find something I could use as the basis for a novel. The initial idea came to me after I read an article in the *Albuquerque Sun* about an accident where a man was killed, and his left foot was severed. My novel had nothing to do with the actual accident, and all I know about it came from the newspaper articles I read. That first book wasn't much of a success. Well, that's not the whole truth—it was a total failure. I almost quit writing. But later, when my first bestseller came along, my publisher reissued it, and it sold pretty well. That was when I started to get these letters. They were from the son of the man killed in that accident back in the 1980s, wanting to know if I knew who killed his dad. They were a little incoherent and demanding. In total I got six letters, and they became more threatening as they went on. Maybe that's who's following me."

"Do you have a name?"

"The man in the accident was Vic Miller, and the letters were from his son, Sam Miller."

"Why don't we find the other women and see if they're

ready to go back to the Inn? Maybe sometime tomorrow we can meet and talk about this some more. But now that I have a name, I can do some research—probably even get a contact number for Sam Miller, and see what he wants."

"Is Stella attractive?"

"What does that have to do with anything?" Vincent had just told Nancy about his day, including the incident with Stella at the writer's conference.

"Just wondering."

"You've been talking to Cindy."

"Maybe."

"Stella *is* attractive, but *I'm* only attracted to you." It was the right thing to say and Vincent was rewarded.

One of the lessons I'm having trouble learning is to keep my mouth shut about contact with other women. Nancy is very tuned in to anything involving me being around another woman. I would never have guessed she was the jealous type, but apparently, she's either jealous or just very protective. A whole new world for me to try to understand.

3

Write When You Get Work

Vincent had already had a busy morning, taking the guests to the convention center, returning to Albuquerque to pick up the supply house order, going back to the Inn to unload the order and drop off the van, and now he was headed to the police station to see if the chief was available. It was busy work, and he didn't want to do it right now. He needed some quiet time to think about the Hill deal, and about how to make contact with Stella's mystery man.

Law enforcement in Santa Fe was a bit convoluted. The city had its own police department, headed by a very professional lawman, Chief Brad Stanton. The county was served by the Santa Fe County Sheriff's department, run by Sheriff Matias Ortega, who in Vincent's opinion was more gangster than cop. Ortega and his lead detective, Tony Sanchez, had made it clear on several occasions that if it were up to them, Vincent would be run out of town, or suffer some other unpleasant fate. Vincent had no friends in the Sheriff's Department.

Chief Stanton, on the other hand, held a certain level of respect for Vincent. Today he would push that a little to see if the chief would help him get information on Sam Miller.

"You wouldn't know this, Vincent, but that accident is famous in New Mexico law enforcement circles. The state police did forensic work on the accident scene and recommended to the governor that a more complete investigation take place regarding the county sheriff's department's handling of the whole matter, but the governor quashed it. The story goes that it was an election year, and the governor didn't want a feud between a rural county and EPSCO to muddy the waters during the election. It's strange that I remember the newspaper accounts of that accident. I was just a kid, but I usually read the morning paper, and the story caught my attention. It wasn't just the accident. There were editorials about the electric company's tactics in building power lines, how the rural people in those areas felt steamrolled. There was also a bunch of TV coverage, too. Not sure why it stuck with me, but it did. And then it came up later, at the police academy. They use that accident as a case study in how *not* to do crime scene preservation."

"Do you think the sheriff covered up a crime?"

"Who knows? It was thirty or so years ago, and a lot of law enforcement, especially rural cops, pretty well ran things by the seat of their pants back then. My guess would be something more along the lines of incompetence than trying to hide something specific. But sheriffs can be very protective of their residents, even the bad ones. So, it's not impossible."

"Do you remember the sheriff's name?"

"Nope. Not sure he was mentioned much in the news stories. I'm sure that'd be easy to find out, though. Research—isn't that supposed to be your forte?"

"Not sure I'd say that. I always thought my strength was my charming personality."

The chief chuckled. "Does the lady writer want to press charges against Sam Miller?"

"No. For one thing, she doesn't know for sure he's the man she's been seeing. She's just making a connection between the letters she got and this guy seemingly following her. It's entirely possible that the letters have made her jumpy about people looking at her, even a little paranoid, and that the guy at the airport and the convention center is just some innocent fellow writer who's admiring her looks. My plan was to call Sam Miller and just ask him why he was bothering Stella. The problem with that plan is I don't have any contact info for him. Would you be able to help me out with a little police magic?"

"Look, you know we don't use our official databases to help private investigators find people." The chief seemed sympathetic to Vincent's situation, but it was also apparent he wasn't going to break the rules on his behalf. "If Ms. Stanton wants to bring those letters in and file a complaint naming Sam Miller, we will investigate, which would involve trying to locate him. But without that, my hands are tied."

Vincent nodded. "Well, let me talk to her and see what she thinks. Like I said, this may be nothing at all, but it definitely has Ms. Stratton spooked. Thanks for the information about the accident—at least that confirms the story she told me. If anything else happens, I'll let you know."

Most of Vincent's interaction with cops over the years had been confrontational, often with good reason. As a PI working for lawyers in Denver, a lot of what he did was try to prove the cops had screwed up, so they were not pleased to see him poking around their investigations. Cops in general were protective and secretive, and they sure as hell didn't want some asshole investigator looking over their shoulders. Chief Stanton was an exception, in Vincent's experience. The guy actually seemed to want to do the job of protecting citizens and enforcing the law. He admired Stanton a great deal for his evenhanded approach to a difficult task.

Vincent left the chief's office and headed toward the Crown Bar, located just off the famous plaza on one of the narrow side streets. His fiancé owned the place, a holdover from a previous stage in her life when she'd been married to a cop. He'd claimed at the time that he bought the bar as a retirement investment, but everyone knew he mostly just enjoyed spending his off hours there. Her husband had made a fatal mistake on a burglary call, so he never had the chance to retire. Nancy, now a widow, started running the bar out of financial necessity, turning it into a Santa Fe landmark in the process. Vincent, who also loved bars, found Nancy attractive all on her own, but the fact she owned a bar was a nice bonus.

"Hey, handsome, how 'bout a beer?"

"If I wasn't already engaged to you, I'd ask you to marry me." Vincent took a seat at the massive wooden bar and immediately felt at home. He had battled drinking problems his entire life, and now felt he had a decent handle on things. But he still loved the atmosphere of a bar. His phone vibrated, an annoying interruption of his happy thoughts. Maybe always being available was something he should give up. He looked at the call—Tucker. "Malone."

"Sent you an email with Hill's list attached. There are five names. Four are fairly normal political types, but one is a little surprising." Tucker paused.

"Okay. The surprising one is . . . ?"

"Our buddy Sheriff Ortega."

"How is Hill connected to that asshole?"

"Don't know. I'm guessing he thinks the guy might be able to win a congressional seat."

"Based on his ability to bully people or his impressive intellect?" Vincent didn't like this turn of events one bit. Investigating Matias Ortega might be fun, but it could also be very dangerous. And it wasn't the kind of thing he'd been expecting when he'd agreed to work for Hill.

"Considering your past dealings with Ortega, might be best to tell Hill you can't handle this one. Just let him know you've butted heads with the guy, and it could blow up if he found out you were snooping around about him."

"Yeah, maybe. On the other hand, I'm a big boy. Might be fun to look into the tyrant's past. And if things get ugly, I can just tell him Hill asked me to do it, and he can take it up with the big shot—not me."

"Well, that's another thing. Hill doesn't want anyone to know he's hired you to do this. He emphasized several times—this has to be hush-hush."

"Anything comes of this, and Hill's going to hang me out to dry, right?"

Tucker paused. "Look, Vincent, there might be too much risk here with one of the targets being Ortega. I think you ought to back out. I can explain something to Hill. Maybe you started drinking again, or something."

"That drinking thing is looking more likely every minute. But if I decide not to do this, I'm going to be honest with him and tell him that I don't trust him, and he can fuck off."

"Always the diplomat." Tucker was silent for bit. "So, what do you think you'll do?"

"Let me look at the list and think about it. I won't do anything rash. I'll give you a call later." He disconnected

Nancy walked up and smiled. "Trouble in paradise?"

"Yep, 'fraid our mangos are going bad. But don't worry, I'll get it all straightened out in a day or two." He gave Nancy a more serious look. "I need to chat with Stella Stratton, want to come along?"

"You need a chaperone?"

"Let's cut to the chase. Stratton is super attractive. I know that, and I'm betting that you know that through Cindy. That doesn't mean anything to me—not because I'm blind, but because I'm in love with you. I sure don't need the grief it might cause if you think I'm doing something wrong. So, please, just come with me so I can discuss some things with her."

"Makes me feel foolish." Nancy looked thoughtful. "Maybe this once, I'll come with you. Who knows, she might be more willing to talk about things if another woman is there."

"Great." That was what he said, but what he was thinking was that he wished she'd said: *No, you go. I trust you completely.*

Oh, well. "Are you okay to leave right now? She's still at the convention center, and this should only take half an hour or so."

"Let's go."

Vincent Malone, big strong, tough guy, and his partner, his mom. He shook his head a little to make the image go away and they headed to the convention center. As they entered the central hall Vincent spotted two of the guests at a table sipping drinks.

"Hello, ladies. I'm looking for Stella. Have you seen her?"

Both ladies eyed Nancy, sizing her up. Elsa Chambers spoke.

"Just saw her a little bit ago at the hot-dog stand. It's right around the corner there." She pointed.

"Thanks."

"More female authors?" Nancy smiled at Vincent.

"Yep." Turning the corner, he saw Stella.

"Hi." Stella smiled at Vincent and rose to greet Nancy.

"Stella, this is Nancy McAllen—she helps me sometimes. Do you have a minute to talk?"

"Sure. Are you the Nancy he's going to marry?" Stella was smiling.

"Yep, that's me."

"Cindy said such wonderful things about you. And she's so excited you two are getting married. It's so romantic."

Within seconds they were chatting like long-lost sisters. Vincent just couldn't understand how women became so comfortable with one another so quickly. It made him feel like he was observing a different species.

"You know; I kind of forced Vincent to bring me along. Mostly I wanted to tell you how much I enjoyed your last book. My women's book club always reads your novels—we just love them. Maybe I could swing by the Inn before you leave and get you to autograph a copy?"

"Sure, that'd be great. It's always nice to meet readers."

Vincent was stunned. He'd thought Nancy had come along to protect her turf, but it seemed she was just a fan—a minor hit to the ego. As the two women stood, talking about books, friends, travel, and who knows what, Vincent took a seat. They both looked at Vincent at the same moment and laughed.

"Maybe you should let Vincent ask you a few questions before he gets upset."

Vincent just smiled. He was off-balance, and didn't have a smartass answer ready. He covered his meeting with the police chief and discussed the difficulty of trying to find someone without more information about the person, preferably an address, or at least a state.

"I didn't bring all the letters with me, but I stuffed the last one in my bag when I opened it—I'm pretty sure it's still in here." She rummaged through her purse, extracted an envelope, and handed it to Vincent.

"Wichita, Kansas, with a street address. That makes everything easier. I guess that's it for now." Vincent got up to go.

"Stella," Nancy said, as she stood, too, "you may not know this, but I own a restaurant and bar downtown, the Crown Bar. If you and the other women don't have plans, maybe you'd like to visit for dinner. I'm sure the Inn can transport you there and back, or you can take a cab. I'd love to have all of you as my guests. What do you say?"

"That sounds wonderful. I'm sure everyone will want to come. And it's so nice, but you don't have to treat us. Do we need reservations?"

"No, we'll have room. Say about eight?" Nancy gave Stella one of her cards.

As they drove back to the bar, Vincent was quiet.

"Mad at me?"

"Nah. I was just thinkin'. I really don't understand how women can become friends in a matter of minutes."

"Not sure I know, either. Stella's a nice person. I'm glad you're helping her."

"Because I'm a nice person, too?"

"Somethin' like that."

4

Dinner at Eight

It didn't take Vincent long to find information on Sam Miller. Getting a cell phone number for him took a few calls to some Denver buddies and a quick transfer of a few hundred bucks. Vincent had been a good customer over the years to two mostly unseen tech guys who could find out almost anything for the right price. The problem with this transaction was that he didn't have a client to pass the cost along to—not smart to lay out money to help a damsel in distress who wasn't paying. He called the cell phone number and got voice mail.

"Mister Miller, my name is Vincent Malone. I'm a private investigator working for an Albuquerque law firm. Need to talk to you about Stella Stratton. At this point we only want to talk. Call me back or this can get ugly." He left his number.

He had dropped Nancy off at the bar, and now was home sitting outside sipping some tea he had found in the fridge. It had a strange flavor—not good at all—he went back inside to get a Tecate. Much better.

Jack Hill worried him. He knew he needed to make some money, and the easiest way was to do some dirty work for Hill. He couldn't just mooch off Nancy, which meant that if he couldn't earn some cash, he would either have to leave Santa Fe completely or go back to the Inn—neither option was what he wanted. He had little choice but to work for Hill. It just made him very nervous. His phone vibrated.

"Malone."

"I don't know what 'get ugly' is supposed to mean. All I wanted was to talk to her, but she keeps running away. She wrote a book about my father's murder, and I just want to know what happened."

"I guess this is Sam Miller?"

"Yeah. Look—I don't want any legal trouble. I could tell I scared her, and I didn't mean to. I was so nervous about approaching her. I know those letters sounded wrong. All I want is information about my father."

"Where are you now?"

"I'm staying at a motel on Cerrillos Road. Can't afford that fancy stuff downtown."

"Can you meet me?"

"I guess. But it needs to be someplace public, okay?"

Vincent paused. "At Cerrillos and St. Francis there's a McDonald's. Say in about thirty minutes?"

"Okay. How will I know you?"

"Big guy." Vincent thought about adding "who is carrying multiple weapons," but there was no reason to make the guy more nervous than he already was.

Cerrillos and St. Francis were both major thoroughfares in Santa Fe, with a lot of traffic, and the McDonald's was busy. Vincent got a coffee and waited. It was a shame he had more or less given up smoking—this would have been a perfect time to enjoy a cigarette. Of course, you couldn't smoke in most places anymore. He sighed and reflected on the changing world, not really sure whether he fit in.

"Malone?"

Vincent looked up from his daydreaming and knew immediately this had to be Sam Miller. He was tall, maybe Malone's height, but slim and balding. He squinted at Vincent in a way that suggested his eyesight wasn't good, but he didn't wear glasses. The impression he made, especially from a distance, might be a little sinister, but no warning bells went off, and Vincent didn't think he was a risk to anyone. "Sam Miller. Have a seat."

He slid into the booth with a huge cup of some kind of soft drink.

"You spooked Miss Stratton pretty good."

Miller looked down at the table and nodded. He spoke without looking up.

"Yeah, sorry about that. I didn't mean to alarm her. I guess I was as nervous as she was, and maybe it came off in a threatening way. I really didn't intend to scare her."

"Why didn't you just call her?"

"I didn't have her phone number. I called her publisher, but they wouldn't tell me anything. I had an email address that I got from one of her books, but I figured it would probably just go to some publicist or something—she'd never even see it. So, I sent those letters. After I sent them, I realized they probably didn't make much sense. I'm not a very good writer. So, then I decided I should just approach her in public somewhere, and explain what I wanted—but of course, that didn't work out."

"Why do you think she knows something about your dad's death?"

"She wrote that book, *Warrior Ghosts*, and it describes the murder. It was a motorcycle gang, and they ran him off the road. I know most of the book is just made-up stuff, but when she described the murder, she included details that hadn't been in the newspaper, things I learned over the years as I tried to find out what happened. I just want to know how she knew."

"What kind of details?" Vincent had a cold feeling. It crossed his mind that maybe lovely Stella was lying.

"She described the gang going after the truck, and how they shot the back window out and it grazed the driver. After years and years of digging, I believe that's exactly how my dad was killed. That can't be something she just dreamed up, can it?"

Vincent was taken by Sam's obvious pain. "How long have you been digging into this stuff about your dad?"

Sam made a visible effort to calm himself down. "I was eight when my dad was killed. My sister Jane was ten. From that day, when the police came and told my mom he was dead, nothing has been right. My mother is in a nursing home, more or less out of her mind—she doesn't even know who I am. My sister Jane killed herself with a drug overdose when she was twenty-eight because she couldn't stand the emotional trauma of taking care of my mother any longer. Since Jane died, I've spent a lot of time and money trying to find out what really happened, as if that can change anything. I know I'm just as nuts as my mom, but I can't stop. It's been ten years, with me obsessing over something that does not matter to anyone but me." He looked up at Vincent. "But it means everything to me. My life stopped when my dad died, and I want to know who caused all that pain."

Vincent just sat a while, not sure what to say. He knew most people had a sad tale or two about themselves or their family, but this was a doozy. "I'm going to get another cup of coffee. Want somethin'?"

Sam shook his head.

Vincent stood in line, wondering how Stella could have known details of an accident all those years ago. He had an inkling that she wasn't telling him everything—but then, why should she? She didn't know Vincent, and had no reason to trust him with anything sensitive. Vincent was an old hand at lying—in some cases, it's your best option. He needed to talk to her, but first he needed more information from Sam. He got his coffee and headed back to the booth.

No Sam. *Fuck.* Why would he leave? He looked around. The place was crowded, but it was easy to see he wasn't there. He checked out the bathroom. Some guy gave him a dirty look, but no Sam. After scouring the parking lot, Vincent headed back downtown to the Crown Bar.

The place was packed. Good for business, but he wasn't in the mood for a crowd. He found a spot at the bar and ordered a Coors on tap. The bartender knew Vincent, and nodded. He looked around but didn't see Nancy. With this rush, she was probably in the kitchen. It was seven-thirty, and he wanted to ask her if the Blue Door Inn guests were still coming for dinner at eight. He wanted another conversation with Stella, though he wasn't sure it would be a good time if she was with her friends. He was anxious about something, that old feeling of danger, not sure why. He thought about Sam some more, but still concluded that the guy probably wasn't dangerous. But if that was true, why was Vincent so nervous? He didn't have an answer.

"Hey, you here to meet your girlfriend?" Nancy was smiling.

"You know you're not funny, right?"

"I thought I *was* funny."

"Just met with that Sam Miller guy, the one who's been trailing around after Stella. A really tragic story about his family, but he seems harmless. He told me enough for me to wonder if she might be lying about something to do with his dad being killed thirty-some odd years ago. Think I should try to talk to her tonight, or wait for some time more private?"

"What does she have to do with a death thirty years ago? She would have been a baby, or not even born." Nancy gave him a quizzical look.

"Well that's just it. I don't know. But it does seem that she included details in her book that this guy Sam says are accurate, but that were never mentioned in any news reports."

"Maybe he's lying."

"Yeah, that's possible, obviously. But when I talked to him about it, he struck me as believable."

"Is anyone paying you to look into this?" Nancy tilted her lovely head in a way that asked him, a little teasingly, just what was he doing. Vincent sighed.

"Nope. Nobody's paying, so why am I doing this? Damn good question. Thanks, Nancy. That cleared everything up for me. I'm going home—see you later."

"Hey, I didn't mean to run you off. Why don't you stay and have dinner? I know the writer ladies would be thrilled." Another mischievous look from the not-so-sweet Nancy.

"How about a green chili cheese burger with fries to go?"

"Not the best dietary selection, but I'll put your order in." Nancy got Vincent another beer and went into the kitchen.

The Crown Bar was the favorite after-hours joint for local law enforcement, a tradition that had started when Nancy's husband ran the place. Him being a cop made it a friendly, safe place for other cops to drink. Vincent looked around and recognized some of the patrons, but he hadn't exactly become pals with the men in blue.

"Hey, Malone. Enjoying your girlfriend's hospitality." Detective Sanchez's remark was accompanied by a sneer.

"Detective." Vincent and Detective Sanchez were not friends. He wasn't sure if they were enemies, but it was likely.

"The sheriff still can't get you off of his mind. You must have really pissed him off when you two met."

"I think your sheriff is easy to piss off. I wouldn't have taken you for the bar type. Not following me or anything stupid like that, are you?"

Sanchez smiled. "Nah, birthday party for one of the guys

I work with. I was just headed out. Malone, I don't know if you're a good guy or a bad guy, but you'd better watch your back. Ortega thinks you're some kind of threat to him, and he doesn't play nice."

"Your leader is a psychopath, which means you're the one who should be watching his back. Can't believe a brute like Ortega can keep getting elected. You ought to run against him and clean up the mess at the Sheriff's Department."

"I'm not that fuckin' stupid. Plus, I don't want to be sheriff. Just want to do my job and go home. Could be Ortega is gettin' ready to move on to bigger and better things, anyway. So, maybe the fine citizens of Santa Fe County will elect him to a better position, and I can live in peace."

Sounded like confirmation that Ortega was going to run for something else, probably the U.S. House of Representatives. Vincent shuddered a little, realizing that the bully could probably win. What a country. "Well, if it'll take him out of the sheriff's department, I might vote for him myself."

Sanchez chuckled and left. Vincent got his burger and went home. He'd decided that causing a scene with Stella in Nancy's bar was a formula for some cold nights at home, and he sure as hell didn't want that.

How is Hill connected with Ortega? Is it just politics? Both men are dangerous, but very different. I'm not sure if I'd rather deal with a bullheaded, I-don't-give-a-fuck bully like Ortega or the smooth and slimy Jack Hill. I don't know if it's the best decision, but I'm going to complete this project for Hill. And I hate to admit it, but it's mostly because I want to know more about Ortega. Maybe there'll be something I can use to keep that madman from trying to run me out of town.

5

Run, Rabbit, Run

Vincent woke with a start. His first thought was to wonder where Nancy was. He relaxed—she was next to him. He hadn't heard her come in the night before, no doubt after a late night with the crowd at the bar. He sat up. Age is a depressing thing. He didn't exactly feel bad, but he was already a little tired, and he hadn't even gotten out of bed yet. In his drinking days, he might have had a morning shot just to get the motor running, but that was then. He ventured into the kitchen to get some coffee brewing instead.

He went to the front porch and retrieved the Albuquerque paper from the steps. The newspaper business was going through some rough times, and the papers kept getting smaller, with less and less meaningful content. Why someone thought it was a good idea to cut down on news in order to survive in the news business was beyond him, although one of the problems was obvious the moment he looked at the front page. He already knew something about each story from television or the internet. Opening the morning paper and getting *new* news just didn't happen anymore. He sighed—something he'd started doing a lot, and hated in himself. He ended up reading about the beginning of a new construction project on I-25—take that, CNN!

After an aspirin and a cup of coffee, he was feeling better. He grabbed his phone, dialed, and got voice mail.

"Sam, don't know why you took off. Still think we should talk. Plus, I think Miss Stratton might be willing to meet with you. I'm going to see her this morning, so give me a call and let's see what we can set up." He left his number.

Why had the guy taken off? Had he gotten a call? Or maybe he'd just decided that he'd said enough. But that didn't make sense. It had been obvious that they were headed toward a plan to get him together with Stella, which is what he wanted. And then he just disappeared. Weird. He tried calling Stella. Voice mail, of course.

"Hey, Stella, this is Vincent. Sorry to call so early, I was hoping you'd be up. I'm driving everyone to the convention center this morning, but I wanted to see if you and I could take just a few minutes to talk. I have some new information on Sam Miller. See you in just a bit."

The investigator's mind hates a coincidence. Could they both have bolted? Nah, that was stupid. Stella was at the Inn, in bed, and probably very annoyed that he'd called so early. Still, it seemed odd. He tried calling Jerry and for once didn't go to voice mail.

"Hey, Vincent, I was going to call you this morning. You beat me to it. Not sure what's going on, but Stella left last night. She was at the Crown, and apparently they were all having a great time, when she got a call. She told Dorothy it was her grandfather, and she had to leave. Took a cab back here, got her stuff, and left. It was late, so we weren't even up, and didn't see her, but she left a note. All it said was that she had to leave, that she'd given Dorothy info on how to contact her if there were any additional charges, and that she would mail the key back to us."

Every alarm bell in Vincent's head was going off. "Do you need me to drive the rest of the guests to the convention center?"

"Nah, I can do that. What do you think is going on?"

Vincent told Jerry about his meeting with Sam Miller. "This could be totally unrelated, but it feels strange. Any idea where her grandfather lives?"

"No, none. I can ask Dorothy. She was just here getting coffee and went back to her room. It's probably nothing, Vincent. And even if it is, there isn't much you can do." Jerry might as well have said that using Nancy's voice—he sounded just like her.

"I know. Nancy's already reminded me I don't have a paying client. So why am I poking my nose into this, anyway? The simple answer is that something about the whole mess has me worried. When I worry, I want to fix whatever's bothering me. I don't know, Jer—sounds like crazy talk, doesn't it?"

"It's not crazy to care about people, and that's what you're saying. You're worried about these people. And you should be. This is odd behavior, and too much of a coincidence to not be related somehow. But at this point, I think all you can do is wait." Jerry sighed a little, but said nothing more.

"Yeah. You're right. If you hear anything, give me a call.

Need my help with anything, let me know." Vincent enjoyed taking to Jerry, and missed seeing him every day. He was a great friend.

"Sure. If anything comes up, or if Dorothy knows anything, I'll call you. Talk to you later."

Nancy walked in as he was putting his phone down. "Early happenings?"

"Did you know Stella left suddenly last night?"

"Left? I know she left the group. Dorothy said she was tired. Was it something else?"

"I think so. She checked out of the Inn, too. Left a note for Jerry she was leaving and would mail the key back. Seems like a weird coincidence she takes off at about the same time that Sam Miller disappears. Probably nothing, but it sure seems odd."

Nancy got herself a big cup of coffee. "Do any good for me to tell you that it's not your problem?"

Vincent chuckled. "Yeah, Jerry already told me the same thing. I know it's not my problem. I guess it just feels like something bad is about to happen, and my instinct is to try to stop it."

"Something bad? Like what?"

"I don't know." Vincent shrugged. "Don't worry. I've already decided there's nothing I can do except wait and see if anything goes 'boom.' It doesn't make me happy, but I'm going to get busy doing other stuff. Today my goal is to rack up some billable hours for good old Mr. Deep Pockets, Jack Hill."

"Perfect. That sounds like an excellent plan." Nancy smiled, but still looked concerned.

Stella was in a panic. She hadn't heard from her grandfather in years. The last time they'd talked, he was in Florida, and had said he wanted to be left alone, that he was there to drink himself to death. Now he'd called and wanted her to come to Las Cruces, saying it was a matter of life and death. Malcolm Benson, her mother's father, always had a flair for the dramatic, but here she was, rushing to Las Cruces, hoping this wasn't some wild goose chase as a result of dear old granddad going on a bender.

Benson had been a legendary professor at New Mexico State University. He'd developed an archeology program for the school in the 1970s. With a reputation that spanned the globe, he was famous on and off campus. His renown had attracted top students to the program, which soon made it one of the most sought-after archeology schools in the country. At the same time, although the university administration held him in high esteem, he also made them nervous. He had questionable ethics, and his parties were the subject of a lot of gossip, as was his attraction to young coeds. Benson's off-campus archeology digs in Northern New Mexico were in huge demand, both for college credit and real-world field experience, although many students also found them attractive due to his lax supervision.

After several scandals in the late 1990s, Benson made the wise decision to retire and make a quick escape from New

Mexico. The last straw for the administration was the claim by a woman young enough to be his granddaughter that he had fathered her child. The school offered the young woman a generous settlement, contingent on her willingness to sign a non-disclosure agreement, but the professor had to go. After that, he severed ties with his family and friends, saying he would live off of the meager royalties he received from several books he'd written. After all, booze didn't cost much, and he didn't expect to live long. He disappeared.

Stella's panic was over more than just her rascal of a grandfather suddenly reappearing in her life. It was the timing. Her grandfather was the person who'd given her the information about the death of the electric company employee that she'd used in her book. First, Sam Miller shows up and spooks her, and now her grandfather calls out of the blue and says she had to come to Las Cruces—how did he even know she was in Santa Fe? She'd tried to ask him what it was about, but he just said she should come immediately or not at all—he didn't give a fuck—and hung up. Benson had never been the stereotypical warm, loving granddad. He was a pain in the butt, and she'd been the only one in the family he would talk to, even years before he disappeared into a bottle in Florida.

After his call, Stella made excuses to the group, headed back to the Inn to get her stuff, and took a cab to the Albuquerque airport, where she rented a car. Now she was driving toward Las Cruces, and the unknown.

It was in the last conversation she'd had with her grandfather before this that he'd told her about the murder in New

Mexico. It was apparent, even over the phone, that he was drunk. Still, he could be very charming when he wanted. She'd told him she'd decided to become a writer. He approved, saying she was very smart, and that whatever she did, she would likely be a success. He said that if she ever wrote a novel, she should consider writing it about the descendants of the Native Americans in Northern New Mexico taking revenge against the descendants of Juan de Oñate. He'd told her about the electric company surveyor, and how he'd been killed by a motorcycle gang—including quite a few details. To him, the murder had been justified, since the electric company was going to destroy their sacred grounds. He'd rambled on, even giving her instructions about doing the necessary research. The last thing he'd said on the topic had been odd: that she must never tell anyone where she'd gotten the information about the murder. He'd made her swear she would never reveal him as her source, and that she'd attribute everything to the newspaper articles he'd told her how to find. It had scared her, but she'd decided he was just drunk and being melodramatic.

The drive to Las Cruces in the middle of the night was making her anxious all over again. It seemed foolish to rush out based on her weird old grandfather's cryptic call. She was on I-25, pretty literally in the middle of nowhere. There were very few cars on the highway—she hadn't seen another vehicle on her side of the road in over an hour. Mountains lined both sides of the road, dark looming masses of nothing. Her imagination was starting to run wild. A sudden bolt of lightning flashed from a mountain storm off to her right, causing her to jump, and she let out a meek scream. She steadied herself, letting her breath out, and started to laugh. She needed to find a place to stop and get some sleep. She saw a sign saying that the famous chile town Hatch was about twenty miles ahead, and decided if there was a motel at the exit, she would stop there and stay the night. Getting closer, she could see nothing at the Hatch exit but darkness. She pulled off, anyway. It seemed to get darker, if that was possible. A couple of miles to her right she could see a few lights, presumably the very small town, and she headed that way.

At the center of town, a single traffic light was blinking yellow. A sign indicated she should turn left to get to Las Cruces. After several miles in deep darkness, she came upon a small motel. It was dark, too, apart from a light dimly illuminating the mostly empty parking lot. She thought it would be rude to wake someone up at such a late hour to check her in, so she pulled into the lot, locked her doors, and tried to get some rest. She was so exhausted that she was soon sound asleep.

6

What's Really Happening?

"Morning, everybody."

"Morning, sheriff."

"Anything goin' on this morning?"

"Very quiet. Have an abandoned car up in Hatch, at that old motel just outside of town. A Budget rental according to the window sticker. Susan has a call in to the rental company now to find out who was driving it. No sign of foul play, so it may be something or may be nothing. Other than that, it's dead quiet. Booked a couple of drunks last night."

"Strange place to abandon a car, rental or not. Did we check to see if it was out of gas?"

"Yeah. Douglas was the deputy up there, and he said he thought it had about a quarter of a tank left. It wasn't locked, and there was nothing personal in it, like luggage or whatnot. So, until we can find out who rented it, we're not sure what to do."

"Okay. As soon as you get a name, send a couple more deputies up there and canvas the area to see if anybody saw anything. Let me know what you find out. I'm headed downtown for a chamber meeting. Should be back in a couple of hours."

Tim Ballinger had been the sheriff of Dona Ana County

for four years. He loved his job, and was considered by almost everyone to be very good at it, including dealing with its unique challenges. Dona Ana County was about the size of some states back east, but its land was sparsely populated. Plus, big chunks of the county were under the control of the federal government, with responsibility in the hands of the Bureau of Land Management or the Army. The U.S. Army managed the vast White Sands Missile Range with the isolationist, no-nonsense approach that comes with any secret military installation, which meant that even the sheriff had very limited access to much of his county. He spent much of his time dealing with the complications created by the diverse interests that existed in it.

Las Cruces was the largest town in Dona Ana County, with a population of over a hundred thousand, not including the twenty-odd-thousand students who attended New Mexico State University, or the people who lived on the military base on the other side of the mountains. Having a major university in a small town had a good side and a bad side for the permanent inhabitants. Without the university, Cruces would return to its agricultural roots, even though it would be alongside a large contingent of rocket scientists spending their days doing something they could never tell you about. People would be growing pecans and chiles on one side of town, and contemplating the destruction of the world on the other. The university created a middle ground.

It was only a short distance from the sheriff's headquarters to the chamber building downtown. Las Cruces was a small town, but it often struck Ballinger how frequently there was traffic congestion. If he had complained about the traffic to his brother, who lived in Dallas, he would have been ridiculed, but here he was, all the same, stuck in traffic. His phone vibrated.

"Ballinger."

"The car was rented to a Stella Stratton at the Albuquerque airport late last night. Based on the time, she must have headed south right away. She listed her destination as Las Cruces, so maybe she took the wrong exit or something. But I have no idea where she is or why she would leave the car. Interesting point—I Googled her, and apparently, she's a bestselling writer. There was a bunch of information about her. Pictures, too. We've run off some copies and have a couple of deputies headed up to Hatch to ask around if anyone has seen her."

"Good, sounds like you're on top of it. If they don't find anything, maybe call her publisher and see if they know what she had planned in Las Cruces. And you might as well check with the university, since she's an author. I bet it has something to do with them. Good work. Keep me informed."

Bestselling author disappears in Hatch, New Mexico, in the middle of the night. That didn't sound like a headline the political leaders in Hatch or Las Cruces would be happy to see. Ballinger felt like there were storm clouds on the horizon. He debated canceling his meeting and heading to Hatch, but decided he would just be in the way. He would let his deputies handle the matter, at least for the next hour or so.

Stella's phone rang. She had forgotten to mute it, and it was loud inside her small rental car in the middle of the night.

"Yes."

"Stella, this is your grandfather. Where are you?"

"My god, Papa, what's wrong? Why are you calling me in the middle of the night?"

"Stella, just tell me where you are." Even at his age, his voice was strong and demanded a response.

"I rented a car and was on my way to Las Cruces. I got too tired, so I pulled off the highway at Hatch, and now I'm in the parking lot of the" she paused to look around "the Traveler's Inn."

"Okay. I know where that is. Just stay there. I'm coming to get you."

"Look, that's silly, I have a car. I can just meet you somewhere."

"That car can be tracked. I'm coming to get you now. Just stay put, and I'll be there in about thirty minutes." He disconnected.

Tracked? What the hell did that mean? Stella sighed. She suddenly felt very alone and in danger. She double-checked that the doors were locked, and waited.

Vincent had already spent much of the day doing online research into the five people on Hill's list. He'd also been in touch with his hacker buddies in Denver to pursue the less visible dirt buried behind electronic walls he couldn't penetrate. While research and digging had been a substantial part of his work as a PI over many years, it wasn't something he enjoyed. He was old school. He would have preferred going out in the field and finding people who would talk, or even just gossip, about his targets. That felt direct and honest to him, while this computer shit felt sneaky and somehow dirty. Drop into Mr. X's favorite bar, and ask the bartender what kind of asshole the bastard was—that felt professional, honorable. This thing of spending hours digging into untold databases looking for clues to something incriminating struck him as low, and made him feel small. He took a shower and decided that he'd visit his wife-to-be at the Crown. He needed a beer and a bar to lean on.

"Looking a little worn around the edges. How 'bout a cold one?" Nancy placed a tall glass of Coors in front of Vincent with a lovely smile.

"I always tell people that research is my thing, but this computer stuff definitely isn't. I need to get out and touch the world to understand what's going on—not sit at home in front of a screen."

"What's stopping you?" Nancy loved her fiancé, and she was the only person who could slap him in just the right way to get his attention.

"Yeah, I know. My fault. I'll do something about it." Vincent sipped his beer and gave the lovely Nancy one of his nicer smiles. "Biggest problem is, I'm not real sure how to proceed. Except for the sheriff, these guys all look like respectable people, so my usual tactic of schmoozing around in bars might not work."

Nancy patted his hand. "You'll think of something."

Vincent was one lucky man—but just then, the lucky man's phone vibrated. "Malone."

It was Hacker #1. "Got some damn good dirt on a couple of your names. This Ortega guy—the sheriff? He was in lots of trouble before he became the people's protector. In Cibola County, New Mexico—wherever the hell that is—he was arrested maybe twenty times for all kinds of offenses. This goes back into the 1980s. One was murder—not exactly the usual path to law enforcement. Also, there's a charge of stealing religious artifacts. Not sure what religion or whose artifacts. But nothing stuck. Most of them were minor offenses, usually involving drinking. But a murder charge and stealing religious artifacts seem to put him soundly on the wrong side of the law. No details about why the charges were dropped, but neither one ever went to trial. He was charged, and then the charges were dismissed. Plus, only someone very talented—ahem— could dig up this stuff, because these files have been sealed. So, you be careful how you use this information. Some small crime may have been committed to get it."

"The murder charge—does it say who was murdered?"

"Nah, no name. This was a charging form with almost no information. Pretty sloppy police work. Maybe that's why the chargers were dropped. But I poked around in some other files and found only one death listed in the coroner's files during that time that might fit with a murder. Eventually the death was classed as accidental, but the original files have it as 'cause unknown.' Really old man named Jake Sullivan bled to death after hitting his head on a rock out near a remote store that he owned. But, like I said, no connection in the files to the Ortega charge."

"Is it possible that someone could have gotten this information a different way than how you got it?"

"Well, the records are electronic now, but at one time they were probably paper documents stored somewhere. Often these types of records aren't destroyed even after they've been converted to a digital format. So, if that happened, then someone who had access to it could take a photocopy or scan it, then give it to whoever was looking for it. It's against the law, but it's not a very serious offense. Not sure why, but the old laws, before computers, seemed to assume that all file clerks were upright and honest, so for a lot of records it was only a misdemeanor to make a copy. Having files stolen by faceless hackers seems to scare people more, so the laws on that are a lot tougher."

"Okay. Why would these records be sealed?"

"Good question. Don't know the answer. It wouldn't be common for this type of situation, after the charges were dropped. That usually happens when there's someone important involved—a judge, a politician, or the local banker. Doesn't come up when it's some regular Joe."

Vincent thought about what that might mean. "You said there was dirt on a couple. Who was the other one?"

"William Jackson. Several arrests for solicitation of male

prostitutes. All in Dallas over a period of about three years. Several charges were dropped, but he was convicted on two. They were misdemeanors, and he paid a fine, although one of the prostitutes later filed a complaint against Jackson because he hadn't been paid back for drugs he bought on Jackson's behalf. The complaint was dropped when the prostitute disappeared. Looks like Mister Jackson's living a secret life. The records I pulled up showed he's a county commissioner in Dona Ana County, New Mexico, with a wife and three kids. A leading citizen having a little out-of-town fun during some convention."

"Great stuff. You're the best. Thanks." Vincent disconnected. Now he had something to dig into. Dirty sheriff? Big shock. And a closeted county commissioner who enjoys drugs? Vincent smiled. The gut instinct that told him most people were only superficially good was confirmed—again. *Although, I guess that's only if I overlook the fact that three out of five are apparently just what they seem to be: good citizens. Maybe I just didn't dig deep enough.* He put the thought aside and called Tucker.

"Vincent, you in a bar somewhere?"

"Yeah, but only because I'm working. Got some dirt for Hill. You want to pass it along or you want me to call?"

"I'll tell him—that way you can continue to pad your hours." Tucker chuckled.

Of course, he wants to pass it on. He wants to know what the dirt is. Vincent shared the details. He didn't tell Tucker how he'd got the information. No reason to challenge his lawyerly ethics.

"Not surprised that there's dirt on Ortega, but murder? And what's this stuff about artifacts? Is that a serious crime?" Tucker shared Vincent's low opinion of the bully sheriff.

"Not sure. Given the location, I'm figuring it was Native American stuff and could be worth a lot, but that's just an educated guess." Vincent made a mental note to himself to spend some more computer time and see if he could figure out more about it.

"Jackson doesn't mean anything to me, but that might have the most interest for Hill. That's exactly the kind of shit you don't want the man you're backing to have hanging around in his past. Hill's out this morning, but I'll get with him right after lunch. He may call you. Any issues with how this bit of news was obtained?"

"I'd prefer not to discuss it." Vincent did not want to trust Hill with any information that could cause him problems.

"Okay, I'll cover you on that. You need to be real cautious with the sheriff. This just confirms my worst fears about the guy—nothing but a gangster with a badge."

"Yep. I'm going to be cautious. I've dealt with a lot of Ortega types in my life, but this is the first one who's a sheriff. That's a deadly combination. Right now, I'm going to enjoy a couple more beers at Nancy's bar, have dinner, and go home to bed. I've got one more source looking into the guys on the list, but I should have all I'm going to get in a day or two."

"Good work, Vincent. Hill will be pleased."

"Not really my main goal, but I'll email you a bill as soon as I'm done."

"Watch your back, Vincent." Tucker was serious.

"Always have."

Matias Ortega charged with murder and stealing artifacts in Cibola County. All charges dropped and the records sealed. It was a bright blinking red light. The same county the EPSCO employee was working in when he died. Coincidence? Maybe, but it's troubling. I'm not often afraid of people, but Ortega is incredibly dangerous, and now I know something that Ortega might kill to cover up. How should I proceed? I hate this fear, and there is only one way to get rid of it: jump in with both feet. Consequences be damned.

7

Some Good, Some Bad, Some Crazy

Vincent was enjoying a tranquil morning, reading the paper and drinking coffee. The feeling of being out of place that he'd experienced from time to time in this new environment was fading—he was starting to feel at home. He smiled as he thought about his new relationship, and how he found this cozy kitchen so comfortable and normal.

Nancy had gone into work early to prepare the bar's weekly payroll. He missed her, but it was nice to have some private time and just relax. He had a lot of things going on, and wasn't sure what his next steps should be, so he sat and waited for some sign that would give him a hint about what to do. His phone vibrated. God calling, maybe?

"Malone." He didn't sound pleased.

"Catch you at a bad time? This is Chief Stanton."

He hadn't expected this. "Nah, I always sound that way in the morning. What's up?"

"Got a call from a police investigator in Durango asking about you."

Vincent wasn't sure what to say to that. He could guess what it was about—he'd had a call from George Younger in

Durango giving him a heads-up—but he decided to keep his mouth shut for the moment. "Oh, really. What about?"

"They're investigating a murder. Guy named Ken Simpson. He said you were connected with a case in Durango where Simpson had filed a complaint against that Flores boy. Also, their research has turned up some Denver records indicating there were various confrontations between you two. Wanted to know if we had any information on you that would help them. I told them I knew you, but there was nothing negative in any of our dealings. I knew you were working as a PI on a couple of matters. That was it—he went away."

Vincent decided—again—to trust the chief. "I knew Ken Simpson." He paused, collecting his thoughts. "We've had some run-ins over the years, the last one some months ago in Denver. I didn't kill him. I did know about his body being found. I worked with an attorney in Durango, guy named George Younger, on that Flores matter up there, and he called and told me. If needed, I'm sure I can provide an alibi, especially since I wasn't anywhere out of Santa Fe around the time he was likely killed, apart from trips to Albuquerque and Las Cruces. I'm thinking the suspicion aimed at me is coming from another lawyer, a guy out of Telluride named Maxwell Franks Junior. Without knowing exactly what I did, it looks like I stepped on someone's influential toes and they're not happy about it."

"The Durango officer hinted there was something political going on, but it was none of his business. Maybe you should stop by sometime in the next few days and give us a sworn statement. Without charging you, there's nothing they can do.

But you need to be careful, Vincent. Don't repeat this, but I hear rumors about Durango that are not a good reflection on law enforcement."

"Thanks, chief. I'll take you up on that, and come by in a day or so and give you a sworn statement. As I'm sure you can guess, I've screwed up a few times in my life, but I haven't murdered anyone. Simpson, if he was still alive, could've filed a complaint against me for assault, but he didn't, and he wouldn't have, because he was a hoodlum. If there were going to be any further entanglements between us, he was going to handle it himself. So, looking at me as a suspect may be good police work, but there's nothing there."

"Well, good to know. Come by and make the statement. Watch yourself out there, Vincent. Lots of snakes in the grass."

The chief clicked off. Vincent called Younger and got his voice mail.

"Police chief here got an inquiry from Durango police about me. He told them I was an upstanding citizen, or maybe just said I hadn't caused any trouble in Santa Fe—yet. See if you can find out when Simpson was killed. With the right time of death, I can firm up my alibi. Call if you learn anything useful."

Simpson being dead didn't bother Vincent at all. Good riddance. He was sure there had to be a long list of suspects, given that almost anyone who knew the guy probably had reason to end his miserable life. So why did his name pop up to the top of the list? Somebody had their finger on the scale. Might be best to stay out of Colorado for a while.

Vincent got dressed for the day. He was very concerned about Stella Stratton and, in an odd way, about Sam Miller. He was reasonably sure Miller wouldn't hurt Stella, but stranger things had happened, and to have them both disappear was worrying. But even while he was troubled, he knew there wasn't much he could do. He decided on researching the sheriff in Cibola County circa 1988. He messed around on the computer for what seemed like hours, though it wasn't, without finding the name he wanted. Finally, he looked up the phone number for the sheriff's department and called.

A very nice lady told him the sheriff back then was a guy name Juan Reyes, but everyone had called him Bud. She said he was sheriff when she'd first started, but that he had died about four or five years ago. Must have been a slow day in Cibola County, because the lady acted like she'd be happy to stay on the phone and answer anything he wanted. Okay, why not?

"Would you happen to know a Matias Ortega who used to live there?"

There was a pause. "Um, yes. Who are you again?"

What changed? "My name is Jack Ward, and I'm doing research for a history book for New Mexico State University. Just tracking down some names that I have listed as important citizens in Cibola County in the 1980s and 1990s."

"Well, I guess that sounds okay. You should call over to the county offices. They can give you all of the information you need about the history of the county. Sorry, I've got to go." And with that, she hung up. Strange. Maybe it was just his imagination, but he was sure that what he'd sensed radiating off the woman had been fear.

When Stella's grandfather came to pick her up in front of the old, broken-down motel in the middle of the night, she was scared. At first, she was glad to see him, but he acted so weird she ended up even more nervous than she'd been to start. She didn't think he would ever harm her, but he wasn't acting even close to normal. And he looked awful, like he was seriously ill.

She went with him to another dilapidated motel, this one closer to Las Cruces. When she tried to ask him what was going on, he told her they would talk later. He drove too fast and seemed distracted, finally parking in front of one of the motel rooms. There were only a few cars in the lot. He gave her the key for the room next door.

"Go get some sleep, and we can talk in the morning, Stella. I'm just too tired to talk right now. I need to lie down. I'm in 401 and you're in 402. I'll knock on your door in a couple of hours and we can go get breakfast. Please, just go rest."

He slammed his room's door, leaving her alone in the dark night. She wanted to scream. He had to be insane. Her hands were shaking so; she could barely get the key into the lock. Once she made it inside, all she could do was sob as she tried to think her way through the nightmare in which she'd suddenly found herself. She took a shower and tried to relax. She might have catnapped some before the knock came at the door, but she hadn't really slept. It was still dark. *If everyone in your family is crazy, what does it say about you?* she wondered. She opened the door.

"Who the hell are you?" The question came from a very old, feeble-looking man, definitely on his last legs. Stella was stunned, but for some reason she was not afraid, maybe because he looked so weak.

"I'm Stella Stratton. Who are you?"

"Stella. Wow, you have really grown up. And you're so pretty. Where the fuck is your grandfather? He said to meet him here, but he just lies about every goddamn thing. Sorry, Stella, I really shouldn't use that kind of language around you. It's just that Malcolm is such an asshole, he makes me a different person even when I just think about him."

Stella stared at the man. "Um, who are you, sir?"

"Oh, I'm sorry. I'm Alex Wallace. I used to work with your granddad, and your father, too, at the university. You were just a little girl at the time. Do you know where your granddad is?"

The name meant something to Stella. She'd heard her parents talking about this man, but she couldn't remember any details. "Are you okay? You don't look well."

Wallace sighed. "Yeah, not doing so good today. Some days are worse than others. I'm going downhill pretty fast. Do you mind if I come in and sit down?"

Even basic common sense would have told her to say no, but Stella let him in, anyway. She was pretty sure she could take him if it came to that—probably with one hand. Wallace dropped into an old stuffed chair, and it was a legitimate question whether he'd be able to get up again without help.

"Your granddad got me in a lot of trouble years ago, and now I need his help. I have no idea why you're here, but if you're helping him, you should know—he's not a good person. I don't know if he's lost his mind or what, but over the phone he sounded pretty loony. 'Course, maybe I sound loony, too. Look, all I want is some money. I'm about to be evicted because I can't pay my property taxes, and Malcolm owes me, big time." The effort of talking took the last bit of energy he had, and he leaned back into the chair, his eyes closed.

Stella stood looking at him, thinking he might have actually dropped off to sleep, but when she reached down and gently shook his shoulder, his eyes opened.

"Mister Wallace, I don't know anything about you and my granddad, but you really don't look well. Do you want me to call an ambulance?"

"No, no, don't do that. Can't afford no fuckin' ambulance. Look, Stella, I just need to talk to your granddad, okay? Then I'll go away, and pretty soon I'll die. I'm not going to kill the bastard, though I should. I just need a little money. Do you know where he is?"

Stella had already made up her mind she wasn't going to tell him her granddad was next door. She didn't know exactly what was going on, but both of these old codgers seemed out of their minds, and she didn't want to see what might happen if they confronted one another. *But what do I do instead?* "How did you get here?" Stella asked in a calming voice.

"I drove. I know I shouldn't, at my age, but I don't live far from here. When I talked to your granddad—yesterday, I think it was, or maybe the day before—he agreed to meet me, and I told him about this place because it's close to my house. He was supposed to check in and then let me know which room he was in, and then we'd meet. He left me a message on my phone with his room number, and said we should meet this morning. I accidently erased the message—I hate these damn smartphones, never got the hang of them—but I was sure it was four hundred and something. When I drove up earlier, your room was the only one with a light on, so I figured it must be Malcolm's room. How come you're here, and not Malcolm?"

Stella ignored the question. "Mister Wallace, why are you and my granddad meeting, and why are you so angry with him?"

"We're meeting so he can give me some money he's been hoarding that came from the stolen artifacts. Why am I angry? I hate the bastard because he lied to the feds. I ended up in prison while he hid in Florida, trying to drink himself to death. He's a goddamn rat and he deserves to die."

There was a loud knock on the door. The sound was aggressive, even angry. Now what? Stella opened the door, and there stood her disheveled grandfather—holding a small pistol. He pushed past her and pointed the gun at the wide-eyed Wallace.

"You hurt my granddaughter, and I will blow your stupid brains all over this room."

Welcome to hell, senior-living style.

8

Welcome to Hell, Additional Parking In The Back

"Go ahead and shoot, you maniac. You think I care? What'll it do? Take a couple days off my miserable life? Be a fuckin' blessing. Shoot!" Wallace was yelling, and it looked like he was drooling slightly. Then he fell back in his chair and grabbed at his chest, looking very pale.

Stella was beyond distraught—she wanted to scream. "I'm calling an ambulance. And put that stupid gun away. What the hell's the matter with you?"

"No, no. Don't call! Jesus. I'm okay. Really. I get these pains, but I just need my medicine. Help me get it out of my pocket."

Stella searched the pockets of his jacket and found a medicine bottle. She opened it and Wallace took out two pills, dry-swallowing them. Stella found a glass and got him some water. He leaned back in his chair, color starting to return to his face.

"Listen, Papa," Stella told her grandfather firmly, "This is nuts. I don't know what is going on here with you and Alex, but I don't want any part of it. If there's any more yelling or threatening I'm calling the police." She was almost yelling, herself.

"Okay, okay," Benson said. "I wasn't going to shoot the old bastard. Stella, I shouldn't have called you. I think it's best if you go back to Santa Fe. Alex and I can work this out." He was still holding the gun, giving the scene a dangerous, out-of-control quality.

"How did you even know I was in Santa Fe?" The circumstances made everything feel conspiratorial, and she was suspicious in a way she wouldn't normally be.

"Calm down, honey. Don't let Alex get you all excited." Malcolm went over to Alex. "Look, Alex, I'm sorry you're having problems. We can work this out, especially the money part. I'll help you, okay?"

"Sure." Alex spoke in a whisper.

Stella pulled her grandfather aside. "Don't sidestep the question. I want to know how you knew I was in Santa Fe." Her voice was low, but it was obvious she was still angry.

"Stella, you don't exactly hide what you're doing. I follow all your social media accounts. Plus, I got a publicity release from your publisher saying you were attending a writers' conference. If you don't want people to know what you're doing, maybe you should get off all that social shit, and do a better job of hiding."

She felt stupid. Of course, her publisher put out a release every time she did anything. And they managed all her social media accounts, ensuring a steady stream of posts about what she was up to. It simply hadn't occurred to her that her grandfather might follow that sort of stuff. And obviously that was how Sam Miller knew about her plans to travel to Santa Fe. She had begun seeing sinister plots around every corner when, in reality, it was just the natural result of her bigmouth publisher trying to keep her name in front of readers—some conspiracy! Her foolishness embarrassed her.

"Okay, Papa. I guess I started seeing enemies everywhere after that guy, Sam Miller, followed me to Santa Fe. He really had me spooked, and then you called acting kind of crazy, and both things together were a bit—"

He cut her off, suddenly crazy all over again. "What the fuck? Sam Miller followed you? When? Where?"

"He followed me from Chicago to Santa Fe. He tried to approach me, but I got scared and hid in the ladies' room. Do you know what he wants?"

"You know who that is, don't you?"

"He wrote me letters—very threatening ones—wanting me to tell him anything I knew about his father's death. So, I guessed he was the guy following me. And then the van driver at the place I was staying made contact with the guy, and found out it was Sam Miller, the son of that guy who was killed, the guy whose story I used as part of my book."

"What van driver? What the hell are you talking about?" Malcolm's face had begun to turn red.

"You know; I've had it with you yelling at me. No more. Take me back to my car, now!" Stella started toward the door.

"You can't go back to that car."

"Why not?" Stella demanded, glaring at her grandfather.

"I've got someone after me, and he's a cop. He might have been following you."

Vincent's first stop was McDonald's. He pulled into the drive-through and ordered a sausage biscuit with egg and a large coffee. Any time he headed out on a morning road trip, his first stop was for his favorite in-the-car breakfast with hotter-than-hell coffee from McDonald's. Best bargain food ever, right at your car window. It was before dawn when he left for Cibola County, and he found it comforting to eat his breakfast as he drove through the darkness, knowing sunrise was only minutes away. It made him feel productive, taking action, and starting bright and early in the morning—or, in this case, a little before early and not yet bright. He still wasn't sure exactly what he was going to do, but he was headed to the source of several things that had caught his attention.

This morning's destination was the city of Grants, New Mexico, the Cibola County seat. The first leg would take him to Albuquerque, after which he'd go west along I-40 to Grants, for a total of about three hours of travel time. Long enough for his coffee to cool to a point that he could drink it.

Many counties in the west are huge, and Cibola is no exception. Approaching the size of Connecticut, with a population under thirty thousand, it's the very definition of sparsely populated. In fact, much of it is virtually uninhabited, replete with mountains and forests but very few people.

As he approached Grants, signs indicated a couple of exits. He took the first one, Route 66, which immediately set the familiar song playing in his head: *get your kicks on Route 66.* He wasn't sure, but he thought it had been recorded by Chuck Berry. Despite the song, it didn't take long to see that this Route 66 wasn't very pretty or inviting—no kicks at all, that he could see. One of the first buildings he spotted housed the Cibola County Sheriff's Department. He debated stopping, but decided to move along, and maybe stop there on the way back. Then something caught his eye: an uglier-than-sin roadside bar. *Information central,* he thought. He pulled into the dirt parking lot.

There were a few bikes and a couple of cars. It was still very early in the day, even for die-hard drinkers. The vehicles might have been left by patrons from the night before, or simply abandoned, each representing some hard-luck story that had already played itself out. The place was called Pete's, and Vincent warmed to it, even if it was a dump. He went in.

"We're not open yet. Come back in an hour or so." The unfriendly voice came from the dark confines somewhere in the back, but he couldn't see who'd spoken.

"Just a couple of questions. Doin' a little research for a book about roadside bars—willing to pay." Vincent delivered his pitch into the darkness and waited for a response.

"Twenty bucks and I'll talk to you for just a few minutes," the mystery voice said after a moment.

"Deal." Vincent made his way to the bar and put down a twenty.

From the shadows in the back came the oldest living human on the planet. If he wasn't a hundred, he sure could fool most people. What had ever happened to retirement? The feeble-looking man made a move as quick as any Vincent had seen, and the twenty disappeared. Might not be as old as he looked, with those reflexes.

"What the fuck you wanna know?"

Okay, we'll skip the friendly chit-chat, Vincent mused. Probably better to cut to the chase before the old bastard died on him. "What do you know about Matias Ortega?"

The old man chuckled, but there wasn't any humor in it. "Don't know who you are, but if you have some kind of death wish, you just keep askin' about Ortega."

"Does he scare you?"

"Scares everybody who ain't dead."

"What do you know about Bud Reyes?"

The old man attempted a smile. "Good guy. Good friend. Long dead. Used to be sheriff here. Did a good job, but couldn't control some of the resident ruffians. Tried the best he could."

"There was an accident here years ago, somewhere north of here actually, where an electric company surveyor died. The sheriff and his people investigated it. Do you know anything about that?"

"Sure, I was here then. Supposed to have been an accident, with the electric guy drinkin' and missin' a turn. Went off the side of the road. Later the rumors were that it might not have been an accident, maybe the guy was killed. Some folks said it might have been just for fun, and others said it was because of the Indian junk those university people were stealin'. Don't know what it really was—probably just an accident, like Bud thought. That was a long time ago, and most of those people are dead. You start stirrin' shit like that up, you might end up dead, too."

"What university people?"

"Back in the 1980s, people from New Mexico State used to be up here all the time, usually with a lot of students. They had digs all around this area. The rumor at that time was that a lot of what they were doin' was taking away artifacts that weren't supposed to be removed. Stealing shit, much of it very valuable shit."

"Was Ortega involved with that?"

The old man held up his hand and rubbed his fingers together in the universal sign for money.

Vincent put down another twenty, but the ancient one went right on gesturing. A second twenty joined the first on the bar, and the two bills vanished. *Good thing I can bill Hill for this.*

"Could be he was involved. He's still a powerful man in this state. If you think you're goin' after him for something, you better be well armed and very brave. Or maybe just stupid. Take my advice and leave Matias Ortega alone. He's a very violent man."

"I've heard stories about an old man who may have known what happened on that mountain road way back when, who died mysteriously. You know anything about that?"

The man looked at him in a new way, with something like admiration. "I don't know how you know this stuff, but whoever killed Jake should rot in hell. If I knew for sure who it was,

I'd kill the bastard myself."

"Wasn't Ortega charged for the old man's murder?"

"Yeah, that's enough. Get the hell out. Take my advice, big man. Get back on I-40 and go home. All you'll find here is grief." He disappeared back into the gloom, conversation over.

Vincent went outside, immediately shielding his eyes from the bright sun. The conversation felt unreal, as if he was hallucinating. Too-strong coffee or something. He debated about going back in and making the old fart tell him everything he knew, but something told him that wasn't a wise move. He'd let that old sleeping dog lie.

Back on Route 66, he headed into town. The main thoroughfares seemed to be First and Second streets, both one-way, cutting through the middle of town. Not much going on—the usual boarded-up storefronts you see in a small town, plus a few restaurants and insurance offices scattered here and there. He hadn't seen it yet, but somewhere there had to be a Wal-Mart that had killed off most of the other downtown businesses, same as in hundreds of other small towns. Free enterprise has its place in the world, but Vincent thought it was sad that it had sucked the life out of so many little communities.

He made a turn onto Roosevelt Avenue and drove a few miles, soon spotting some county buildings and the Grants Police Station. He decided to visit the county courthouse first.

All courthouses, even those in the smallest, shittiest places in the country, seem to have a regal bearing to them. Why spend so much money on buildings that were seldom used, and often misused when they were occupied? Vincent didn't know. Maybe it was meant to say something to people about justice, but even when he'd spent most of his days in buildings like this one, he'd seldom seen it. There was a counter toward the back of the building, and behind the counter, a middle-aged woman typed on her computer. Vincent approached the counter, but the woman kept typing. He cleared his throat, but got no reaction.

"Excuse me ma'am." The lady jumped a good foot off of her chair. Vincent was surprised she didn't scream.

"Oh, my god. I'm so sorry, you just scared the daylights out of me. Almost no one ever comes to this counter." She laughed at herself. She was still breathing hard. "How can I help you?"

"If I wanted to research some old cases, how would I go about that?"

She gave Vincent a blank stare. "You mean court cases?"

"Yeah. Some of these would go back to the 1980s."

"I'm not sure. But I don't think you can do that." She had begun to frown, and looked concerned.

"Well I guess these are public records, so there must be some way to access them." Vincent smiled, but he could see she was becoming nervous, and wasn't sure what she should do.

"Hmm. Public records. I don't know. Wait just a minute, and I'll go ask the judge." She got up quickly and went out through one of several doors.

Vincent hadn't expected that. In his experience, a judge was the last person to know anything about administrative matters. When she returned, she seemed more in control.

"The judge says that we don't have any public records, and

you should go away." It seemed like she might finish with "so there," but she didn't.

Vincent chuckled. "I guess the judge must have misunderstood. All courts have public records. I just want to know how to access them."

"The judge said if you were disruptive, I should call the police." She gave him a challenging look that made it clear she'd be happy to sic the cops on him if he didn't leave immediately. Vincent held up his hands in a gesture meant to show that he wasn't picking a fight.

"Is it okay if I ask the judge's name?"

"Judge Wilcox. Now, leave."

He did. Okay, small town justice can have its oddities, but a total absence of public records and chasing him out of the courthouse's public areas, all on the word of a judge, didn't sound very American. He had a sneaky feeling the police were being notified despite his prompt exit, and decided to stop by the police station to save them some trouble.

9

Heard It Through the Grapevine

"Good morning. I'm in your town doing a little investigative work, and I thought I'd stop by and introduce myself. Any chance the police chief is in?" Vincent gave the rather young man behind the counter his best smile.

"You're the asshole who was bothering the judge's secretary. Right?" The young officer gave Vincent an ugly look that seemed to hurt his face muscles, screwing his mouth into a pained expression.

"Well, I don't know about bothering her. I asked her how I could go about accessing public records. She seemed to think that there aren't any public records—but, of course, there are. She asked me to leave, and I did. How is that bothering?"

"What's your name, asshole?"

"I think it'd be better if you stopped calling me asshole."

"Oh, is that what you think, asshole?" The young man's face now went from ugly and angry to ugly but bemused.

"See this little button on my collar? That's a camera. I'm live-streaming this conversation, so you might want to hide your name tag, Jack Mitchell, or be a little bit more courteous."

"You can't do that. That's against the law." The face went

from bemused to tearful—it was quite a show.

"What the hell is going on in here?" An older man—probably the police chief, Vincent thought—stepped out of an office in the back.

"This guy says he's live-streaming our conversation. He can't do that, can he?"

"What'd you want, mister?" The police chief ignored his young charge.

"My name's Vincent Malone. I'm a licensed investigator and I'm doing some research in your town, so I stopped in to introduce myself. And at this point, I don't think I want anything."

The chief looked at Vincent for a long moment, presumably trying to decide on his best course of action. "What happened at the courthouse?" His tone made it clear he wasn't going to be a friend.

"I asked the lady behind the counter how I could access public records. She seemed confused, went into a back room, and then came out and told me the judge said I should leave. So, I left. I'd still like to access public records, but I'll go back to Albuquerque and tell my client—the law firm of Johnson, Johnson and Hill—that there are no public records in Cibola County. Now my contact there, Peter Tucker, may well think that's odd. Cibola's part of the good old USA, so you'd think they'd have public records, like most counties. But, hell, I'm sure he'll be able to find a judge in Albuquerque who can set him straight. Now, regarding your assistant here, Mister Mitchell, I walked in and he called me an asshole three times before I could even tell him what I wanted. Your hospitality sucks, and unless you think you have something to charge me with, I'm leaving. And for future reference, it's legal in New Mexico for me to record our conversation without your permission. Have a nice day."

Vincent went to his car. There was always some chance these people were stupid enough to try to arrest him for something, but nothing happened, and he drove off. So far, all he'd learned was that Grants, New Mexico, was not a very welcoming place. He knew he wasn't supposed to use Hill's name, but he sure as hell wasn't going to be small-towned into some phony charge without mentioning it as an insurance policy against police mischief. In this situation, he didn't give a fuck what Hill thought. He was giving serious thought to calling it a day, when he saw the local sheriff's office. Might as well go for the trifecta.

The Sheriff's Department building was much larger than the police station, which he was discovering was common in these large counties, where the sheriff often had a larger force. Once again, there was a counter with a young man working on his computer.

"Good morning. My name's Vincent Malone. I'm a PI working for a law firm in Albuquerque, and I was in your county doing some research, and wanted to stop by and introduce myself."

"Well, that's interesting." The young man's tone didn't sound sarcastic, and he stood and offered a hand to Vincent. "Let me go get the Sheriff. I'm sure he'll want to talk to you.

Just have a seat."

In the world of cynics—where Vincent was a long-time resident, and maybe even something of a fixture—this seemed too good to be true. Maybe it was a trap. The chief might have called ahead and warned the sheriff about the marauding PI in their midst. But even Vincent found that almost too crazy to believe. He waited to see what would happen.

"Mister Malone, hello. My name's Clyde Begay, and I'm the sheriff. Come on back, and let's chat." Begay was a large, friendly-looking Native American with a strong handshake. Vincent followed him into a somewhat cluttered office filled with pictures of family and baseball teams.

"Looks like you were a professional ballplayer. Where'd you play?" Vincent examined the photos on the wall.

"All over Texas and Oklahoma. Never made it out of the minors, but spent some great years trying to make it as a pro. The curveball did me in. I could hit any fastball a human could throw, but toss me a curveball, and I looked like a ten-year-old swinging at gnats. Finally gave up my dream and came home, ran for sheriff. Tell me about this research you're doing."

His instincts said he could trust the sheriff, at least up to a point, so he decided to give him a version of the story that was very nearly true, beginning with his interest in the accident that had killed an electric company employee some years ago. He said he was gathering data for a law firm in Albuquerque, though he didn't say which one, and indicated that it involved some kind of family conflict. Begay nodded as Vincent talked.

"Mister Malone, I'm sure there is an element of truth in

what you just told me. I'm also sure that you left out a lot of details about what you're looking into. I'm a pretty direct kind of guy, so I don't play games with people. We got a call from the police chief about your visit with them and the judge. Thought you might stop in to see us, so I made a few quick calls. You won't like this, but one of those calls was to Sheriff Ortega. He and I aren't exactly buddies, but we know each other. When I mentioned your name, he exploded. Completely lost it. At one point in our brief conversation he was *threatening me*. So, I'd say you have one very powerful, dangerous enemy. But all I really learned in my calls, apart from the fact that Ortega hates your guts, is that you're a licensed PI, and a Mister Tucker told me that you work for the largest law firm in the state. So, let me be clear: I'm not your enemy. I just don't want any trouble in my county. So, if you don't mean to cause trouble, you're welcome here."

Vincent chuckled. You have to admire talent when you see it. "That's a lot of work in a short amount of time." Begay smiled, and Vincent smiled back. "I sure didn't come here to cause trouble. As I said, I'm interested in the old case involving the electric company employee's death, and I was trying to find out about a murder charge that was brought against Matias Ortega."

"What's your interest in Ortega?"

"This is political research for a client. That's all I'm going to say about it, except to mention that it's entirely legal, and that all I was trying to get was access to public records."

"I'm not aware of any murder charge against Ortega. When

was this?" The sheriff seemed genuinely interested.

"Around the same time as the accident, in the late 1980s. The charge was dropped, so I don't know what kind of records there would be."

"How do you know about this?"

"I think it's reliable information, but it might turn out to be just a rumor."

"I wasn't around at that time, so I don't have any information about Ortega being charged with murder. I would think if that was true, I'd have heard about it, but there were a lot of things that happened back then that people don't talk about. I do know that Matias Ortega grew up here and was something of a problem for law enforcement around the time that you're looking into. But it was my impression that the problems were all minor—basically a young guy sowing some wild oats. He may have spent a few nights in county jail, but I don't think there was anything serious. Definitely not murder."

"There was an old man who was killed about that same time up by San Mateo. He owned a local store and gas station, and I think his name was Jake. Do you know anything about that?"

"You've got some good sources, although they may not be very accurate. I've heard that story about the old store owner and yes, I know it's connected with the Miller accident. I've looked at our records, and before he died, I talked to Bud Reyes, who was sheriff at that time. The records support what he told me: that the guy up there, Jake something-or-other, died due to an accident. He was very old. Fell off of the front porch at his store and hit his head. An accident, not murder. You may think we're backward people, living in these small towns, but Sheriff Reyes was one of the best lawmen in this whole state. If something else had happened in San Mateo, he would've been all over it. But he told me it was an accident, and I believed him." Sheriff Begay gave Vincent a look that said there wasn't going to be any more discussion about the topic—case closed.

"Sheriff, I appreciate you taking time to talk to me. I'm headed back to Albuquerque. Please give my apologies to anyone I might have somehow offended. That was never my intention, just looking for information. Thanks again."

They shook hands and Vincent left. He still didn't have the whole story, but it was probably as good as he was going to get. Now he had to think about Ortega and what was going to happen next.

Vincent and Nancy were sitting in their small back yard having a glass of wine while he told her about his day in Grants.

"Do you think the old man was killed?"

"No way of knowing. I think the current sheriff believes it was an accident, but that also allows him to not deal with it, which I'm pretty sure is what he wants. It's old news, and bringing it up just causes problems. He was an old man, and old men fall and die sometimes. But it's a pretty big coincidence, with the Miller death happening in the same area at the same time. Of course, it could be exactly that—just a coincidence."

"Every single cop in this county knows Ortega is a dangerous goon. What are you going to do, Vincent?" Nancy was on the verge of crying, obviously afraid.

"I think he's a bully. Beyond that, I don't know. Bullies always have a more threatening reputation than the facts warrant. It's how they live—all bluster and threats. But what has he actually done? I don't know of anything other than being an asshole. Plus, I'm not without resources. I think the police chief is becoming a friend. Jack Hill is going to be angry I dropped his name in a few spots, but he won't let Ortega go into full criminal mode if he thinks the guy has any chance as a politician. And don't forget—I can take care of myself."

He was trying to reassure Nancy, but inwardly he had to admit that he was a little nervous about Ortega, too. A misstep on his part might genuinely make the guy dangerous. The biggest problem he saw with Ortega was the man's ambition, and the fact that if any of the ugly possibilities about his past turned out to be true, he was done as a politician. How far might he go to protect that?

"Have you heard anything about Stella?"

"No. But there's no reason I would. She was a guest at the Inn for few days, and I met her and helped a little. That's not a connection. We don't even know why she left. Could have been some kind of book publishing emergency, nothing to do with the Miller stuff. She just went home to take care of business. She doesn't owe anyone here an explanation." He was trying to convince himself, as much as anything.

"You don't believe that, do you?" Nancy thought the lady

was in some kind of trouble, and it worried her.

"Nope, I don't. There seems to be a connection with New Mexico State. Stella went to school there. Based on that, I think she might have gone to Las Cruces. During some of my visits to Cruces, I met some local cops. Maybe I'll give them a call tomorrow and see if anything's happened there that might point to Stella. Other than that, there's probably nothing we can do." Vincent was getting tired and was ready to call it a day.

"You should firm up your deal with Jack Hill. I know you think he's dirty in some way, but if you're going to keep doing your investigative work, you need an ongoing source of clients and money. I think Jack Hill's that source, bad guy or not. Plus, Tucker's there, and you need their backing to keep you out of trouble." Nancy delivered this as a statement as fact, not something open for discussion.

Vincent paused and looked at her. Once again, he realized how lucky he was to have her in his life. He smiled. "You're absolutely right. Thank you for making that clear. I'll get that handled tomorrow." He took her hand and they went inside.

Never needed anyone's help before. That was my motto in life: take care of yourself and screw the world. You're on your own. Now I need help—I even want help. Nancy's made me a better person, and I want her to help me continue to grow. I'm an old man learning how to be a more complete person, thanks to this thoughtful, generous woman. The woman I love. Will wonders never cease?

10

Follow The Bouncing Ball

Stella had gone outside to get away from her grandfather and his friend—who also seemed to be his enemy, partner, co-conspirator, and loony chum—for a bit. If she'd been a smoker, she'd be smoking and thinking. Instead, she was just thinking.

What a screwed-up mess! My ancient-as-hell grandfather is involved in some kind of criminal enterprise involving Indian artifacts with the help of this other crazy professor. Insanity! It's like a bad movie.

Benson came out to join her. "Look, Stella, honey—I know this sounds bad. So, okay, maybe I stole some artifacts to make a little extra money. Somehow, I rationalized the whole thing. I knew those bastards in administration were going to fire me over my little affairs—which were all absolutely consensual, by the way. I sure as hell wasn't forcing myself on anyone. Stealing the artifacts seemed like stealing from the dean, who was about to take my job away. It doesn't sound too convincing now, but it seemed solid to me back then. And I didn't kill anyone, I didn't harm anyone, okay? It was that stupid motorcycle gang—they were the ones who killed that guy."

Stella stared at her grandfather with her mouth agape.

Motorcycle gangs, killing, stealing. My god, he was a university professor, not some crime lord. What had started out weird was turning into something truly bizarre—and scary. "I want you to take me back to my car. I'm leaving. I can't help you. You need to get some help. Papa, you might be crazy. Please, go see a doctor. Now take me to my car!"

"If you don't help me, he'll kill me!" Benson was waving his arms and pacing back and forth, looking manic.

"Alex?" Stella demanded, yelling. "He won't kill you. I don't even think he can get up. Now, take me to my car!"

"Not Alex. Ortega. *He* will kill me." Benson was angry, glaring at Stella, but he was obviously also frightened. "Forget it. I'm not taking you anywhere, get the hell out of here. I'm done with you." He went back into the room and slammed the door.

Stella didn't know what to do. She wanted to cry or run away. *Who the hell is Ortega?* she wondered, feeling even more out of her depth as a new puzzle piece appeared. But she stood still, staring at the closed door. Then she heard a car pull into the parking lot and turned to look. It was a Las Cruces police car. She thought she might faint. Stella glanced behind her to see if her grandfather had come out at the sound of the car. He hadn't. She was alone. Two officers got out of the car, one maintaining cover behind his door. The other approached Stella. Both had their hands on their guns.

"Ma'am we received a call about a disturbance here. What's your name?"

"Stella Stratton." She had begun to shake.

"Are you staying in that room behind you?"

"No. Well I mean, yes; sort of." She knew she sounded out of her mind, but she was so scared she could barely speak.

"What are you doing here?"

Stella suddenly flashed on her grandfather coming out the door with his pistol drawn. He would die, she would die. She almost collapsed. She had to decide what to do, and if she picked the wrong option it was going to be bad.

"My grandfather and a friend of his are in that room. They're both very old and they might not be thinking clearly. I was trying to help them settle some differences, and it's gotten out of hand. They both used to be university professors. They're not gangsters or anything—I don't believe they will hurt anybody, but you should know that my grandfather has a gun. Please, don't hurt him. If you let me go into the room, I can talk to him and have him come out without the gun. Please let me do that."

Both officers drew their guns. "Ma'am are you in any danger?"

She wasn't clear on why he was asking. "No. He's my grandfather. He won't hurt me. Please, can I go in and bring him out? The other man is sick, and I don't think he can walk at the moment."

The police officers exchanged a glance, and that brief hesitation gave Stella the chance she needed. She turned and went into the room before they could stop her. She heard them calling out to her and cussing as she shut the door.

"The police are here with guns drawn," she announced. "If

you want to die, go out there with your gun—you'll be dead in seconds. But I told them you'd come out with me, and without your gun. If you do that, nobody will be killed. Papa, I don't want to die."

Stella had started out stern, but now she began to cry. Benson took the gun out of his pocket and placed it carefully on the coffee table.

"I'm sorry, Stella. I'm a useless old man. Let's go." He took her arm and they went outside together.

The officers relaxed once they saw Benson. He was exactly as the lady had said—an old man who looked completely harmless. One of the officers approached them, and had Malcolm move over to the police car and lean on the hood to be searched, then handcuffed him. Stella began crying again. The other officer went into the motel room. When he came back out, he said he'd called an ambulance for Wallace, whom he thought had just died. Stella cried harder.

Stella and Malcolm were placed in a small detention room where they could be interviewed by detectives. No one had been charged, and they'd removed Benson's cuffs. He leaned over to Stella and whispered to her.

"Don't say anything about the artifacts. There's a lot I haven't told you yet. We need to go to Santa Fe. Please, Stella, I need your help."

Stella looked at her grandfather with a blank expression. She was exhausted and felt hollow. She nodded and closed her eyes.

Vincent had just finished giving his sworn statement to a Santa Fe Police Department stenographer. He signed the document and was heading out, when the chief waved at him to come back to his office.

"Hey, chief, thanks for letting me give you my statement. Hopefully nothing comes of this, but it feels better to establish what I know. Really appreciate you thinking about that before something happened."

"Sure, no problem. I've talked to several people today about your travels yesterday. Seems you are making quite a reputation for yourself across the entire state."

Vincent grinned a little. "Yeah. Not sure I learned much, but I definitely seem to have stirred things up a bit. Any chance one of those calls was from Sheriff Ortega?"

"Yep. He was not happy. Probably could have heard him without even using the phone. Did you accuse him of murder?"

"I didn't accuse him of anything. I had information that back in the 1980s in Cibola County he was charged with murder, but that the charge was dropped. I was trying to determine if it was true, and ran into a Grants city brick wall. Those records may have been sealed, but all I was asking for was access to public records, and all of a sudden, I became public enemy number one. Still don't know how I upset people—I was my most charming self the whole day. Got along great with the current sheriff over there, but not so much with the police chief and with a judge I never actually met."

Chief Stanton began to laugh. He was clearly trying to control his strange burst of good humor, but wasn't having a lot of success. "Sorry, Vincent. But I know some of those people, and they're not used to anyone asking questions." He continued to laugh, and Vincent smiled—sort of. The chief finally managed to calm himself some. "I also talked to Clyde Begay, he's one of the true professionals in this state. He and I go back to police academy in Albuquerque. He told me you weren't doing anything wrong, that folks just overreacted. He said if you needed his help in the future to just call him. He's a good guy, always tries to do his job by the book."

"Well, that's good to know. What is Ortega saying? That my days are numbered?" Vincent was still a little annoyed with the chief's cavalier attitude.

"He didn't say that exactly, but he's definitely not a fan of yours. Apparently, Jack Hill's name came up, and that has him restrained for the moment. He thinks you're a bully and a goon and should be locked up, but I get the feeling that he'll ignore you for now and see how this affects his political plans. Might be in your best interests to see what you can do to get him elected to Congress and off to Washington, D.C."

"He doesn't exactly fit my image of a good congressman, but maybe I'll toss my support in his direction just for the sake of local peace and harmony." Vincent was feeling better about the Ortega risk, although now he'd have to deal with some fallout from Hill. He left the police station and decided to walk over to the Crown and have a midmorning coffee with his lovely wife-to-be. As he entered the downtown plaza area, he could see a crowd gathering around some police officers who were dealing with a disturbance. It looked like the cops had pulled two men apart after some kind of altercation and were giving each of them a lecture. They didn't arrest anyone, just shooed each man off in a different direction after giving them a dressing-down. One was Sam Miller. He looked like he'd been living outside and seemed oblivious to his surroundings. He stared at the ground, and when the cops said the men could leave, he headed off down one of the side streets. Vincent held back some, then followed. After a few blocks Vincent decided Miller was just walking, heading nowhere in particular.

"Hey, Sam," he called out.

Sam took off at a run. Vincent hadn't been expecting that, and debated whether or not to give chase, but with no paying client he wasn't about to sprint after anyone—especially Sam, who looked fast. *Why did he run?*

He arrived at the Crown, took a seat at the massive bar, and ordered a Coors draft. He loved his soon-to-be wife, and he loved her bar. He smiled, a happy man.

"What are you grinning about?" Nancy sounded surprised, and a little alarmed, to find him just sitting, looking pleased with life.

"I know this'll shock you, but I just realized how happy I am." He smiled again.

"Vincent, you're starting to scare me."

=—⊕—

Stella's experience with the police was exhausting, but it ended with her and Malcolm being released without any charges. Alex's body was taken away by the coroner's office. He had been a citizen of Las Cruces, with a local address, and the medical people said he had died of natural causes, and those two facts, taken together, seemed to reassure the police. Stella and Malcolm returned to the motel to retrieve his car and belongings, including his gun. The police had run a check on the firearm and had found that it was registered to Malcolm and legal in New Mexico. Stella would have preferred that the cops took it, but there was no legal reason for them to do so.

They retrieved Stella's rental from the Hatch police department, paying a small fine and storage fee. She had explained that her grandfather had met her there, and that they'd left in his car to see his friend who was ill. Then the friend died, and she hadn't been able to go back and get the car. The story made sense, and came naturally, because it was sort of the truth. Malcolm turned in his rental car at a large hotel, where the national rental company had an office, insisting he could do that part on his own. Stella didn't argue, but thought his behavior was getting odd again. She saw him talking on his phone and wanted to ask who he was talking to, but also didn't want to know.

Unbeknownst to her, Malcolm called Jackson Smith, his long-lost son, but got no answer. He left a voice mail saying he was leaving the car in the Hilton parking lot, that Jackson should turn it in at the desk, and that he couldn't do it himself because it was in Jackson's name. They didn't need the car anymore, he said, and he would call Jackson later, but Jackson should not call him.

Stella and Malcolm drove along Interstate 25 in silence. How was she supposed to start a conversation with him? Her grandfather had pulled a gun and threatened to kill a man. Then, for completely unrelated reasons, that same man died. She'd never even been in a police station before, much less questioned by frowning detectives. She didn't even know where to begin, but she had to start somewhere, so she plunged in.

"Don't lie to me anymore. What is this all about? You owe me an answer. And why are we going to Santa Fe?"

"It's about all the mistakes I've made. I've screwed up a lot of people's lives, and it's coming home to roost. I'm sorry I called you, but I didn't know what to do."

"You're still haven't told me what's actually happening. That's just gibberish. What the hell's going on? Who's Ortega?"

"It's about money, sex, bastard children, murder, years of lying, fear—all of it because I'm so weak and selfish. First, you should know that the story you used in your book, the one about the man being killed by the motorcycle gang, was true. That actually happened. The people who did it were working for me. I used them as guards so I could steal artifacts. It's so ugly." Malcolm began to cry and soon he was sobbing.

Stella thought maybe she should stop and make sure he was okay, but before she could decide, in just a few short minutes, he'd fallen sleep. She still wasn't sure what he'd gotten her involved in. Was he just making stuff up? Was this dementia? Was he losing his mind? And now, of all things, he'd gone to sleep. She knew he must be exhausted, but right in the middle of confessing his sins? It was her turn to start crying, but she kept driving. Maybe there would be answers in Santa Fe.

11

Blessed Are The Misfits

Vincent had enjoyed his early morning coffee and the newspaper, a ritual still important to him even if the paper was more ads than news. Now it was time to call Tucker. Always deal with the most difficult task first thing in the morning, hoping, of course, that you would get voice mail and not have to talk to your "task."

"Morning, Tucker. Just wanted to let you know that Hill's name somehow got dropped yesterday while doing some in-field research in Grants. There's a chance—well, a good chance—that Ortega was made aware of that little slip-up. Also wanted to talk to you about me making my arrangement with Hill a bit more formal, with a retainer maybe. Give me a call when you get a chance, and we can talk about some of the things I learned in Grants."

He followed up his voice mail with an invoice by email to Tucker. Money hadn't been a driving force in his life after his downfall in Dallas. Back then he'd been a hard-charging guy, for whom money and status were all that mattered, but after his life imploded, he'd become a just-enough-to-get-by sort of person. Now, though, money meant he could be with

Nancy. Without a reliable flow of funds, he knew he'd have to leave—he wasn't going to burden her with his failed life—so, his new goal was to make a steady income doing dirty work for Jack Hill. He wasn't sure he liked the idea, but it was his best option, and he trusted Tucker. His phone vibrated.

"Malone."

"So, you want a full-time job working for a con man? Have you been drinking this morning?" Tucker always got right to the point.

"Not yet. I know it kind of contradicts some of what I said before, but I need to work for someone so I can support myself. I'm still suspicious of Hill, but he's the best game in town, so why not join and see how it goes?"

"I'm fairly sure he'll agree to a retainer against an hourly rate. He's got lots of work, and for some reason, he likes you. Plus, he's impressed with some of the things you've done on other matters since you came to Santa Fe. Yet another plus; he had you checked out in Denver. He asked me the other day about your reliability because of your health problems. I told him you were drinking less and taking medicine for the gout. He just nodded and walked off, but he was obviously thinking about using you more. I haven't heard anything about you divulging his name, so it could be that no one's said anything to him. He was very pleased with your info about the commissioner in Las Cruces and his closeted baggage. And the timing's probably good, so you want me to propose something to him?"

"Tell him I'm interested and would like his thoughts. Don't

mention any amounts and see what he comes up with." Vincent didn't want to accidentally lowball his own pay.

"Will do. How's pre-married life treating you?" Tucker had already told Vincent he might be the luckiest man alive to end up with Nancy, at his age and with his attitude.

"I sure wouldn't want to jinx anything, but it's about as good as it gets." Vincent couldn't help himself—he smiled. He went on to cover what he had and hadn't learned in Grants. While there were probably some questionable things in Ortega's past, at least at this point he couldn't say for sure that anyone would find anything. The bad stuff seemed to be well hidden, and might not be true, anyway.

"My opinion of Ortega is still that he's a hooligan with a badge, but in the crazy world we live in these days, that might actually be an asset if you're running for office. Nobody's going to be able to intimidate Ortega, and he has an ego the size of a small building."

"Yeah, he might just be a leader. I'll discuss this with Hill and let you know." Tucker clicked off.

Stella took the first exit for Santa Fe. "Where to now?"

Her granddad had been awake for a while, but had said very little. "I think we should go to the church." Malcolm spoke in a soft voice, apparently still tired.

"Okay, and which church is that?"

"San Miguel Chapel. It's on Old Santa Fe Trail, but I'm

not sure how to get there from here."

Malcolm closed his eyes again, leaving the problem of navigation to Stella. She decided to pull into a parking lot of a small shopping center and used her smartphone to get directions to the church. It wasn't far, and after a short drive they could see the majestic old adobe structure. Stella found a parking spot on the street.

"Why are we here?"

"I need to see Father Joseph."

Stella was getting annoyed again. Now Malcolm was answering every question with the bare minimum of words, never telling her the whole story.

"Okay, Papa, I understand that we're here to see someone. But, why?"

"I can't tell you right now."

Malcolm opened the door and got out. He started off toward the ornate carved wooden doors of the church, leaving Stella standing by the car, glaring at his back. Then she followed.

As she entered the small chapel, she was stunned by its beauty. The place was clearly very old, with a surprising majesty. The walls were decorated with artifacts that appeared to be as old as the church, and the overall effect was to induce a respectful quiet in the visitor. When she recovered herself a little, she saw her grandfather talking to a young priest near the front of the church. She began to walk toward them, but he abruptly broke off his conversation and started toward her.

"We need to get out of here—now. Thought I told you to

wait in the car." He seemed angry.

"You didn't tell me to wait in the car. What's the matter?"

Malcolm left the church and headed for the car. Stella followed, pausing to wonder if she should go back in and ask the priest what was going on. Would a priest lie? She decided she wasn't really sure she wanted to know. She went to the car and got in. "Was that Father Joseph you were talking to?"

"No. He said Father Joseph left some years ago, and nobody knows where he is. They're worried he had some kind of mental breakdown, and said that if I found him, I should ask him to call them to let them know he's okay."

"Look, I don't know why you're being so mysterious. Maybe there's even a good reason. But I'm not going to play this game anymore. I'm calling Mom to tell her what's going on, and that you need help—then I'm leaving. If you need someone to help you, you should ask her, not me. I won't be treated like a ten-year old. So," she paused for a breath, "where do you want me to take you so you can get a room, or a car, or whatever it is you need?"

"You can't call your mother. She wouldn't help me, anyway—probably just call the cops. She hates me. But you're right, you should go on with your life. I'm sorry I got you involved. I just panicked because I thought Ortega might try to hurt you. You should drop me at a motel. Get on a plane and leave. I can handle this."

She rested her head on the steering wheel and shut her eyes. Her older-than-dirt grandpa was the one acting like a ten-year old. What to do? "Okay, look—I can't just leave you. I know someone to call. He's somebody I met here in Santa Fe. You need to talk to him and tell him what's going on, and then maybe he can help you."

"You just don't get it, do you? This isn't me being nuts. This is a massive cluster-fuck in the real world, and if you bring in some do-gooder, they'll call the cops, and I'll end up in jail. And if I'm in jail, I'll be dead in a week. Probably less. So, just take me someplace where I can get a drink, and then go. Go, go! I can take care of myself."

Stella headed toward the Crown. He could get a drink and eat something, and maybe she could figure out a way to get her granddad to talk to Vincent. She wasn't sure what she wanted Vincent to do—she knew she was pushing her tenuous connection with him to the breaking point—but she sure as hell needed someone who could give her advice, and didn't see any other option. Vincent sometimes did work as an investigator, and she had plenty of money, so maybe she could just hire him to fix whatever horrible mess her granddad had gotten caught up in. All she knew for sure was that she couldn't deal with him anymore. She parked.

"It's only a short walk. I know the owner of this bar, she's a fan of my books. You can get a drink and something to eat, okay?"

"Sure, whatever."

She wasn't going to hear "thank you, Stella" any time soon. She sighed and forced a smile at her granddad. After they'd walked a couple of blocks, she pointed out the Crown. Once inside, her granddad seemed to cheer up. The crowd seemed to be half drinkers and half late-lunch diners. It was a joyful atmosphere, and a little loud, and Malcolm immediately felt at home. They found a back booth and slid in. Malcolm ordered a gin and tonic and began scanning the menu. Stella smiled at the attractive waitress. "Any chance Nancy might be here?"

She got a smile back. "Oh, I'm sure she's here somewhere. Are you a friend?"

"Sort of. We met a few days ago. I'm an author, and I was here for a writer's conference. Would you mind telling her that Stella's here, and would like to talk to her?"

"Sure, no problem. You want to order now?"

Malcolm ordered a cheeseburger with fries, while Stella got a small salad and iced tea. The waitress left.

"You know, at your age, you shouldn't be eating cheeseburgers and french fries." Stella sounded like a nag, even to herself.

"I'm sorry you think you have to babysit me. You shouldn't worry, my dear. I've already outlived most of my contemporaries, and for my entire life I've more or less done what I wanted, consequences be damned. I regret a lot of that, because of the harm that it's caused others. But not once have I regretted eating a good cheeseburger with fries, especially in a rowdy bar."

Stella smiled despite herself. He was old—very old, actually—and here she was, telling him to eat better? "Maybe you're right, Papa. Enjoy your cheeseburger."

"Well, Stella, hello." Nancy was pleased to see Stella, but knew almost immediately that something was wrong.

"Oh, Nancy. It's so good to see you again." Stella stood and gave Nancy a hug. "This is my grandfather, Malcolm Benson." Nancy reached out and shook his hand. He held on too long and gave her a look she'd seen many a time in her life. Granddad was clearly a lecher.

"Nice to meet you, Mister Benson. I just love your granddaughter's books. She's a great writer."

"Yes, she is. Not sure where she got that talent. Although I guess I was a pretty good storyteller myself." Malcolm smiled, clearly thinking he'd said something clever. "You've got a great bar here."

The waitress arrived with the food. Stella excused herself from her granddad and pulled Nancy aside. "I know, he's an old fool. I saw the way he leered at you—sorry."

"Oh, it's okay. I took it as a compliment. I bet he was something when he was younger."

"Yeah, he was. I think he's still somethin', just don't know what. I think he's in some kind of trouble, something serious, but he just hints at things, and won't tell me the whole story. I know this is going to sound weird, but do you think I could hire Vincent to help me find out what's going on with my granddad?"

Nancy was surprised at the question. "Well, I know Vincent was worried about you when you left so suddenly. But you know, he's an investigator, not a counselor or anything like that."

"I think my granddad has committed a crime in the past, and now he has people after him because he stole something. He mentioned someone from Santa Fe named Ortega who wants to kill him. I just don't know if he's lost his mind or if some of it might actually be true."

Nancy knew her mouth was open and that she should shut it, but she kept staring at Stella with the same dumb look on her face, nonetheless. Ortega! From Santa Fe? Wanted to kill her grandfather? Jeez, should Vincent even get involved? She gathered her senses. "Stella, let me call Vincent. Just sit back down and enjoy your dinner, and I'll be right back."

12

Cry Me A River

"Back up. You want me to come down to the Crown to talk to Stella's grandfather, who maybe committed a crime of some kind, and Matias Ortega maybe wants to kill him, and maybe Stella will pay me. Is that right? That sounds like an awful lot of damned maybes, to me."

"That's pretty much it." Nancy was smiling. She liked it when Vincent went into his Brooklyn gangster voice.

"You know, the only crime that might connect those people is the dead EPSCO employee from the 1980s. Is that what we're talking about?"

"Vincent, lower your voice—this is me you're talking to."

"Okay, yeah, sorry. Do you think that's what they're talking about?"

"I don't know, but it almost has to be. Her granddad must be in his nineties, or close to it, but he's still kind of feisty. I get the feeling that if I get to know him better, I won't have much trouble believing he's broken the law here and there. But it's really Stella who needs the help. Generally, I'd advise you to leave the situation alone. It sounds like family trouble, and there's no way to win in that kind of scenario. But she's says she'll pay, and she's a bestselling author, so she can actually do it. Plus, I think she's in way over her head, which means she could get hurt if she doesn't have anyone to help her. So, Mister White Knight, I think you should at least talk to her—and bad grandpa, too."

"Okay, but I should get something out of this besides the promise of a payday, someday, maybe."

"How about I promise you a good time with a very attractive lady named Nancy?"

"I'll be there in fifteen minutes."

Vincent entered the Crown right on time and spotted Nancy and Stella sitting in a booth with an older man. "Good evening. Stella, it's good to see you. I was worried after you left so abruptly. Glad to see you're okay."

Stella looked up and smiled weakly. She seemed on edge. "Yes. I'm sure it seemed odd to leave so quickly." She apparently didn't have anything else to say about her sudden departure, and changed the subject. "Mister Malone, this is my grandfather, Malcolm Benson." Benson looked up and nodded, then went back to his fries, ignoring everyone.

"Nice to meet you Mister Benson." The conversation was becoming increasingly awkward, with Stella looking apprehensive and the granddad ignoring them all. Vincent decided to grab the reins and guide them back on course. "Nancy, why don't you show Stella your office? I'll sit with Mister Benson." In other words, would you ladies get lost so I can talk to this annoying old fart? Maybe, if they didn't have an audience, he'd even get a straight answer out the guy.

"Sure. It's not much, but it's where I spend a lot of time."
They got up and left. Malcolm didn't even seem to notice.

Vincent slid into the booth.

"Malcolm, you might not have caught it, but my name is Vincent Malone. I'm a private investigator. Do most of my work for attorneys, working on their cases. I used to be a lawyer, too, but I ran into some trouble and got my ass disbarred. I've seen more fuckin' grief than you can shake a stick at, and I don't take shit off people. So, if you want me to help you, you should make an effort to not treat me like dog poop."

Benson looked up at Vincent. A moment later he smiled. "A no-bullshitter. I like that." He reached out and shook Vincent's hand. "Are you working for my granddaughter?"

"She's said that she'd pay me to help you. If I decide to do that, then she'll be the money, but you'll be the client. I'd be working for you, not her."

"If I tell you stuff, will it be confidential?" Now Malcolm was paying attention.

"Nope. I'm not an attorney, so anything you tell me will definitely not be confidential. If the stuff we talk about involves illegal activity, I can't hide it from the police. I have an obligation to tell them—at least, if they ask. If you think you have some criminal liability, you should hire an attorney. I know some, if you don't. Let me say that again, Malcolm. If this is a legal matter, you need an attorney. Is this about a crime?"

Malcolm was quiet. He was obviously turning things over in his head. Vincent waited.

"Yes, a lot of my problems involve crimes. Some of them

are probably way beyond the statute of limitations, but some might not be. I know I should hire an attorney, but I don't generally like lawyers. You seem like a decent guy who won't bullshit me. I think I want to tell you my story."

"Maybe we should go somewhere more private. Where are you staying?"

Malcolm seemed confused again. "Not sure. Maybe Stella made some kind of arrangements, I don't really know."

"That's okay. Let me talk to her. Will you be okay by yourself?" Vincent didn't want to leave him alone very long.

"Sure. I'm fine. Might get another gin and tonic." Malcolm smiled.

Vincent waved over the waitress and ordered his drink. "Be right back." He found Stella at the end of the bar, out of earshot distance, but where she could still keep an eye on Malcolm.

"He wants to talk to me. But I think it would be best if it was somewhere more private. Do you have a place to stay tonight?"

"No. I haven't made any arrangements. I've been so upset and confused. Is there someplace downtown?"

It was a silly question—Santa Fe was crammed full of hotels and motels, with many of the most expensive close to the Plaza. "Sure, there's a bunch near the Plaza. They're going to be on the high end, though."

"That's okay. Money's not a problem. What would you recommend?"

"Well the Hilton's right around the corner. It's huge, so unless there's a convention or something, they'll have some rooms. Pricey, but nice—and convenient, too."

"Okay." Stella pulled out her phone and began searching. In a surprisingly short time, she booked two rooms at the Hilton. "All set. Our car is just a short walk from here. Let us go get checked in, and then maybe you can come over there and talk to granddad in his room. Does that work?"

"Perfect. Just call me when you're ready."

Stella went back to the booth, and Vincent saw her talking to Malcolm. He didn't look pleased to be going, but he slugged his drink. Stella put money on the table, and they got up and left. Nancy approached Vincent. "What's going on?"

"Malcolm wants to talk about whatever it is that's going on, this mess he's in. They're going over to the Hilton to get a room. Once they're settled, I'm going to meet up with him and hear his story."

"Do you have any idea what her granddad could have been mixed up in so long ago? And in an out-of-the-way place like Cibola County?"

"I might. I know there were active digs—archeology sites, where they were finding artifacts—around that area at the time, and that New Mexico State University professors ran the sites. Apparently, Malcolm was a professor over there, but beyond that I really don't know how it all fits together. My guess is that the information she had about the murder of Sam Miller's dad came from her grandfather. But how he knew any of that, and why he would tell her, I have no idea."

"How do you know about those university digs?" Nancy seemed to be asking more out of curiosity than anything else.

"I have my sources," Vincent said, trying not to smile.

"Your source is a bartender, isn't it?"

Vincent shrugged, trying to give nothing away, but he smiled.

Vincent was just about to give up on Stella and go home when his phone vibrated.

"Sorry. My granddad decided he wanted to go to bed, but I've convinced him to talk to you in the morning, is that okay?"

"Sure, that's fine. I'll call you in the morning when I get there. Then he and I can meet downstairs for breakfast. Unless he wants to meet in his room."

"Breakfast might be a good idea, but have it in his room. And you should make it early—he gets up early. I won't be there, right?"

"Right. It would be best if it was just me and your grand-dad. Talk to you tomorrow." He found Nancy in the back and gave her an update. "Think I'm headed home."

"I should be home in about an hour, in case you want your Nancy reward." Her look nearly made Vincent blush. He smiled all the way home.

Vincent knocked on the door of room 1408 and waited. In a moment, Stella opened it.

"I'm in 1410," she said. "When you're done, call me, okay?" She walked out past him into the hall.

Vincent entered. Malcolm sat at a small table with a coffee service and some breakfast rolls. "Want some coffee?"

"Thanks." The old rogue seemed more alert than the night before. A good sleep will help anyone, but it can do wonders for the elderly.

"I've done some bad things," Malcolm began without preamble. "But I've never murdered anyone, and never asked anyone to kill anybody. Ortega's threatened me because he thinks I ordered his dumber-than-a-doorknob brother to kill someone. I didn't. He was paid, but it sure as hell wasn't to hurt anyone. Him and his gang of morons were supposed to keep tourists and other nosy folks away from our digs. And he was supposed to let us know if there were any EPSCO linemen or surveyors in the area. I don't know why they decided to attack that surveyor, but they did. I think it was more that they hated EPSCO than anything to do with me. When I heard about it, I challenged Santiago, and the dumb SOB said he didn't shoot the bastard—just shot out his back window, and the guy crashed. I really think he actually thought that was okay, that if he was only trying to scare him, then it wasn't really his fault." Malcolm looked furious. "Of course, that just messed up everything. As soon as that happened, we had to close everything down and leave. I never wanted to hear about any of that business again."

"Were you stealing Native American artifacts?" Vincent was always amazed at how effectively people could rationalize away concerns about their own stupid actions so they could feel better about themselves. Malcolm, he was pretty sure, was a pro at it.

"Well, yeah. You know, they don't really give a shit about that stuff, anyway. They want the damn government to give them money and land because of their past, but the truth is they could care less about their heritage. I was doing them a favor, selling that stuff to true collectors who really appreciated it, and would preserve it."

"Did you sell all the items you took?" He couldn't help it— he was really starting to dislike Malcolm Benson.

"Well, you know, it wasn't just me. There were three of us. Alex Wallace, the guy who just died in Cruces. He was involved. He was never at the sites, but he had the contacts, the buyers. He was always nervous about it, and he'd talk about how it was wrong, the hypocrite. But he did it, just like me and Zangari."

"Who's Zangari?"

"Patrick Zangari. I think he's dead, too. He was with me at the digs. We did all the hard work."

"How much money are we talking about?"

"Oh, quite a bit. That stuff's really in demand all over the world. I think over that one summer we probably sold maybe two hundred thousand dollars' worth. But hell, the stuff we didn't sell would have been worth even more."

"So, you didn't sell it all?"

"Nah, that was the plan. We sold some of the hotter items to get some money, and then we were going to sell it off a little at a time to keep prices up. You flood the damn market with all of it, the prices drop. Then I got fired, though, and everything got really screwed up."

"Why did you get fired?"

Malcolm smiled. "Even in my not-so-young days, I had an eye for the ladies. I was a popular professor, known internationally, and the students loved me—some of them a bit too much, very attractive young ladies. My wife had died years before, and I guess I kind of went overboard on romantic encounters with some co-eds. Willing ones, of course. But one of the little darlings got pregnant and raised holy hell. Big-time professor or not, the administration came down on me like a ton of bricks. They made some kind of deal with the girl, paid her off. And then, without even a hearing, they fired me."

"Did you ever hear from the girl again?"

"No, but I heard from the kid—hell, he's a grown man, now. I guess she told him who his father was, so suddenly last year he drops out of the sky, calls me up. We met, but I felt threatened. That's why I came to Las Cruces to find Alex."

Vincent wasn't sure what the truth was, but he could tell that Malcolm was lying.

"Back up a minute. You said you didn't sell all the artifacts, so where are they now?"

"That's what Alex wanted to know. Then the dumb bastard contacted Ortega and told him I was in Cruces, which was exactly what Ortega wanted to know. After that, I'm not telling anyone where that shit is." Benson had a defiant look on his face, or maybe crazy.

My god, Vincent thought, *this old man is a ticking time bomb.* "Why would Alex call Ortega?"

"Ortega knew about the cache of artifacts from when he was just a lowlife back in San Mateo. He heard it through his brother, who'd helped move the stuff. When his brother was killed in an accident, Ortega went kind of nuts, threatened to kill me. But he also wanted the artifacts. That's why I disappeared to Florida. I really thought he'd kill me unless I gave it all to him. I know he threatened Alex, and I think he may have killed Zangari. But they couldn't tell him where the stuff was hidden, because they didn't know—I do. He's a dangerous, two-bit hoodlum, and now he's the damned sheriff. What a screwed-up world."

Vincent wasn't about to argue—he'd reached the same conclusion years before. He shook his head at the maze of connections and complications, of lies and stupidity, that seemed to close in on Benson like a net.

13

Oh What A Tangled Web We Weave

"What makes you think Zangari's dead?"

"Well for one thing, we're about the same age, and I'm almost dead. Do you mean, like, do I know somebody killed him or something? I don't. He went to California a year or two after I ran off, and I never heard from him again. Or heard anything about him, either. But he hasn't turned up demanding my scalp, so I'm going to go out on a limb, and assume he's dead."

"What about your son, what did he want? And what's his name, by the way?"

"Jackson Smith. What a stupid name. I don't really know what he wanted. But we talked a while, and I guess he decided he didn't like me. And I decided I wasn't going to hang around in case he got it into his head to end my miserable life, so I left."

"When did you see him last?"

"I guess it's been about two weeks now. I met him in Miami at a bar. He seemed shocked that I was so old—excuse me for aging, you little whelp. Told me about his mother, how hard her life has been, and his, too. Maybe I didn't come across as sorry enough for him. Anyway, when he went to the men's room, I left."

"Do you think he'd follow you here?"

"I don't know how he could. Anyway, he hasn't turned up, so I'm guessing he went home to live out his useless life."

Vincent stared at Malcolm Benson for a beat. "You know, Malcolm, that's a lot of people who might wish you harm. Might be in your best interests to go to the cops and tell them your story. I bet you could work a plea deal and not serve any time if you return the artifacts—the ones you're still hiding. That might go a long way toward keeping any of these people from hurting you. And there's something else you need to consider. There's a man named Sam Miller, the son of the EPSCO employee who died in the accident. I don't know if he knows about you or not, but he's been digging into his father's death for years. If he finds out about you and your role in it, he might be one more person who wouldn't mind seeing you dead."

Malcolm hung his head. "I really never meant to do anything that would make people hate me. I didn't intend to hurt anyone. And that guy who died in the accident—I had nothing to do with that. Why hate *me?* I guess it might help to give the artifacts back and work some kind of deal, but there's a problem. I don't know where they are."

"What do you mean? Didn't you hide them?"

"I had help. Someone else has kept them hidden, and now that person's gone."

"Who the hell are we talking about?" Any more pieces to this puzzle, and Vincent was going to scream.

"Father Joseph. The artifacts were supposed to be hidden

in an outbuilding at the church. But now he's gone, and I don't know where. The outbuilding was torn down years ago, and the priest there now didn't know anything about any crates that might have been inside it."

"Which church?"

"The San Miguel Chapel, here in Santa Fe. Father Joseph took a bunch of the artifacts and used them to decorate the church. In exchange, he was hiding the rest until I came to get them. But now he's disappeared, and so have the artifacts. Although most of the ones he took for himself are still on the walls of the church."

Vincent pondered the twisted tale for a moment, wondering if it added up to anything more than nonsense. Maybe this old man was on some kind of lark, just making shit up as he went along.

"Why did you tell your granddaughter the details of the accident back in Cibola county?"

"Yeah, shouldn't have done that. I was drinking a lot back then. She told me she wanted to be an author, but didn't know what to write about. For some stupid reason, I told her what I knew about the accident. Obviously, I left out specific names and things, but I told her most of what I knew. I thought that if she tied that into a plot based around Native Americans taking revenge against the conquerors who made their ancestors' lives so miserable, it would make an interesting story. But I never really believed she'd not only write it, but manage to get it published, too. I was shit-faced, so I didn't really think it through. I was a little worried when she actually wrote about it, but the book was a huge flop—maybe twenty people read it—so I figured nothing was going to happen. I didn't mean to get her involved in any of this. She's the only family member I care about. Do you think someone might hurt her?"

"Probably not. There are a few people who probably wouldn't mind hurting you, but unless she knows where the artifacts are, no one's likely to do anything to her."

"I hope not. You know, I don't want one of my asshole enemies killing me, but the truth is, I'm not real sure how much I care. I'm pretty well at the end."

"I know this has been a tough conversation for you. I'm going to talk to Stella. I'll protect your secrets as best I can, but if she needs to know something to protect herself, then I'm going to tell her. I still recommend that you hire a lawyer, and approach the proper law enforcement agency and tell them your story. Even without the remaining artifacts, I don't think they'll prosecute you." Vincent paused. "Might be best if you lie down and rest. You're looking pretty tired."

"You do what you think is best. I'm going to take a nap. Tell Stella I'll do whatever you two decide." Malcolm rose slowly and headed to the bedroom.

Stella and Vincent were in the lobby café.

"What should I do?" she asked.

"Your grandfather has made some enemies. Based on what he's told me, some of them may want to harm him. There are also some very valuable Indian artifacts that are hidden, and that might be motivating people to threaten him, too, so they can find out where the loot is. At his age, it all seems kind of bizarre. I don't believe that he's criminally liable any longer for what he did back when he was working for the university. He told me he stole a lot of artifacts and sold them. If that's all that happened, then that crime is long past the statute of limitations—no one can touch him for it. But if he hid some, or had other people hide them, then he still could be in legal jeopardy. Possession of stolen items is a crime, too. But I'm not real sure what actually happened. One thing for sure; those missing artifacts could be a real problem. If I understand what your grandfather said correctly, I think that stuff might be worth a million dollars or more. A lot of money. He says the artifacts are missing—something to do with a priest taking them, or moving them, or something. Whatever the details, he says he doesn't know where they are now. You may have heard him mention the name, Ortega. I know who that is, and he's a very dangerous man. To make things worse, he's sheriff of this county. There's a history between those two, and there could be reasons beyond money that Ortega might want to hurt your granddad, but my guess is that the primary motivation for Ortega is money—a lot of money. I think what you should do is talk your grandfather into going somewhere and checking into some kind of health care center or retirement home. Somewhere he can be taken care of, and do it under an assumed name. He seems to think he won't live long, so it might be best to just hide for whatever time he has left. Of course, that takes money. The bottom line is, I don't think he's in danger of being arrested, but he might well be in danger of getting himself hurt or killed, and he should be where he can be hidden or protected, or both."

Vincent was quickly getting tired of thinking about Malcolm. He deliberately didn't tell Stella about the son who might or might not wish Malcolm harm. It seemed like an unnecessary detail, at least for the moment, and she had enough to deal with.

She slumped. "My god, what a mess. His family—including my mother, his daughter—have disowned him. Nobody's going to help him. I'm not sure how much money we're talking about, and whether I can cover it. Shit, shit, shit. What a nightmare. Do you really think someone would kill him?"

"Stella, there's something else you should consider. Some of what your granddad has told me is at least based loosely on the truth, but some of it could be a lie, or maybe he can't tell the lies from the truth anymore. Maybe Ortega had harsh words for him because he thought he was responsible for the eventual death of his brother. But, who knows about the artifacts and the priest and a bunch of other stuff he told me? It may all just be in his head." Vincent smiled, trying to relieve the tension. "If it was me, and I had a little money, I'd try to find a nice place somewhere close to where you live, where he could stay and be provided care. Not the top-of-the-line, not the most expensive, but something reasonable. Move him there. I wouldn't try to deal with any of the threats, since they may not even be real, or even if they were, the circumstances may have changed. I would make him as comfortable as possible, and then get on with my life."

"I actually may know a place in Chicago. It's a group home where a friend's mom lives. She told me it was very reasonable. I don't know if he'd agree to it, but I guess if he says no, he's on his own." Stella gave Vincent a firm look, suggesting it was going to be her way or the highway. "Let's go talk to him."

Stella knocked on the door. No answer. She knocked again, a little louder this time. No answer. She had an extra key and used it to open the door, but they both knew that the room would be empty. On the small table by the window lay a note.

Father Joseph called. He said he wants to talk to me. I'm going to meet him at the church. I took some money from your purse earlier, sorry. I'm taking a cab. Back soon. Papa

"Damn. What is wrong with him?"

"Do you want me to go see if he's at the church?" Vincent asked.

"Yes, but I want to come along, okay?"

"Sure."

They took Vincent's Mustang for the short drive. There was no way to tell from the note how much of a head start Malcolm had—they'd been in the café a long time. Vincent maneuvered the car through the narrow streets of downtown, made a quick turn onto Old Santa Fe Trail, and all they could see were police cars, an ambulance and fire trucks in front of the church, emergencies lights all flashing.

Stella drew in a breath. "Oh, my god. Something has happened."

Vincent parked a few blocks short of all of the activity. "Stay here until I can find out what is going on."

She nodded, not looking up.

Vincent spotted the police chief. "Hello, Chief. What's going on?"

"Is this an incredible coincidence, or are you actually attracted by emergency vehicles?" The chief was smiling, but it might still be a serious question.

"Someone I know was looking for her grandfather, and we thought he might be at this church."

"Tall man with grey-brown hair, maybe close to ninety?"

"Yeah. What's happened?"

"He was shot. He's dead. Do you have a name?"

"Malcolm Benson."

"That was the ID on the body. Do you know what this might be about?"

"Not really, chief." Vincent knew that the chief knew he was lying, but at this point he wasn't sure what else to say.

"Well, we've arrested a suspect. Found him holding the murder weapon, standing over the body. Is the dead man some relation to Stella Stratton?"

"Yes. He's her grandfather."

"The man we arrested is Sam Miller."

14

Some Days Are Worse Than Others

"Dead! Oh my god. Why? What happened?" Stella began to cry. It made Vincent feel helpless.

"I don't think you should be alone. I'm calling Nancy to see if she can meet us at her house, okay?"

She looked at Vincent as if she didn't understand what he was saying, saying nothing. Vincent stepped away from the car.

"Where are you, Vincent?" Nancy sounded worried. "I haven't seen you all day."

"Met with Stella's grandfather. Turned into more time than I thought. But right now, I've got a problem. Malcolm's been shot—he's dead. Stella seems strange, like she's going to explode. Is there any way you could meet us at home and stay with her while I come back and find out what has happened?"

"Dead. Her grandfather? Are you all right? Is Stella all right?"

"Yeah. I'll tell you what I know in a little bit. I just need someone to watch Stella and make sure she's okay."

As soon as they arrived, Stella completely broke down. Nancy led her into the back bedroom, reappearing a few minutes later. "You were right. She shouldn't be alone. You can go back now. She said Sam Miller killed her grandfather?"

"That's what the police say. He was standing over the body with the gun. Don't know much more than that right now. I'm headed back to see what I can learn." They hugged. Vincent didn't want to leave, but he did.

"Hey, Malone, you know we don't allow amateur investigators to snoop around a crime scene." The chief was smiling, but the words hurt anyway—*Amateur, my ass!*

"Stella Stratton asked me to get as much information as possible. We were with Malcolm just before this happened, over at the Hilton. He left a note saying he got a call from a Father Joseph, who used to be the priest here, and he was going to meet him at the church. As soon as we found the note, we headed here. But it was too late."

"I know Father Joseph. He retired and moved someplace else, years ago."

"Well, I'm just reporting what the note said, that they were going to meet. You sure Sam Miller shot him?"

"This is an active investigation, so you know I'm not going to discuss it with you. But we have a pretty strong case, given that the first officers on the scene found him standing over the body holding the gun. Damn gun may still have been smoking."

"What's Miller say?"

"Nice try, Vincent, but nope—that's all you get. I need you to clear out so we can finish our forensics."

"See ya later."

Vincent called Tucker.

"Just got off the phone with Hill," Tucker answered,

abruptly. "He's putting together a proposal for you. I think it'll be generous, so don't screw it up, Vincent."

"You're supposed to say hello, then talk."

"Hello, what the fuck do you want?"

"There's been a murder in Santa Fe. The dead guy is one Malcolm Benson, once a professor at New Mexico State. He has some connection to the accident—or murder—long ago in Cibola County that's tied to Ortega. He's also the grandfather of Stella Stratton, who believed she was being stalked by the son of the man who got killed in that little mishap. Benson was shot at an historic church, and the prime suspect is Sam Miller, the son of the long-ago accident victim. When the cops showed up, he was still hanging around, holding the gun—not a very bright killer."

"Sounds like the esteemed Santa Fe Police Department should have that wrapped up in a couple of hours. Did he do it?"

"I don't know, but I think maybe not. I've met this guy and I'd never peg him for a killer. He might kill in the heat of the moment, but most people can do that—this isn't a guy who would plan a killing. Plus, he may not be bright, but if you were the killer, why would you just stand there waiting on the cops? Benson had a lot of enemies who were more likely to end his existence than Miller. The guy's going to get railroaded, though, unless someone steps in and helps with his defense."

"Oh, no, no, no. Don't even go there. I don't do charity cases. Is he a multi-millionaire? Then talk to me. Is he famous, so the case will draw a lot of attention? Then talk to me. Otherwise, leave me out of your do-gooder world."

"This case? This is the kind of stuff you have to do to make up for all of the crap you did to make your millions. This is penance, and you really need to cleanse your soul. Don't take the case to trial or anything, but represent him for a while so the cops don't close the case in the next hour."

"Vincent, this is one of those cases where you can only get the guy off if you can find the killer. That's leg work, PI work—it's a job for you, not me. If you want to do this for nothing, go right ahead. You could probably use a little cleansing yourself."

"No, you're absolutely right. We have to have a client if we're going to do anything about this. Let me see what I can do."

Vincent clicked off and headed home. A short drive later, he found Stella and Nancy in the kitchen having tea, both looking forlorn. He related what little he'd been able to learn at the crime scene.

"What'll happen now?" Stella asked softly.

"The police will move fast. They have enough to charge Miller with murder, which I think they'll do today or tomorrow. Once that's done, they'll stop looking for anyone else. Miller will be arraigned, and things will begin moving toward a trial."

"You don't think he did it, do you?" This came from Nancy, giving the conversation a little momentum.

"No, I don't. I could obviously be wrong, but I just don't see him as a killer. I think Miller knew a lot more than he was telling us, and it's very possible that he was trying to find your granddad all along. He might even have been following you because he thought you might lead him to your grandfather.

The only way he'd kill Malcolm would be if he thought Malcolm was involved in killing his dad, but he knew already about the motorcycle gangs, and I'm guessing he also knew about the archeological digs. With all that, he'd know your granddad was involved, but he'd also know Malcolm wasn't behind his father's death. He might want to talk to him, but I can't see him wanting to kill him."

"But you said he was standing over my granddad holding the gun. How do you explain that?" It sounded like a valid question rather than a challenge.

"People react in strange ways in the middle of trauma. It's not uncommon for people to pick up a weapon. Some kind of reflex. If he fired the gun, there would be gunshot residue on his hand, but holding the gun isn't the same as shooting the gun. The forensic people will look for that, which could clear him, or convict him. Malcolm got a call from the priest. That's why he was at the church. But why was Miller at the same church at the same time? To me, it sounds like some sort of setup. Someone directed Miller there, so he could be charged with the crime."

"So, Miller will have to hire a lawyer?" Once again, Nancy edged the conversation forward.

"My guess is he doesn't have money. More than likely, he'll end up with a public defender."

"Is that bad?" Stella asked.

"Not always, but it may be in this case. Public defenders are usually very good at what they do. When you're guilty, and the goal is to work toward the best deal you can get on a sentence, they often actually have an advantage over outside lawyers. Public defenders are basically co-workers with the judges and prosecutors, so they communicate easily. The problem comes in if he's innocent. To get someone off on a murder charge, you have to give the jury alternative suspects—people who might have been the killer, other than your client. The better job you do in providing a reasonable alternative, the better the chance of a not-guilty verdict. And to do that, you have to have resources—money to hire investigators, to pay for expert witnesses, that kind of thing. Public defenders have very limited funds to work with."

Stella looked concerned. "Do you know someone who could represent Miller?"

"Sure. They might even do it cheap, or even for free, if I can shame them into it."

"What if I paid?" Now she looked thoughtful.

"Why would you do that?" This came from Nancy, but this time it seemed like she really wanted an answer rather than just trying to move the conversation forward.

"Because I don't think he did it, either. It's just too perfect. Somebody shot my granddad, and they should be punished. I don't mean to brag, but I've made a lot of money with my books. Maybe I should pay for his defense. Would that look weird?"

"Might," Vincent replied. "But wanting justice isn't weird. I know everything is happening fast, and if you need to be alone, or don't want to talk about this, I'll understand."

Stella sat up a little straighter. "I'm sad about my granddad.

But at his age, this isn't a tragedy. I wish things had been different, but I'm okay."

"Do you know if your granddad had a will?"

"Strange you should ask. I know he did, because he gave me a copy of it. He also gave me the name of an attorney in Florida who filed the will and has the original. I didn't think too much about it at the time, but he left everything to me. Until now, I thought that was zero. Do you think there's anything of value?"

"Who knows? If those artifacts exist, and you could prove a claim to them, they're probably worth millions. But your grandfather stole them, so I don't think you'd have any right to that part of his estate."

"Well, I don't need any more money than I have, and I don't want to be rewarded for my granddad being a thief. But maybe that's the rationale I can use to explain fronting the cost of Miller's defense. If anybody deserves some benefit from the crimes of the past, it's Sam Miller. Who's this lawyer I should hire?"

"Peter Tucker."

Vincent and Nancy lay in bed, not saying anything, but awake.

"Tucker told me Hill is preparing a work proposal for me. He said he thought it would be generous." Vincent sighed a little.

"Is that a problem?"

"Shouldn't be, should it? But I guess it made me feel small. Not sure why."

Nancy raised herself up on an elbow. "Because you can be bought?"

Vincent chuckled. He really loved this woman. "Yeah, I guess that's it. A knight in shining armor who can be bought by the highest bidder. Somehow it just doesn't feel right."

"You're still in control. He's going to pay you to do what you want to do, so how is that bad? And if you get one hint of something not smelling right, you'll tell him to go to hell. And I'll back you, right down the line."

Vincent actually laughed out loud. "You know I love you?"

"I know."

My life gets more complicated every day. Not long ago I was contemplating a quiet, do-nothing retirement. Just waiting to die. Now I have a whole new world that's incredibly important to me. Never, ever give up—you never know what might happen. Now, the prospect of digging into a new murder case, with my buddy Tucker defending an innocent man—what kind of fun might this be? Energized, excited, and in love. My goodness, life can be wonderful. Next I just need a list of possible killers. What fun!

15

We Are All Sinners, Except For Me

Stella signed the financial agreement, and Tucker signed for the firm.

"I'll contact Miller right away and get him to sign a representation agreement. If he says no—which can happen, you never know—then this financial agreement will be void," he told her in the lobby of the Hilton. "A couple of things I want to make sure you understand. First, you've agreed to pay for Miller's legal defense within the limits set forth in the contract, but that doesn't give you the right to make any decisions about his defense—what I do on his behalf is solely up to him. Second, his communications with me are privileged, and I won't breach that privilege and share anything with you without his written consent, despite the fact that you're the one paying my fees."

"Yes, Vincent explained all that to me. Look, I'm making the funeral arrangements for my granddad, and then I'm going home. You may think it's funny, Mister Tucker, but I trust Vincent to handle this matter and find out what really happened."

"I don't find it funny at all. I trust him, too."

Stella handed Tucker a check for the initial retainer. She

was ready to forget all the ugly details of the last few days, arrange for the cremation her grandfather had requested, and go home. She had talked to her mother, who had been subdued and maybe even sad about her father, but willing to let Stella handle whatever needed handling. It felt like something between her and Malcolm had been broken, and wouldn't heal anytime soon.

"I wish you good luck. Are you writing a new book now?" Tucker was the world's worst at small talk, but he tried.

"You know; my last four books have been huge bestsellers. I've made a ton of money, and in a way, I guess I'm famous. I came to this writer's conference because I was lonely and had stopped writing. Before I had all this success, it seemed like there were hundreds of books I wanted to write—I just didn't have enough time to get everything down on paper. Now, I don't know—it's like I'm burned out, I have no energy. Most of my old friends seem to resent my success. My mom just married a new guy—I hate him, and he hates me. I don't know, Mister Tucker, maybe I'm just a crybaby. I want one thing until I get it, and then I want the opposite."

Tucker surprised himself by telling Stella the truth. "When I was a young lawyer, all I wanted was money. I couldn't get enough. Money and fame, that was my entire life. Somewhere in the middle of my successful run as an asshole attorney, I realized that I didn't want the money or fame, anymore. What I wanted was someone to love, a family, a real life—but it was too late. Now I'm at the end of my life, and I'd give back all that money if I had someone who I loved and who loved me. Being alone isn't good or healthy. Go make up with your mom. Overlook the bum she married—she must have seen something in him. Find a guy, or, today, I guess, it might be a gal. Anyway, find someone to love. Take care of yourself, and the writing will happen when you're ready."

Stella rewarded Tucker with a large smile and a hug.

"Thank you. You're right. I should go see my mom. I miss her. And I think she's very sad about her dad, and needs to talk about it with me. It's hard, though. Thank you so much." She gave him another hug, and Tucker smiled.

Tucker and Vincent waited for Sam Miller to be brought into the county jail consultation room.

"How long is our list of alternative suspects?" Tucker seemed in a good mood—or what passed for a good mood in his world.

"Well, I think I can get to five pretty quick, without much work. Placing any of them in Santa Fe at the church is going to be harder. The first thing anyone's going to want to know from Miller is why was he there, and why in the hell was he holding the gun. I know I pushed you into this defense because I said I thought he didn't do it, and that's still true. But until we can get some answers from him that make sense, he's still the number one suspect, logically speaking."

"Are you fuckin' with me, Vincent? Our client is the number one suspect?"

Vincent chuckled. "Okay, maybe that's not fair. I'll keep him on the list at number six."

The door opened, and a sheriff's deputy brought in Sam Miller, who looked like he'd been run over by a small bus, with bruises on his face and cuts around his eyes and mouth. There was dried blood all over his civilian clothes, and he was bleeding from his right ear. He looked dazed as the guard shoved him into the room, then started to leave.

An explosion occurred. "Wait one goddamned minute, you prick!" Tucker bellowed at a volume that could have been heard blocks away. "What in the fuck has happened to our client? Why is he bleeding, you son-of-a-bitch? The fuckin' sheriff's department suddenly sign up for enhanced interrogation techniques? I want to see the *goddamned* sheriff and the *goddamned* police chief this *goddamned* second!"

The guard stepped back into the room and made a move toward Tucker, actually reaching for his weapon and starting to pull it. Vincent rose—this was going to get ugly, fast. The guard raised the gun toward Tucker, and Vincent punched him with such speed the guard didn't even see it coming. His momentum was interrupted, and Vincent shoved him into the wall with such force, something cracked. The man went down, out cold. Vincent stepped over him into the hall.

"You need to call nine-one-one and get an ambulance, now," he called out. "Also, we want to see the police chief."

Within moments, multiple guards arrived at full speed. They secured Vincent and Tucker in a different detention room and locked the door. The two waited.

"Thanks. I thought that idiot was actually going to shoot me. Can you believe this shit?"

"It's a fucked-up world."

Vincent was angry, but also sad. And he still had the urge to hit someone. His thoughts were interrupted when Chief Stanton entered the room.

"I just watched the video from the detention room and saw what happened. You're lucky we have cameras in those rooms. There won't be any charges. Miller's been taken to a hospital to get treatment. The guard is one of the sheriff's goons, claims the sheriff ordered him to welcome Miller to the jail. Have no idea why, exactly. Anyway, he's in a cell being treated by the jail medics. I called Ortega, but he hasn't gotten back to me. Could this have something to do with your feud with him?" The chief was looking at Vincent.

"I'm not having a feud with the goddamned sheriff. He's a fucking goon with a badge. Why don't you go ask him if this is part of his one-sided feud with me?"

"I will." The chief didn't look happy, but he also sensed this wasn't a good time to grill Vincent.

Tucker stood. "As soon as you release us, I'm filing a complaint. And I'm filing a motion with the court to have that tape placed in court custody. This isn't going to end with that bastard giving some fake apology! That son-of-a-bitch pointed his gun at me, and if Vincent hadn't stepped in, I think there's a real chance he would have killed me. This is going to get loud, and it's going to get messy. I may not be the bulldozer attorney I once was, but I've got connections, and this is going to be the ugliest shit-storm you've ever seen. A civil suit and assault charge for the attack on me, and a civil suit and attempted murder for the one on my client. And it's not going be just that Neanderthal of a guard who answers for this. That killer clown of a sheriff is going to feel the heat, too. And you, as well. Hell, the mood I'm in right now, I'd sue every person in this god-damned county if I could, up one side of town and down the other. Now I want out of here, immediately!"

The chief, showing a lot of good sense, stepped aside, and Tucker left. "Sorry, Vincent. You know some of my problems dealing with this joint operation of the jail. But I'm not going to try to dodge this—it's a right royal fuckup. Try to tell Tucker when he's calmer that this isn't how I run things. Not that I'm asking for anything. Just let him know I'm not his enemy."

"I'll tell him, for all of the good it'll do. But why would Ortega do this? That's what's so strange. I know he's part hoodlum, but why now, and why here? Doesn't seem to make much sense."

"I know. Something's missing." The chief looked thoughtful. "Let's hope this doesn't get worse."

Tucker was waiting outside. Vincent passed along the peace offering from the chief, but Tucker waved it away. "Let's run by the Hilton. They'll let me use one of their small conference rooms. I want to file something with the court immediately. We need a guard on Miller while he's in the hospital, and I'm going to ask that it be handled by the Santa Fe Police Department. Once he's released from the hospital, I want him transferred to Albuquerque until his trial. Not sure a judge will agree with it, but I can sure as hell ask."

"The police department has some cells of its own that are normally used as short-term holding cells, for a few hours or maybe a day. You could ask that he be held there. I know you're angry with everyone at the moment, but I do trust the police chief. This is Ortega. It had nothing to do with Stanton."

"Yeah, well, maybe. For right now, I'm going to bust everybody's balls. Why would Ortega have Miller roughed up?" Tucker had already started walking, ready to get to work.

"My car's in about the middle," Vincent noted. "Might be just as easy to walk to the Hilton and leave the vehicle where it is."

"Sure. I need to burn off some energy, anyway."

"I can only guess at Ortega's motives. We haven't had a chance to talk about everything I've learned on this case. But a big part of what's going on has to do with money. There seems to be a valuable stash of artifacts that were stolen in the '80s that are still missing. I get the sense it could be worth millions. My guess about Ortega is, he thought Miller might know where that stuff was hidden. I don't think Miller knows, and that might explain why that goon at the jail did such a number on him—he didn't spill the beans because he didn't have any to spill, so the guy beat the crap out him."

"This is the Ortega that our pal Hill wants to back for the U.S. Congress?"

"Same guy. How do you explain that?"

Tucker shrugged. "Human beings are fucked up?"

"Yep, that's as good an analysis as any. Looking at it another way, Ortega may want to stop this whole mess from moving forward. His political ambitions would take a major hit if there was a big-time scandal right now."

"You don't think Ortega had anything to do with Benson's killing, do you?" Tucker stopped walking and looked at Vincent.

"His name's on the list. I told you I doubt Miller has what it takes to carry out a cold-blooded murder. To the same degree, I'm confident that Ortega's capable of almost anything, including killing someone."

"What sort of shit-pile have you walked me into?" Tucker was grinning.

"You're going to love this case. It's got every human sin you can dream of, wrapped up into a nice, neat package. Greed, lust, wrath, envy, pride—aren't there seven of them? Could be gluttony and sloth aren't involved. Benson was so self-absorbed; I don't believe he thought he was doing anything wrong. But he left an impressive trail of grief."

"Yeah, I was sort of picking up on that point. Guy was a real asshole. How does such a loser end up with such a great granddaughter?"

"I think he avoided her for most of her life. That might have helped."

They spent the rest of the walk to the Hilton in silence. Tucker was on a mission to spread some grief. And he loved electronic court filings.

"Lots of chatter in the bar about the confrontation in the county jail. The gossip says you were the hero. Apparently, the guard you hit is the most hated person in the sheriff's department, which is quite an achievement." Nancy clearly wasn't happy with Vincent and his adventures.

"Well, I sure didn't plan it this way. The deputy went nuts after Tucker yelled at him. I still don't know if he was going to shoot him or not. I just don't know anymore; you know? Some of these people in law enforcement are way scarier than the criminals. Their very first reaction is to pull out a sidearm and kill. Can you imagine if they hadn't had video?" Vincent shivered a little. "I know it's not everybody in law enforcement who's like that, but it's a scary world, right now."

Nancy looked sad. She knew there were real problems in law enforcement, but she had so many friends who were cops. The thought was like a punch to the gut. "What's Tucker going to do?"

"Mostly raise hell. And he'll protect Miller as best he can from any more bullshit. I'm not sure there's anything of consequence he can do, but he'll try to make as many people uncomfortable as possible. The downside to this is Hill. He doesn't like public battles—he's a behind-the-scenes kind of guy, which means that Tucker going after everyone in sight could cause a rift in their relationship. And, of course, that might mean grief for me."

"What would you do?"

"Not sure. Still haven't seen the proposal Hill is supposedly putting together, but if Tucker has a break with Hill, then I guess I will, too. With Tucker inside, I felt comfortable around Hill. Without that, I'd walk."

"What would you do then?"

"Would you hire me as a bartender?"

"Nope."

"That's not very nice. Why not?"

"You don't want to be a bartender. You'd quit in a week. There are other law firms. You'd get work. Maybe Tucker would start his own firm again."

"You wouldn't hire me as a bartender? Not even if I asked nicely?"

"Nope." Nancy smiled and gave Vincent a kiss. "I've decided I'll only hire female bartenders from now on."

"Isn't that discrimination?"

"I think it's just good business. About two-thirds of my customers are men. Who would you rather buy a drink from, yourself or a very attractive young lady who smiled a lot?"

"That really is discrimination! But, yeah, I agree—young women are the answer."

There was a time when all I cared about was money. It felt like I was trapped in a cycle of making money, spending money, and then spending more and borrowing more, and on and on. Then it all went away, and suddenly I felt free. Maybe it's because I've never had the opportunity to make big money again, but I've never fallen back into that trap. I ran a one-man business and more or less did exactly what I wanted. Of course, I never had a family, a wife or a couple extra mouths to feed, but I gave very little thought to money. Now responsibility feels like a burden, but I want to be sure to carry my own weight with Nancy, so if Hill and Tucker have some kind of breakup, guess I look for work. I wonder if the police chief would hire me—nah, that's going too far.

16

Here Comes Da Judge

Vincent was in the middle of his morning routine, combining strong coffee with a weak newspaper, when his phone vibrated.

"Malone."

"Got an emergency hearing set with our old friend Judge Nathanial at one this afternoon. Can you make it?" Tucker seemed to begin every phone call in the middle.

"Sure. Man, that was quick." Vincent was impressed.

"Called in some favors. Something you should be aware of—got a strange reaction from Hill about the dustup at the jail. Just got off the phone with him—someone told him I was beating my war drum. His advice was to let the matter cool off before taking any action. I strongly disagreed and said it was personal. He was not pleased; said we should discuss it later. Vincent, you should know that I came within an inch of telling him to fuck off. Too old to take shit off some smart-ass lawyer who thinks he's a political operative. Whatever I do could affect your new deal with Hill, so if that's really important to you, then you might be wise to keep your distance during this latest crusade of mine."

"If you're on a crusade, so am I. I'll worry about any impact with Hill later, or maybe never. How do you feel about a split with him?"

"Not what I'd choose, but if it happens, I have some options. Another firm in town has approached me about becoming a named partner. My first reaction was no—it sounded like they wanted me to actually work, and I'm not sure how I feel about that. Anyway, if this blows up with Hill, I'll land on my feet. And I'm sure you will, too."

"Who's the other firm?"

"A couple of young lawyers who think a partnership with an old warhorse like me would give them the gravitas they need to become the best criminal firm in the state. To them, Hill is a political whore who doesn't practice anything close to the law anymore."

"Hard to argue with them on that. Maybe it's time we both tell Hill to fuck off." Vincent was feeling better about his life already.

"Could be. It'd be best not to make an enemy of him, if possible, but it might be unavoidable. For now, I just wanted to let you know there might be some changes that come out of this Miller thing. If it comes to that, I'm sure Miller and Stella would switch firms if we asked them to."

"What's the plan for the hearing?"

"First part of the plan is to make noise—lots of it. I'll be asking for a restraining order against Ortega. This will start a real battle. Have no idea what Judge Nathanial will do with that request, but my guess is it won't be much. I think the next step will be scheduling another hearing with Ortega in attendance. What I want is visibility. No more secret beatings. With the court involved, Ortega will have no choice but to back off or suffer the consequences. The emergency part of my filing was because I believed Miller's life was at risk. The judge might view that as an overstatement, so he might not want to do anything immediately, but with some photos of the damage, I don't think the judge can just sit on his hands. If you can run by the hospital and take those photos for us before court, that would help."

"Can do. I know this isn't your style, but you might consider calling the police chief and letting him know about the hearing. He might even surprise you and offer to be there. I really think he's on our side, at least on this." Vincent didn't want this incident to turn into a war with the chief.

Tucker was silent for a moment, thinking. "You're right. I'll do that as soon as we're done here. I don't plan to call him as a witness, and I don't think the judge would want any evidence from him in this hearing, but I'll call the chief and just give him a heads-up about the hearing, in case he wants to be there. Sounds like a good strategic move. Call me if anything comes up. Otherwise, see ya in court."

"Sounded like a Tucker call." Nancy walked into the kitchen.

"Yeah. He's already got things stirred up. There's a hearing at one today in front of Judge Nathanial. Tucker had to pull some strings to get it scheduled so quickly." Vincent was smiling.

Nancy wasn't smiling. "You do realize that sometimes the obvious answer is the correct answer? That Miller shot Benson?"

"Yep, I know. The jail incident has clouded over some stuff we need to know as soon as possible. The big one is whether the gun was Miller's. If not, whose was it? We need forensic evidence, too. Was there GSR on Miller? Lots of questions. I still don't think he did it, but I could be completely wrong. Maybe he did, case closed." Vincent was thinking about all of the information he needed to gather, which was one more reason not to piss off the police chief.

Nancy's expression segued into a smile. "You really enjoy this, don't you?"

"Yeah, I do. You're right, I would have quit that bartender's job within a week." Vincent stood and gave his future wife a hug. "Shouldn't we set a date or something?"

"We're doing fine. A long engagement has some benefits, and when it's right, we'll set the date."

"Not changing your mind, are you?" Vincent sounded clingy, and he hated himself for it.

"Nope. Relax, it'll happen. Plus, what we have now is pretty good."

Nancy gave him another hug, then went to get dressed. After she'd left for work, Vincent headed to Saint Vincent's, the smaller of the two hospitals in town—its name always made this particular Vincent smile. He quickly located Miller's room and spotted a Santa Fe police officer outside the door. As Vincent approached, the officer arose and blocked his path.

"My name's Malone. I'm working with the attorney representing Miller, Peter Tucker. I'm here to take some photos of Mister Miller." He was pleased to see there was actually security in place.

"Sorry. No one goes in without permission from the chief." The cop gave Vincent a blank expression, the kind that says there's nothing further to discuss. Vincent nodded, but kept talking.

"Sure, but he has a right to consult with his attorney, the guy I work for. Why don't you call the chief? I'm sure he'll give his permission for me to see Miller."

"I can't do that. If you want to see him, you have to contact the department and get permission, and after that they'll tell me to let you in. I don't get the permission, you do."

This guy was getting annoying. Vincent suppressed an urge to do something to the guard. Attacking two cops in a span of just a few hours might not look good. He pulled out his phone instead. On the chief's direct line, he got voice mail. "Chief, this is Vincent. I'm at the hospital and want to take some photos of Mister Miller. The guard says I have to have your permission to enter the room. Could you call him and let him know that it's okay? Thanks."

His next call was to Tucker. More voice mail. "The good news is that Miller's being guarded closely by the Santa Fe police. Unfortunately, the bad news is *also* that he's being guarded closely by the Santa Fe police—the cop at the door won't let me into the room without the chief's permission. I put a call in to the chief and left a message. Might want to file something with the court for us to be allowed access to our own goddamned client. I have no pictures so far. Rather than just stand here glaring at the cop, I'm heading over to the police station.

Give me a call."

Vincent glared for a moment, anyway, then left, driving back downtown to police headquarters. The chief wasn't in, and his assistant didn't know when he would be back. Vincent walked over to the plaza, found a bench, and tried to calm himself. After a while he felt more relaxed, and decided to head back to the hospital and wait. His phone vibrated.

"Malone."

"Sorry, Vincent. I've talked to the guard and he'll let you in to see your client now, as well as taking photos. I wasn't trying to stop you, but I was worried about possible danger to Miller for obvious reasons, so I told the guard, no exceptions. Just didn't occur to me that you might be there this morning. Not trying to interfere, just worried about safety." The chief sounded tired.

"Sure, no problem. I'll head back over there. Thanks for calling."

"Talked to Tucker. A hearing happening this fast? He really must have contacts, and not little ones. I told him that if he needed me to give evidence in court about what happened to Miller, I could, but would prefer not to at this point. He said he didn't think it would be necessary. I suggested that the three of us meet tomorrow and we could go over all the evidence we have so far."

"That sounds great. One quick question: have you determined who the murder weapon belonged to?"

"Not yet. Looks like someone tried to file off the serial number, which would almost certainly mean an illegal gun. I can tell you there's no record that Miller has a gun registered in his name. But we can go into that more tomorrow. I gotta run." He clicked off.

Back at the hospital, the guard looked annoyed that Vincent was now allowed into Miller's room, but Vincent just ignored him. Miller looked better after being cleaned up, but he was still a heck of a mess, with bandages and tubes running here, there, and everywhere. Vincent used his phone to take numerous photos from various angles. Miller was deeply sedated and motionless, and his breathing so shallow you couldn't even see it. If it hadn't been for the beeping of the monitors, Vincent might have thought he was dead. Once he had the photos, he didn't linger. As he left, the guard gave him yet another dirty look—he apparently had an endless supply of them.

Vincent grabbed a large coffee from a kiosk in the courthouse lobby and headed upstairs to the courtroom. He was early, and took a seat on a bench in the hall. Ever since he'd become a lawyer—so long ago now—he'd always been comfortable in courthouses. Something about the environment that made him feel safe, even though he was well aware of the injustice often imposed in the halls of justice. It had been a long time since he'd felt sad not to be a lawyer anymore, but he felt it again now.

"Hey Vincent, glad you're a little early. Did you get the pictures?" Tucker had walked up unnoticed.

"Yep, they're on my phone."

"Can you email them to this address? That way the judge will have them to look at before court starts."

Vincent keyed in the email address Tucker had given him, attached all the photos, and hit "send."

"Had a brief conversation with the chief. We have a meeting with him tomorrow. He said the gun looks like it's illegal, no registration. So, I guess the good news is that it's not registered to our client, though the bad news is that it doesn't mean it wasn't his."

"Well," Tucker said, "at this point I'll take ambiguity as a win."

They entered the courtroom, then had a short wait before proceedings began.

"Please rise," the bailiff said loudly as the judge entered. "The Court of the First Judicial District in now in session, the Honorable Judge Walter Nathanial presiding."

"Please be seated," the judge said, arranging some papers, then looking up. "Mister Tucker, emergency hearings are kind of unusual in my court, but your request was both compelling and—I have to admit—intriguing. You're seeking a restraining order against Sheriff Ortega, I see, and you also want your client held in protective custody in Albuquerque until his trial. Your reason for this is, according to your pleadings, a risk to your client from Sheriff Ortega or his agents. Have I got that right, Mister Tucker?"

"That puts it succinctly, Your Honor."

"Well, I've got several problems with this request, but I take the safety of prisoners very seriously. It's my understanding that Mister Miller will be, or has been, charged with first-degree murder, obviously a very serious matter. This will mean that, more than likely, he won't be granted bail, so he'll be in custody for an extended period of time. So, if there's a risk to keeping him in the local jail, other arrangements will have to be made. But I can't simply accept your claim of risk without hearing testimony from all parties, and that will take time. We can schedule another hearing fairly quickly, but not immediately. So, what to do in the interim? First, I'm reluctant to grant a restraining order naming Sheriff Ortega without first having a full hearing. Sheriff Ortega's a public servant, and he has a difficult, demanding job. I'm not going to rule on this matter, or accept any allegation of risk, without some evidence. It's also my understanding that Mister Miller is currently in the hospital. I received the photos you sent, Mister Tucker, and they're very disturbing. The hospital is in the jurisdiction of the Santa Fe Police Department, and I understand that they have guards protecting Mister Miller for the moment. So, taking everything into account, I'm going to issue a court order that Mister Miller is now in the exclusive custody of the Santa Fe Police Department, and that they are solely responsible for his safety. If and when he's able to leave the hospital, the SFPD will not return Mister Miller to the joint-operated county jail, but hold him in their short-term holding cells. A longer-term solution, if needed, can be decided after a full hearing with all parties in attendance. I'll schedule another hearing on this matter one week from today. Is that agreeable, Mister Tucker?"

"Yes, your honor. There was one other matter that I filed regarding our access to our client. It seems that was the result of an administrative glitch in communication, so it doesn't appear to be an issue at this time."

"Very well. I see that the police chief joined us today, so hopefully everyone's clear about how to proceed. I'll just add that the court is very interested in the events that precipitated this hearing. A prisoner beaten while in custody will never be tolerated in my jurisdiction. This may well trigger a full investigation by the state police regarding the operation of the county jail—it's not just going to go away. Court is adjourned."

"I'd say that was a win, Mister Tucker." The police chief extended his hand and Tucker shook it.

"Sorry if this felt like an attack on you. It wasn't intended that way. I'm glad the judge put you in charge."

"I want this resolved even more than you do. A lot of issues are going to come to the forefront because of this disaster, and maybe that's a good thing." The chief gave a weak smile and left.

"He seems like a good guy." Tucker didn't sound entirely sure, but maybe leaning that way.

"I think he is. I also think he's our best chance of finding out what really happened to Malcolm Benson." Vincent knew he needed Stanton's help if this crime was going to be solved. "I was headed to the Crown. Buy you a beer?"

"Sounds tempting, but I think I'll head back to Albuquerque. Is Miller safe?"

"In my opinion, yes. The cop on guard duty isn't friendly, but he seems competent, and Stanton won't let anything happen to Miller. His job is probably on the line."

"Good. Say hi to Nancy for me." Tucker headed out.

Vincent was sure Miller was safe, but decided to swing by the hospital, anyway.

17

Confused And Bewildered

Vincent's phone vibrated.

"Malone."

"Overlooked something. Never got a signed rep agreement from Miller. Nobody questioned it today, but at this point, technically, we don't represent him. It's a minor issue unless he says no. I'm headed back to Albuquerque, but I can email you the agreement I prepared. Can you get him to sign it?"

"I'm headed to the hospital right now. Decided to drop by and see if he was awake. Can you send it to my phone? Maybe I can just copy it out by hand and then he can sign that?"

"That'll work. I'll pull off up here and see if I can figure out how to get it to you. If I can't do it now, I'll get it to you in about an hour." Tucker clicked off.

Entering the hospital, Vincent headed to Miller's room. Once in the hall, he could see there was no guard. He sped up, arriving to find the room empty. He went to the nurse's station and asked what had happened.

"He was moved into a more secure area on the fourth floor," said a very large, unsmiling nurse, who had plainly had a very long day. "I think you have to have special permission to get into that area. You should check with admissions downstairs."

Going downstairs to get upstairs seemed illogical to Vincent, and he decided to ignore her instructions for the moment. He found some stairs and proceeded up two flights to the fourth floor. The door out of the stairwell was locked, with a polite sign asking him to "go to admissions downstairs." God, he hated following the rules. He went down one flight to the third floor and took the elevator to the ground floor.

Apparently, the twin of the nurse he'd just spoken to worked in admissions, and her day hadn't gone well, either. Vincent sighed.

"I'm here to see Mister Miller, who I've been told was moved to the fourth floor. But I need to do something to get access to that floor, can you help me?"

"Who are you?" The nurse's tone suggested that she didn't actually care—he was bothering her, so he was an enemy by definition.

"Vincent Malone. I'm assisting Mister Miller's attorney, Peter Tucker, and I need Mister Miller to sign a document."

The nurse entered something into the computer and waited for a response. "No one's allowed on that floor without approval from the police."

Conversation over, now leave. Malone gritted his teeth. "How do you know I don't have permission?" It was a wiseass response, but Vincent was curious.

"I have a list, and you're not on it." Conversation over, now leave.

"How do I get on the list?"

"I don't know." Conversation over, now leave.

Reviewing his options, including strangling the woman, Vincent pulled out his phone and called Chief Stanton. He got voice mail.

"Apparently you moved Miller into a secure area in the hospital. The hospital staff says I have to be on a list if I'm going to get into see Miller, but they don't know how I get on the list. I'm assuming this isn't some kind of sick joke, so I'm requesting that Peter Tucker and I be added to the list so we can consult with our client. Thanks."

He disconnected, gave a nod to the nurse and left, still debating the more satisfying option of strangling her. It seemed odd that Miller would be moved so soon, and then put in a secure area, without Stanton adding his and Tucker's name to the list of people allowed to enter. He couldn't imagine that Stanton was playing games, and he wasn't incompetent. It was doubly strange, given all the noise in court today. Outside, he called Tucker, noticing as he did that he'd received the rep agreement via email. Yet again, he got voice mail.

"Miller's been moved into a secure area in the hospital and they just denied me access because I'm not on the list, which comes from the police department. Just left a voice mail for Stanton to put you and me on the stupid list. I'm sure I'll hear from him in a bit. Bottom line is that I didn't see Miller, and of course, didn't get the rep agreement signed. At this point I can't even say that he's actually in the hospital, since I didn't see him, but I'm sure everything's okay. As soon as I hear from Stanton, I'll come back here and get Miller to sign. If I don't hear something, I'll give you a call and you can raise hell."

Vincent drove to the Crown Bar. Once seated at the bar in a place that by now felt like a second home, he ordered a Tecate from a very attractive young female bartender, whom he hadn't seen before. He took a long pull on the cold beer and sighed.

"Tough day?" Nancy had walked up behind him.

"Hey. Nice to see you. Looks like you're implementing your sex-sells-beer strategy." Vincent nodded in the direction of the new bartender.

"In business these days, you have to act quick or you'll miss your chance." Nancy took a stool next to Vincent and gave him a one-armed hug. "You look like something didn't go well."

He told her about what had happened in court, followed by his hospital experience. "I don't know if I'm just becoming paranoid or what, but not being able to see Miller sure seemed suspicious. Stanton was right there in court, so to set up a restricted area and not have his attorney on the access list seems really un-Stanton-like." Vincent's phone vibrated and he reached for it. "Malone."

"I didn't order him moved. I know nothing about that." The police chief sounded very upset. "Headed to the hospital right now, should be there in about ten minutes. I'll let you know what I find."

"I'm not far from there," Vincent told him. "I'll be there in about the same time."

"Bad news?" Nancy was holding Vincent's arm.

"That was the chief. He wasn't the one who had Miller moved. Not sure what that means, but it's nothing good. Going back to the hospital and see what I can find out." He kissed her on the cheek and left.

Vincent saw the chief's car parked in the emergency entrance, the door left open. He parked in a vacant spot and went inside. He saw the chief talking to the same large nurse he'd met earlier at the admissions desk.

"Vincent," he greeted him. "Not sure what has happened, but somebody instructed the hospital to move Miller. I just talked to our officer, and he's upstairs with Miller. Miller's okay. We can go up now, and you and Tucker have been added to the list."

"What do you mean, 'Somebody had him moved?'"

"Don't get all excited. I don't know what that means right now. I called the hospital administrator as I was headed over here, and he told me they got a call from my office and were told to make these arrangements. I don't know who did that, but I can guarantee you it wasn't actually my office, so somebody is messing with me—or maybe you. I just don't know, right now. The good news is that Miller's here, and my guard is still watching him."

They got on the elevator and went to the fourth floor, which was different from other areas of the hospital. It was clearly designed to create a secure environment, either to prevent access or to keep people from leaving. They were greeted by a locked door when they stepped off of the elevator, with Stanton's guard seated there outside it.

"Why didn't you call me when they moved you?" Stanton was clearly annoyed, but he kept his tone calm.

"Thought you'd ordered it. Was I supposed to call and say, 'You sure you want to do this chief?'" The guard looked defensive.

"No, of course not." Stanton nodded and smiled. The man should have been more careful, but he wasn't the real villain here—someone had ordered Miller moved, and it wasn't Stanton.

Once past the secure door, the area looked more like a normal hospital ward. There was a small nurse's station, with no one behind the desk, beyond which were several rooms.

The only one occupied held Sam Miller, who waved at Vincent. "Hey, it's good to see someone. I was beginning to wonder what was going on. Mister Malone, I need an attorney, I need help. That damn jail guard almost killed me. He kept asking about artifacts, where I'd hidden them. Every time I told him I had no idea what he was talking about, he got angry all over again and hit me some more. Who runs that jail, anyway? I thought the guy was going to kill me. Now I'm in some kind of prison hospital or something, and no one will tell me anything. What the heck's going on?"

Vincent walked over to the bed. "It's okay, Sam. A lot's gone wrong, but you're safe now. This is a real hospital, although you're in a secure area. You've been arrested for the murder of Malcolm Benson. Do you remember that?"

"Yeah. That was bad. I didn't kill him, though. He was dead when I got there."

Vincent held up his hand. "You shouldn't talk right now. Your attorney is Peter Tucker, and you need to talk to him in private."

The chief walked up. "Mister Miller, my name is Stanton, I'm the police chief. You asked who ran the jail. Well, I'm one of the people who runs it, and I want to apologize for what happened to you. We're investigating that right now, and the guard who beat you is being held in jail himself. We'll need to talk to you about what happened, at some point, as well as what happened between you and Mister Benson. But Vincent's right, you should have your attorney present for those conversations. Now, you were read your rights when you were arrested, but you seemed a little out of it—maybe you were in shock or something—so I'm going to read those rights to you again in front of Mister Malone." The chief pulled out a rights card and read it to Miller. "At this time, I'm going to leave so you can have a private conversation with Mister Malone. Once again, I apologize for what happened in the jail, and I want to assure you that you're safe now." Stanton nodded to them and left.

"Sam," Vincent said, "you're going to need an attorney, and the best lawyer in this state, or possibly the country, to defend a murder charge is a man named Peter Tucker. Who also happens to be a friend of mine. I have a representation agreement you'll need to sign if you want Tucker to defend you."

"I don't have money for some high-toned attorney."

"This may seem strange, but Stella Stratton has agreed to pay your legal fees."

"Why would she do that?" Sam sounded suspicious.

"I told her I didn't think you killed her grandfather, and I explained that if the police thought you did, they would stop looking for who did it—they'd never find the real killer. She wants real answers, so she decided to pay your legal fees as long as Tucker and I look into who might have actually done this. Plus, she's a good person, and she has the money. I think she just thought that, if you're innocent, it was the right thing to do."

Sam looked thoughtful. "She would do that for me? That's awfully nice of her, right or not." He smiled.

"The rep agreement is on my phone, and I'm not sure I can get it printed until the morning, but you could read it and then sign something that states you read it and agree to sign once a printed agreement is available. Is that agreeable?"

"Sure."

Vincent found the document on his phone. He had Sam scan it, then explained what it meant just to be sure. He found a piece of paper with instructions for ordering food, and on the blank back of the page he wrote out a statement saying that Sam agreed with the rep agreement and would sign the actual document as soon as a printed copy was available. Sam signed the statement.

"Do you have a dollar?"

The question got Vincent an odd look from Sam. "Why?"

"You need to give some consideration, some kind of payment, to make the agreement binding. If you don't have a dollar, I can give you one."

"Seems kind of silly."

"Yeah, well, lawyers—you know how they are. D'you have a dollar?"

"Not sure where my clothes are."

Vincent looked around but couldn't find them. He gave Sam a dollar and Sam gave it back.

"Consideration received. You now have an attorney. I'm going to call Tucker and put him on the phone."

Vincent called Tucker just outside of earshot from Miller. He brought the lawyer up to date on what had happened at the hospital, and what he'd done to work around not having a printed copy of the rep agreement. Tucker had Vincent put him on the speaker.

"Sam, this is Peter Tucker. I'll be there in the morning for our first session. I just wanted to go over a couple of things before tomorrow. First, you should never talk to anyone about the case without me being present. That includes Vincent. Anything you say to me is privileged, meaning I can't be forced to tell the police or a judge what you told me. Same for anything you tell Vincent, but only if I'm in the room. But those are the only situations where privilege applies, so they're the only situations where you should discuss anything even remotely related to the case. You want to order lunch, or talk about baseball, fine—you can do that around other people—pretty much everything else, you save it to talk to me. Now, before we get together tomorrow, let me ask a quick question. And you need to tell me the truth—do not lie. If you lie to me, you're going to damage my ability to defend you. Did you kill Benson?"

"No, I didn't. He was dead when I got there."

"Perfect. Now, get some rest and I'll be there in the morning. I'm the best defense lawyer alive, so don't worry. This will work out." Vincent clicked off the phone.

"I'll also be here in the morning. I'm very interested in hearing your story, too. Now get some rest. Good night."

Vincent left. The guard was on duty as he left the fourth floor, and Vincent's thoughts returned to the mystery of who had called, pretending to be the police, and ordered Miller to be moved. Who would even know the hospital had a secure area?

"What do you think Miller will say tomorrow?" Nancy was just getting into bed.

Vincent had been staring at the ceiling, asking himself the same question. "Not sure. But my guess is that he knows a lot more than he's admitted so far. How he knows, is something that'll be interesting to find out. But there doesn't seem to be much doubt that he knew about Benson, and probably a lot more."

"I think it was Ortega who had Miller moved. He would know that the hospital had a secure area, and I think he'd do that just to rub the chief's nose in it a little. No real reason, just to be an irritant."

"Hmm. I think you could be right. It's exactly the stupid sort of thing that Ortega would think was clever. How would you like to be my investigative assistant?"

"Can I carry a gun?"

"Uh, not so sure about that. I think it would be best if I was the only one with a gun."

"Sexist pig, I quit!" She rolled over toward Vincent and

they made up. Later he said she could carry a gun, after all.

I can't help it. I love cases like this where there are so many threads to pull. It's an adult-size puzzle with pieces made from real life. Can't wait to hear Miller's story—there are bound to be some surprises.

18

It's My Story, Not Yours

Vincent and Tucker met at the entrance to the hospital, dealt with the woman at admissions, and got permission to proceed to the fourth floor. The police officer on guard knew Vincent, and had heard the stories about the day before. So, there were no issues, just nods.

Sam Miller was sitting up in bed, finishing what appeared to be a large breakfast. He looked much better than he had even the day before. Food and rest help everyone. Introductions were made, and they got down to business.

"We won't be taking notes today," Tucker said, speaking a little softly. Miller seemed better, but still fragile. "But I'll be recording our conversation. As I've already indicated, this communication, this conversation, is privileged, and no one else will have access to this recording, so please speak freely. Now, the reason you even knew about Malcolm Benson and his granddaughter has to do with your father being killed in 1988 in Cibola County, New Mexico. That obviously led to a lot of suffering for your family, and it also led you to spend a good deal of time and energy trying to uncover what happened. Maybe you could tell us what sort of things you've done to uncover details about your father's death."

"Well," Miller began, "my sister committed suicide about ten years ago. After that, I stopped almost everything else and spent hours trying to find out what happened to my dad. I had done some work on it before, like reading all the newspaper stories and doing some online research. But after her death, that was my complete focus. I was convinced pretty early on that he'd been killed, that it wasn't an accident, because he wasn't a drinker. To say he was drunk and ran off the road was just not likely to be true. My mother told us from the beginning that something else had happened. I talked to several people in New Mexico, and the publisher of the local Grants paper became a great source—don't remember his name, but he was real helpful. He was the first person who told me about the New Mexico State University digs in the area. He was worried that those digs had something to do with my dad's death. He said there was a lot of anger locally toward EPSCO because of the way they were treating the residents regarding the routes of the high-power lines, plus the university people were upset because it was going to destroy sensitive archeological sites. After that, I started searching other local papers in their archives online. The Las Cruces paper had lots of stories about the university, of course, but also a surprising number about the off-campus archeological sites in Cibola County, which is where I got Malcolm Benson's name. He was always mentioned, and there were lots of photos, usually of him and young women. He was a real star at the school, and almost every month there was something that included a reference to him, so I started looking at him specifically. From that, I found out about his family, which led me to his granddaughter and lots of information about her writing career. I purchased an e-book of her novel, *Warrior Ghosts,* and I was shocked that the accident in her book fit exactly with what happened to my dad. But the thing that really blew my mind was that she had details that had never been mentioned in the newspaper reports. And in her account, he was murdered. Of course, this was fiction, but I couldn't really believe that she'd just made it up. The details matched too well. And there was a possible connection, too, because her grandfather was in Cibola County at the time that my dad died." Miller paused and took a sip of water.

"So, at that point, you had done everything either over the phone or online?" Vincent wanted to give him a minute to gather his thoughts.

"Yeah, mostly. I also used the local library for access to old newspapers. I had stacks and stacks of things I'd printed, and I kept a detailed file of everything, but I hadn't gone anywhere or anything like that. Malcolm Benson became an obsession. I decided he was the key to understanding what happened. If my dad didn't die in an accident, then someone killed him, but the question was why. Robbery didn't make sense. Those surveyors wouldn't have anything worth stealing. Hatred of EPSCO was also a possibility, but that seemed like a reach. Nobody likes the electric company, but killing a random, low-level worker just didn't make any sense. The digs, and the artifacts they must have been finding, suddenly gave me a motive. He was killed because he'd stumbled onto something. I imagined all sorts of evil possibilities, and they all centered around Benson."

"How much time had you spent on all this when you reached that conclusion?" Tucker was listening intently.

"Almost seven years after my sister's death. I was still working odd jobs, and I spent a lot of time taking care of my mom, so it wasn't like that was all I was doing. It was all I thought about, but I could only work on it when I had time. But then my mom got worse, and I couldn't deal with her any longer. I found a place that would accept her and that Medicaid would pay for. That was a very hard thing for me to do. I went into a pretty deep depression. Then I got fired from my crappy job, too. I was living in my mom's old house, which she'd given me some years before. I decided to sell the house. Selling the house gave me the money that allowed me to do nothing but look into what happened to my dad, full-time. It became as much about my mental health as anything else. I was probably a little crazy by then." Miller paused, lost in his thoughts.

"Is your mother still alive?" Unnecessary question, but Vincent asked, anyway.

"Yeah. You know, it's funny. I thought I had done this horrible thing, putting her in that old folks' home, but she seemed to actually thrive there. Odd how things work out, sometimes."

"So, what did you do then?"

"I decided I would go to Cibola County and snoop. I wasn't completely nuts. It's not like I thought I was a detective or something. But I thought if I was actually there, I might pick up on something I'd never find by doing online searches. I drove my old car to Grants, and just kind of hung around for a while, mostly living in the car, although once in a while I'd rent a motel room. It was miserable, but it also felt like I was doing something. Got a job at the Whataburger and kind of fell into a routine. Rented a room by the week at an old, rundown motel, and started to blend in. There was an ancient bar run by this old coot named Tank Cooper, place called Pete's. I started going there, just having a few beers, and it turned out Tank was a talker. He would talk, and talk, and talk, and I would listen. After several months, I was a regular and pretty much invisible, just part of the place. It was from Tank that I learned that the university people might have been stealing artifacts. He said that he knew for a fact that they were, and that the stuff was worth millions. I had no idea if Tank was nuts or if he really knew something, but I had a motive for the killing, now. This was also the first time I heard about the Ortega brothers. They were the most evil people in the county, or maybe the entire fuckin' world, according to Tank, and everyone had been afraid of them back in my dad's time, including the sheriff, who was one of Tank's buddies. I never met the sheriff, he'd died in the meantime—Bud something-or-other. Anyway, according to Tank, Bud was not the kind of man who would scare easily. I stayed on in Grants for a few more months, even though I probably had all the information I was going to get. It was weird, but I almost felt comfortable there. I liked the people at the Whataburger, and I'd made some friends. Really unexpected, but I didn't want to leave."

"Did Tank ever mention a friend of his named Jake?" Vincent knew Miller was telling the truth, at least about Pete's and Tank.

"Yeah. How did you know that?" Vincent shrugged, and Miller went on. "Jake died at his country store up by San Mateo. Tank said he was killed by one of the Ortega brothers on account of Jake knowing they'd killed my dad. He said Jake had told him about an encounter at his station between my dad and Santiago Ortega, the younger brother. But when he told me what Jake had said, it was obvious that he didn't actually have anything more than a suspicion. The sheriff said Jake died because he tripped and fell off the front porch of his store, and bled to death before anyone found him, but Tank thought that was bullshit. I was never too sure about any of that, about what was real and what was just gossip, but it definitely put the Ortega brothers on my radar."

"Do you know what happened to the Ortega brothers?"

"Sure, and so do you. One of them is dead, and one is the sheriff of Santa Fe County. Santiago died in a bar fight in Ruidoso not too long after my father was killed. Matias Ortega has been the sheriff here for years. I never approached him, though. Based on what I'd learned from Tank, and from the way everyone in Cibola County behaved at the mere mention of his name, I figured he might just kill me."

"What did you do when you left Grants?" Vincent was keeping Miller focused, trying to get the whole story.

"I decided to go home. I had a lot of leads, and some okay theories about what might have happened, but I was reluctant to confront anyone. By this time, I knew Benson had been fired because of his affairs with his students, and that he'd disappeared. I knew where his daughter and granddaughter lived, but they seemed innocent to me. And I was afraid to confront Ortega. So, I went home. I'd sold the house, and my mother was so far gone that she didn't even recognize me. I hung around a few months, then left again, this time to Oklahoma City; for no particular reason. Got a job at a Wendy's, found a cheap apartment, and just lived. I started drinking, which was a mistake. It was the drinking that led me to send those letters to Stella. That was so stupid. It was because of the alcohol that I made the decision to follow her to Santa Fe, too. In my drunken state, I decided that Benson was the mastermind behind all of my troubles, and that he was going to meet his granddaughter in Santa Fe—I believed the artifacts were in Santa Fe, so that made a drunken kind of sense. I had the names of his two co-conspirators in the theft of the artifacts. I was still doing lots of computer digging. I knew that one of them, who had gone to jail, had just been released from prison, and in my state, it made sense that he might head to Santa Fe as well. And now Benson's granddaughter was going to Santa Fe for a writer's conference that seemed targeted at independent writers, even though she had a big-time publisher, so it seemed odd that she'd be attending. Everything seemed to point to the possibility that something was going to happen in Santa Fe."

"How did you know she was going to the conference?" Vincent was actually beginning to admire Sam's computer skills, and his diligence, though he questioned his stability.

"I followed her on social media, and kept up with her website. It was obvious that her publisher was the one posting the stuff, but there were constant updates, so there was a post saying she'd be attending the conference. That's when I really made a bad decision. I knew she wouldn't talk to me after I sent those stupid drunken letters, but I thought that if I could just casually meet her in a public place, and she could see that I was not any kind of threat, she'd talk to me. It was really foolish, but based on that theory, I went to Chicago and got on the same flight she was taking to Albuquerque."

"Who were the two partners?"

"Oh, right. One was Alex Wallace—he was the one who went to jail. The other one was a professor at NMSU named Patrick Zangari. He disappeared a long time ago."

"I think we need a break." Tucker looked worn out.

19

Paths Of Infamy

"What do ya think?" Vincent asked. He and Tucker had gone to a main floor vending machine.

"We have lots of connections between Benson and others who might have wished him harm. But our client is right in the middle of all of it, especially since he knew so much. How all that fits together, I'm not sure. I don't think Miller killed him. We'll have to get into that next. We need to answer the questions of why he was there, and for damn sure, why he picked up the gun. How about Benson's supposed partners? Do you know anything about them?" Tucker had gotten coffee, and was making a face while he drank it.

"Alex Wallace was the guy who died in Cruces. He'd be a suspect, but he's dead. The other guy, Zangari, I've heard of, but Benson thought he was probably dead, too. If he's actually alive, then I'm not sure I can find him, but I'll try. There's another element, as well. Benson was fired from the university—not for stealing, but because he fathered a child with one of his students. She threatened a lawsuit against the university and they reached a settlement. He told me that the child, his son, had recently contacted him and threatened him. It was the reason he left Florida and went to Las Cruces—the guy scared him. The father and son reunion hadn't gone well."

Tucker stared at Vincent. "Wow. Whoever killed Benson might have done a lot of people a big favor."

"There's more. He came from Las Cruces with his daughter to see a priest, Father Joseph, at the church where he was killed. He thought the priest was still working there, but when he arrived, he discovered the priest had left years ago, and was in retirement somewhere. He said he'd given the priest some artifacts to use in the church as payment for hiding a stash of others. Benson left a note for Stella saying he'd received a call from Father Joseph and was going to meet him at the church. Stella gave the note to the police. Obviously, I don't know if this Joseph person actually called him. It could have been someone else pretending to be Joseph—it had been a lot of years since Benson talked to him, so it might have been possible to fool him. Or maybe Benson just lied. He seemed good at it. In any case, I need to track down Father Joseph, if possible."

"What about Ortega? Have you had any contact with him about any of this?" Tucker was looking a little confused.

"Not directly. I know he's aware of me being in Grants, asking questions about the death back in the '80s, and about him. And, of course, Miller's beating by Ortega's man. He's out there, and he's dangerous, but I haven't discussed anything with the hoodlum." Vincent's adrenaline was kicking in just talking about Ortega

Tucker had paused and was thinking. "Do you think he's telling us everything he knows?"

"You're sensing that, too? No. He's telling us what's safe. He's leaving out some of his story. Can't say why I think that, but I do. Could be some of the things he did were legally questionable, or something like that. But whatever it is, he's holding back."

"Okay. Let's get back upstairs and finish. Then it looks like you need to get to work. The arraignment is in three days, but there's almost no chance of bail, so it'll just be procedural. Still, I want to be as ready as we can, just in case."

"Yep. I've got things to do."

Sam had his eyes closed, but opened them when Vincent and Tucker entered the room.

"Ready to continue?" Tucker was anxious to get going again.

"Sure."

"Why were you at the church when you discovered Benson?"

"Got a call. The voice was muffled, so I'm not real sure if it was a man or a woman. They said Benson wanted to talk, and he could tell me about my dad. Said I should go to the San Miguel Chapel on Old Santa Fe Trail, and he would be there, waiting on me. They hung up before I could ask any questions. I hesitated, of course. It felt like a trap. I'd never thought that Benson would hurt me, but some of the people in this drama, like Ortega, could be a risk, for sure. Like I've already told you, this isn't the kind of stuff I do—tracking down killers and thieves—so I was really nervous. But I went. When I got there, I didn't see anyone. I almost left, but this was supposed to give me the thing I wanted so badly—a chance to talk to

Benson, who I thought knew what really happened to my dad and why. I looked around and then saw the body. My instinct was to run, but I didn't. I knew immediately that I'd been set up, but my mind was in a fog. I was afraid, but I was also furious. These people had ruined my whole family. My sister, the most important person in my life, had killed herself because of these animals. And now they were playing games with me, and they'd killed the man I wanted so badly to talk to. I think for a few minutes I lost my mind. I can't even tell you when I picked up the gun—I don't remember doing that. Maybe I wanted to kill him again, or something crazy like that, I don't know. Within minutes, there were cops everywhere. Whoever called them must have been watching, because it was timed perfectly. I froze, and I'm damned lucky they didn't shoot me. I dropped the gun, which probably saved my life. After that, everything is kind of a blur. The guard beating me was like a dream—or I guess, a nightmare—it just didn't seem real. He kept asking me where I had hidden 'the Indian shit.' At the time I thought he was as crazy as I was. It was only later, after I'd been taken to the hospital, that I realized he was talking about the artifacts. How could I have hidden them? I never had them. It was crazy."

"Do you remember what kind of gun it was?" Tucker inquired.

"No. I'm not a gun person. It seemed small, but it was heavy."

Tucker quizzed Miller some more to get details about the church, the arrest, the guard, and his time in the hospital. After a few minutes, Miller said he needed to rest.

"How did things go today?" Nancy asked as she served Vincent a Coors—her favorite, not Vincent's.

"It was tiring. Miller has suffered a lot, so it's hard not to feel sorry for him, but at the same time he seems to put himself in situations where he's asking for trouble. There's no question he was set up to take the fall for Benson's murder, but by whom? We know some likely suspects, but we don't know how, or why. Someone might well have killed Benson out of hate or greed. There are several people we know who probably hated him enough, and there are likely others we don't even know about. And if those artifacts are really worth millions, then greed is definitely in the running as motive. But either way, why kill him at the church, and frame Miller? I need to get a lot more information and find a lot of people. But, hey, it's a paying job. How about I buy you a beer to celebrate my riches?"

"Sounds good to me, Mister Moneybags. But I don't want a Tecate."

"Absolutely. Barkeep, a Tecate for this handsome woman."

Father Bill Joseph had gone through several transformations in his life. He'd been a heavy-drinking lowlife street ruffian who watched his best friend die at the hands of a competing street gang when he was only sixteen. It was that experience that eventually led to him being ordained as a Catholic priest. He knew in his heart he was a phony, but the comfort of belonging was too strong for him to turn away from. He had almost lost his mind after that dark day so long ago, and it was the priests who'd taken him in and kept him from going to prison, and he'd repaid them by joining their order. It seemed like the thing to do. He had mimicked them and said the words, but his actual faith had been nonexistent. He'd just been exhausted from living on the street.

Time had passed, and Father Joseph had been moved to a number of different churches. He was always polite and dutiful, but not well liked. He would move on in a few years to a new group of believers, never joining their ranks, but feeling safe among them. The stop in Santa Fe had intrigued him. He'd loved the old church, and his flock, who were mostly tourists passing through. It wasn't like the other parishes, where he was supposed to get to know people in some depth and help them with serious issues. Here, he was mostly a tour guide, and he was very good at it.

He'd made every effort to make San Miguel a success so he could stay there, and it worked. He had grown old pretending to be something he wasn't, and eventually he'd started to dream about being able to just be himself. No more Father Joseph, just Bill. It was during this time he'd met Malcolm Benson. Benson was a brash blowhard who had come to the church to research some artifacts uncovered in local digs, west of Santa Fe. He'd been told by some Indians that there were similar artifacts on the walls of the church. Joseph knew a lot about the artifacts that decorated the place. One of his plans involved stealing the art as his retirement fund, and now this guy was talking about *crates* of it, which Joseph suspected could be worth millions. And the thief and braggart seemed to trust the pretend priest.

After much wine, they'd made a deal. For the "gift" of a couple of pieces, Joseph would allow Benson to store several crates in the church's outbuildings. It was hard to tell if Benson actually believed that Joseph could be bought with a few pieces to decorate his church, or if he just didn't have enough sense to be suspicious of him. Whichever it was, Joseph felt like he'd hit the jackpot. Over several weeks, Benson and some of his workers brought in several loads of artifacts. Joseph made sure they were hidden in a place no one could accidently stumble across. Then, he waited.

The years passed, but Father Joseph hadn't heard anything from Benson—or anyone else—about the treasure. He'd sold a few pieces over the years on the black market, enough to buy a mountain home in Telluride, where he turned into William Hamilton, a retired history professor from California. He'd met some locals and let it be known he was writing several books on historical matters, requiring him to be away for long periods to do research. Soon the appeal of solitude in Telluride became too much for him to resist. He'd started selling more and more artifacts, accumulating a tidy sum of money. Then he secured the remaining ones into two large storage crates. He'd debated having them shipped, but eventually decided there was too much risk, so he rented a car and trailer under his real name. It was something he hadn't wanted to do, but he didn't have ID that would match his new name. He drove the goods to Telluride himself.

Within weeks of moving the cache of artifacts, he'd turned in his resignation. His leaders had been shocked. They'd thought he would probably stay until he died, but he had told them he needed time alone to reach a great oneness with his God, and of course they'd said they understood. They hadn't asked where he was going—it didn't seem right to pry. He disappeared, and so did all traces of the artifacts.

During the first year, he was looking over his shoulder constantly, expecting someone to show up and demand answers, but it never happened. He didn't sell any more artifacts—his life was simple, and he had ample money. He was the happiest he had ever been. Alone.

Then the letter came. Addressed to Bill Joseph. How had they found him? It was from someone named Sam Miller, and it was devastating. The writer knew about the artifacts, and knew where they were. He suddenly felt like he was being watched. He had gone from a life of joy to one of fear in a matter of minutes. Who the hell was Sam Miller? Miller even included his phone number. Should he call? He knew his life would never go back to the way it had been such a short time before, unless he took action.

20

Tying Yourself Into Knots

Vincent's goal for the morning was to try to track down Zangari, one of Benson's partners in the artifact-stealing business of long ago. Locating people with limited information is harder than most people think. Zangari wasn't a common name, but if you're looking at a database of millions it can still be hard to pull out specific information about one individual. Especially if that individual wants to hide.

The university data was easy. Vincent made phone calls using various lies to access information going back to the 1980s, when Zangari had worked for New Mexico State. From that he had managed to glean Zangari's first name, Patrick, and a last known address in Las Cruces from the 1990s. Nothing newer—roughly twenty-five years of nothing.

After spending way too much time on the computer without success, Vincent contacted his cyber guys in Denver and agreed to a fee that he hoped he'd be able to include with the legal out-of-pocket costs for reimbursement, then waited. It was an ongoing frustration in his world that there was often not an actual path he could take to learn what he wanted to know except through the mysterious, convoluted world of the internet. If the internet had been a person, Vincent would have punched it in its damned nose.

Back in reality, though, he decided to read the paper some more and have another cup of coffee. It was something to do while waiting. He knew the most likely outcome of his search for Zangari, apart from discovering nothing at all, was to be told he'd died. He was about Benson's age, so being dead, maybe even long dead, wouldn't be a surprise. But expected or not, it would be a big problem for the Miller defense team. He needed someone he could talk to, so he could find out what had gone on years before, and what it might mean to the world right now. His phone vibrated.

"Malone."

"Not sure what I have. Had to make some assumptions, otherwise the numbers are too big. So, you said the rumor was that he moved to California. I isolated California and then focused on the southern part of the state. I have no basis for that other than the fact that, if I was going to move to California, I would go to the southern part. You can see why any result I get based on this scanty information is suspect. Anyway, I came up with several hundred Zangari's of about the right age. The name Patrick didn't pop, so I tried some variations."

Jeez. Vincent's eyes rolled. Just give me the results. Vincent knew the search was the game these guys played, and they could talk about it forever, but he was only interested in the outcome. Still, he kept quiet and waited.

"Best match was just Pat. Best match based on when the name first showed up in California is a Pat Zangari in Van

Nuys. That's a part of L.A. Not the best part, in most cases, but might have been better and affordable about the time you think this guy moved there. Anyway, I sure as hell can't guarantee anything, but I've got an address and a phone number. Phone number is for a mobile, so even if he's moved, you might still get him. Remember, it's about a ninety percent chance that this isn't your guy, just based on my approach, but unless you can give me more data to go on, it's about the best I can do." He gave Vincent the details.

"Thanks, you're a genius." Vincent doubted his own words, but the guy had certainly done far better than he could have. He called the number, got voice mail.

"Mister Zangari, my name is Vincent Malone, I'm an investigator working on a case in Santa Fe, New Mexico, involving the death of Malcolm Benson. Your name has come up as an associate of Benson's at New Mexico State University back in the 1980s and maybe 1990s. Just wanted to ask some background questions if you have some time. Please give me a call." Vincent left his number and clicked off. More waiting, damn it.

Then he had an idea. He called the genius back. "If this is a mobile number, can you track where it's currently located?"

"Yep, for a small extra charge, and it'll take a bit of time."

The genius quoted him a price. It was highway robbery, internet-style, but what else was he going to do?

"I'll transfer the money right now. Let me know the minute you get something."

"I've had it with that son-of-a-bitch. Maybe I should just shoot the bastard. What do ya think?"

Detective Sanchez nodded as if he agreed. He'd learned a long time ago that the best thing to do when the sheriff started yelling about Vincent Malone was just to nod and go to your happy place. Ortega and Malone had started butting heads almost the moment Malone arrived in Santa Fe. Sanchez had been caught in the middle, and didn't like it. Now the top law enforcement official in the county was threatening to shoot a citizen over something Sanchez wasn't sure he even understood. He knew Sheriff Ortega was a violent, brutish man, but had recently come to suspect he might also be crazy. And the guy was his boss.

"Goddamned bastard was in Grants investigating me. Can you believe that? How the fuck does he think he can investigate me and still live in this county?" Ortega was a very large man, a prime candidate for a heart attack, and at this moment his face was beet red and his neck veins were bulging.

"You should calm down, sir. This isn't good for your health."

Ortega looked at his top detective, whom he secretly hated. "Fuck you. I'll calm down when that bastard is gone and I have my county back again."

Sanchez had news that he should have already given to the sheriff, but he knew the asshole was going to yell at him like it was his fault, which it wasn't. When Ortega had sent one of his goons to pound on a prisoner in the county jail—for reasons Sanchez didn't understand and didn't actually want to know about—it had created problems for the whole department, including the sheriff himself. He had inside information that he should be passing along to Ortega at this very moment, but given the man's mood and the color of his face, Sanchez hesitated a moment longer before deciding to take the plunge and get it over with.

"You're not going to like this, but you need to know—the state police are investigating the incident in the jail. They called me and requested that I make myself available tomorrow for an interview. The police chief also called me and said he was meeting with the state police tomorrow and they wanted to tour the facility. And they're going to interview the guard, who's dumber than a bag of rocks—he won't even hire an attorney. Thought you should know."

"Fuck the police chief. What the hell does he have to do with it?" The sheriff looked thoughtful despite his cursing, maybe even worried. He was a dangerous man under any circumstances, but if he felt trapped, Sanchez was sure he would be lethal. Not sure how to respond, Sanchez remained quiet. "I'm going to Albuquerque," the sheriff blurted out after an uncomfortable pause. "Anybody comes looking for me, tell them to go to hell."

The sheriff left, and Sanchez breathed a sigh of relief. He couldn't believe this buffoon was being considered by the Democratic party to run for Congress. *What the hell is wrong with this country?* he wondered. But his phone rang, and he left the question unanswered.

"Detective Sanchez."

"This is Vincent Malone. I need to meet with you to discuss the matter of the prisoner beating in the jail and your loony boss. I know you hate me almost as much as he does, but I think it's in the best interest of everyone if you and I talk. Can you meet me at the Crown?"

Sanchez's goal in life was to reach retirement—just a few short years away—and spend the years afterward with his wife, never having to think about Ortega again. He was risk-averse in the extreme, but something told him there was a greater risk in taking no action in this case than in meeting with Malone.

"Sure. When?"

They agreed on a time.

"I probably shouldn't say this, but there's a chance the sheriff isn't sane." Sanchez sipped his iced tea.

Vincent smiled. "Well, you know detective, there's probably a chance that none of us are." Vincent sipped his beer. Sanchez was probably an okay guy, just one who was trapped in a really bad situation. "He made a serious mistake with what happened at the jail. At some point, that guard is going to take care of himself, and spill his guts to the state police. You know that, I know that, and the sheriff knows that. What's he going to do then?"

This conversation was clearly making Sanchez nervous.

"Why did you want to talk to me?"

"There's a connection between the sheriff and the man who was killed at the church. The sheriff may even have been involved in the murder." Vincent waited for Sanchez to react.

"If it was you that turned up dead in that church yard, I'd already have arrested the sheriff—he hates your guts."

Vincent gave Sanchez a pained look. "Not funny."

"But it wasn't you, it was some guy from out of town. So, why would the sheriff be involved?"

"It goes back to his old stomping grounds in Cibola County. Benson, the guy who was shot, used to organize archeological digs in that area for New Mexico State University back in the 1980s. Benson hired Matias' brother, Santiago, to provide security for those sites. He was supposed to keep people away, and he was also supposed to let Benson know if any EPSCO workers came around the area. There was some kind of local feud between the residents and EPSCO about a high-power line that was going to go through the area. One of the EPSCO surveyors died in an accident out there. The Cibola County sheriff determined it was an accident—he thought the guy had been drinking while driving, missed a turn, and went off into a ravine. But there are folks who disagree, who think the driver was murdered, and in most people's minds, the most likely suspect is Santiago Ortega. Our Ortega, Matias, thought Benson was responsible for his brother's troubles, for the fact that he eventually felt he had to leave, and for the fact that he was ultimately killed in a bar fight in Ruidoso. So, Ortega definitely knew Malcolm Benson, and hated him."

Ted Clifton

"Do you think the sheriff might have killed this guy because of something that happened thirty-some years ago?" Sanchez wasn't buying it. "I know Ortega, and he might kill someone because of his temper, but I don't think he'd kill a very old man over something that long ago. Especially since I don't really see the connection his brother's death in a bar fight would have with some university guy."

Sanchez was a good detective. Vincent hadn't told him about the Indian artifacts, possibly worth millions of dollars, and as a result, the story didn't really hang together. Even so, he wasn't inclined to tell Sanchez everything he knew.

"Well, I only said it was a possibility. They knew each other, and Ortega has threatened Benson in the past."

Sanchez was quiet, thinking about what Vincent had said. "Does this have anything to do with Father Joseph?"

That surprised Vincent. "It could—not sure at this point. He was the priest at the church where Benson was killed. He left a long time ago, but he did know Benson. I think he may have been given some Indian artifacts that Benson found at his archeological digs to display in the church. Do you know what happened to Father Joseph?"

"Not long ago, Ortega asked me to do a special project for him. He wanted to locate the priest from the San Miguel Chapel for the church. He said the church leaders had lost track of him, and had asked Ortega if he could help them find Joseph. Said it was some church-related matter, and they just needed to talk to him. It took me some time, but I was finally able to track him down, and it was weird. He was living in Telluride,

197

Colorado, under a different name. I found him from records of a trailer and truck he rented when he left town. With that, I was able to contact the sheriff's department in Telluride and they helped me out. Once I had an address, I gave it to Ortega and forgot about it. What the hell's going on here?"

Vincent made up his mind. He needed an ally, and he decided to trust the man who'd been an enemy up until now with the truth. "Apparently, Benson and some of his co-workers were stealing Indian artifacts. And not just a few—a lot. I've been told by people who know that the stuff could be worth millions. I think Ortega knows about those artifacts, and he's looking for them."

"Still doesn't make sense for him to kill Benson. It's starting to make sense why he had a guard give Sam Miller a roughing up, though. How's Miller involved?"

"He's the son of the EPSCO driver who was killed in Cibola County."

"Shit. Shit, no. I don't want to deal with this, Vincent. You need to talk to the state police or to Stanton, not me. I'm just a worker, and I don't do anything that might bring trouble down on my head. My whole life I've avoided butting heads with the big boys, and there's nobody bigger than Ortega. You get me involved in this shit, and I could die. Leave me the fuck alone." Sanchez stood and started to say something else, but left instead. He looked scared.

"Well, Mister Malone, looks like your drinking buddy didn't like what you had to say." Nancy brought Vincent another beer.

"Yeah. I may have awakened his conscience, and he didn't like it one bit." Vincent took a sip of beer. "But I'm betting he has more courage than he thinks he has. I sure hope so."

I know that poking the bad bear of a sheriff will eventually end in some kind of confrontation. If he wasn't the sheriff, I'd deal with this head-on. As it is, I'm not sure how to manage the risk, and that has me worried. Sanchez may be the answer, but only if he'll come through. My guess is that he knows a whole shitload of bad things about Ortega, and may even have evidence to back them up. But will he do something about it or not? The other possible angle is Hill. Hill wants the sheriff to run for a higher office, for reasons I sure don't understand, so maybe he could temper Ortega, calm him down—in other words, tell him not to kill me.

21

Bribes and Threats

Malone's favorite tactic was to shake the trees. He knew it was an old, tired, clichéd sort of method, mostly favored by over-the-hill, out-of-touch investigators—but hell, wasn't that him? Besides, it worked. When he'd first started as a private investigator, he'd thought it would be cool to be a modern Sherlock Holmes, though without the stupid hat. He quickly found out that wasn't how it worked. The real world didn't leave handy, well-defined clues, just waiting to be discovered. So, he developed his own style. He visited the places the bad guys frequented, and he bribed people—sometimes, even threatened them. There were quite a few days when he was as bad as the bad people were. But, it was a living.

He called Stella, expecting to get voice mail. He was surprised when she answered. They exchanged pleasantries, but she seemed guarded.

"Arraignment hearing for Sam Miller today. Not much will happen, but we should get our first impression of how the judge is going to lean on the question of bail and the issue of possibly transferring Sam to Albuquerque. Wasn't sure if you wanted updates or not."

"Not really. I guess, Mister Malone, I want to help find out what happened to my granddad but—and I know this will sound awful—I'm not really sure how much I care about what happens to Sam Miller. Is that terrible?"

"No, it's not. You have no real connection to Miller, and you're doing him a huge favor paying for his legal defense. Let's just agree that if anything big happens, something I think you should know about, I'll call. Otherwise, I'll just wait for you to call me, okay?"

"Yeah. That's probably best. I'm getting ready for a book tour since my new novel is about to be released, so I'm pretty busy."

"There is one thing, though." Vincent hesitated, but went on, "Malcolm told me about being contacted by his son, the child from his relationship with a student at New Mexico State. He said the man threatened him, and that was why he left Florida. He said the son's name was Jackson Smith. Do you know anything about that?"

There was a long pause. "No, not really. I heard something from my mother about his affairs at the university, and I think she said one of the girls got pregnant, but even the information she had was more gossip than anything else. Do you think this man could have had something to do with his death?"

"Don't know. Probably not. But Malcolm said his son had threatened him, and that he'd left because of it. For me to try to track down someone named Jackson Smith, who may or may not be a resident of Florida, would be almost impossible. I was wondering if you or your mother would happen to know the name of the girl Malcolm was involved with."

"You mean, this guy's mother?"

"Yeah. Do you know her name, or where she might be living?"

"I don't. I can ask my mother, but she might just yell at me, even if she does know. She thinks my paying for Miller's defense is the dumbest thing she's ever heard. Said she didn't want to talk to me anymore about anything to do with Granddad."

"Sorry to hear that. I'm sure both of you would just as soon forget the whole thing. But if you could help me find a name, and any other information that might help me track Smith, it could be important."

Another long pause. "I'll try. I have to run now." She clicked off.

Vincent thought he might not hear from Stella Stratton ever again. He sure hoped she paid those legal bills when they showed up. He had just resumed his walk to the courthouse when his phone vibrated.

"Malone."

"Located Zangari's phone. This process isn't very accurate, but it looks like the phone is in Las Cruces, New Mexico. Does that help?" Cyber guy had earned his money.

"Not sure. But, thanks." He clicked off and wondered what that meant. He passed through security and immediately saw Tucker in the hall, talking on his phone. As he got closer, Tucker disconnected.

"Hill wants to talk to you. Don't have all the details, but apparently Ortega wants to kill you, while Hill thinks it's probably a bad political move." Tucker looked annoyed, perhaps at Hill, or Ortega, or maybe even Vincent. It could have been all three.

"Not sure I take much solace in my death being bad for Ortega's political ambitions, but I guess it's something. What does Hill want?" Vincent grinned at Tucker, who smiled.

"As best as I could determine, he wants to broker a truce between the two warring parties. All of this, apparently, is driven by his desire to see Matias Ortega run for Congress. Why he thinks that's a good idea, I cannot fathom. Maybe the inner workings of politics are beyond my understanding? But if it was me, I'd be running, as fast as I could, away from the sheriff." Tucker wasn't a moralist, but he was very pragmatic.

"Any chance the sheriff has compromising information on Hill?" There had to be something behind the connection, and Vincent suspected it was something huge. Hill wouldn't tie himself to that piece of shit without a very good reason.

"Who knows? Hill's been rolling in the mud for years, so maybe some of it stuck. This may be the last straw for me. There's no way I'm going to suck up to some two-bit sheriff. I know *real* thugs—this guy's just a goddamned hoodlum."

Vincent was curious as to what the distinction was, but decided not to ask, since Tucker seemed ready to jump down someone's throat.

They entered the courtroom and found it empty. Most preliminary court matters took place in a hectic, crowded environment, where all the participants were scheduled at eight or nine a.m., and the judge would just work their way through the list. Usually, that would have been the case today.

"Well, shit. What does this mean?" Tucker didn't like surprises, especially in court.

Just as he was going to head to the judge's office downstairs, the judge's clerk came into the room. "Appears we have a problem, Mister Tucker. Miller was being transported from the hospital and they had an accident, just a minor one. But during the confusion, Miller escaped." She shrugged.

"Fuck."

"Funny, that's what the judge said."

"Guess bail is out of the question." Vincent knew he shouldn't be tossing out one-liners, but he couldn't help himself. Neither the clerk or Tucker seemed to find it funny, but he did.

Sitting at the bar at the Crown, which suited him so well, Vincent wondered what might happen next. If Miller was innocent, would he run? Well, he might. Innocent people often got spooked by the criminal justice system, and sometimes tried to just disappear, hoping they would never be tracked down. But it wasn't common, so maybe Vincent had misread him, and the guy really was guilty. If that was so, then his failed judgment had dragged Stella into a bad situation, too. What was she going to think about funding a defense for man who might actually have killed her granddad?

"Too early for a beer?"

"Is there actually such a time?"

His wiseass remark was rewarded with a Coors. Not his favorite, but he suspected Nancy was getting some kind of discount on kegs of the stuff.

"So, your innocent man flew the coop. Bet Tucker's not pleased." Nancy was smiling for some reason, maybe just to annoy her beloved.

"Yeah. I'm staying away from him for at least a few hours. He doesn't care if Miller's guilty or innocent—but interfere with his court proceedings, and he gets pissed. All of his well-planned strategies were just tossed out the window."

"I'm a little surprised the cops didn't capture him immediately."

"Me, too. There's something about Miller that keeps not quite fitting into the nice, neat picture we have of him. It's possible I misread him." Vincent didn't look happy.

"Say it ain't so! You? Misjudge someone?" His lovely, soon-to-be wife had a mean streak.

"Yep, 'fraid so. I saw him once being hassled by the cops in the plaza. He'd been in an argument with a street person. The cops let them go after giving them both a warning, and when I tried to talk to him, he ran off. He looked different, like he was pretending to be a street person. I wondered at the time what that was about, and now I'm wondering twice as hard. This isn't New York or L.A.—disappearing in a small city like Santa Fe isn't that easy. If you were a stranger here, I wouldn't think you could manage it. Disappearing requires contacts. But that's what the cops are saying—that he just vanished. I know it's sad to hear this about your hero, but I think I may have been fooled."

Nancy came around the bar and gave him a big hug and kiss. "You're still my hero."

After a call from Tucker, saying Hill was in town and wanted to meet, Vincent went to the La Fonda bar and waited. He debated whether or not it was wise, but he showed up, anyway. He even thought about having one of the massive margaritas the La Fonda was famous for, but thought better of it. He ordered a cup of coffee instead. It was likely to be a sober meeting.

"Hill won't be here," he heard behind him, and Tucker appeared. "He called and talked to me on his way back to Albuquerque. Something came up he had to deal with. He's pissed at me, at you, and especially at Ortega." Tucker was clearly upset, possibly with Miller, possibly with Hill. He pulled out an agreement and gave it to Vincent. "That's the independent contractor's agreement for your investigative services, signed. No one's real pleased right now, but Hill wanted me to tell you that he definitely wants you on his side, whatever the fuck that means. Are we forming teams now? Shirts and skins?" Tucker was obviously getting close to telling Hill what he thought about him and his whole operation.

"Do I want to work for this guy?" Vincent asked.

Tucker looked serious. "Probably. Look, Vincent, we know one another. I trust you and you trust me. That's not the deal with Hill. He can't be trusted, because I don't think even he knows what he's going to do in a given situation. He has no bearings—just does whatever makes the most economic sense at that moment. The only reason you should stick with him is the same reason that I do: he's got the clients and the money. So, yes, you want to work for him. But watch your back. Something else to consider—Hill has influence over Ortega. As long as Ortega and Hill are plotting the sheriff's climb into national politics, that particular pain in the ass will leave you alone. That's not an insignificant benefit."

Vincent debated telling Tucker about his conversation with Detective Sanchez, but decided to wait until another time. "Yeah, that's a real benefit, all right. I'm planning on volunteering for his campaign. Phone calls, door-to-door canvassing—whatever the man needs, I'll be there to offer my support."

"You know you're a real wiseass, right?"

Vincent reached out and shook Tucker's hand. "You're a good friend. I haven't had that many in my life. Thank you."

"What the—sentimentality? I don't need that shit." The old war-horse seemed embarrassed, making him defensive. Vincent almost apologized for upsetting Tucker, but just smiled instead. "We work well together, Vincent. Big fuckin' deal. Let's just don't let this Hill bastard and his pet sheriff get us screwed. So, let's get down to business. What the hell was Miller thinking? Do you think he's actually guilty?"

Talking about murder put them on much safer ground than a touchy subject like friendship. Vincent nodded. "I've been giving it a lot of thought. He could be the killer, but he might just have more involvement than we know. We've already talked about the possibility that he's only told us what he wants us to know, that he's conveniently left out a lot. My guess at the moment is that he's aware of the scale of the money involved, and he wants a shot at it. That's the only thing that makes sense to me."

"I agree. That fits. He told us a partial truth, but not everything. So, what about him pulling this disappearing act? How'd he manage that?"

"He had help—I have no doubt about it—but I don't know who. I never asked anyone whether he had any visitors when he was at the hospital, because it didn't seem relevant to anything, but now I have to wonder. I also wonder if he got his phone back. I need to talk to the police chief." Vincent went on, describing his conversation with Stella when he'd asked her for information about the son, Smith, or his mother. "The more I learn about the people Benson was involved with, the more I get the feeling that Miller's been there before me, several steps ahead. I just don't know what his endgame is."

"I think he fooled us both."

"I wouldn't have thought that was possible," Vincent said, ever the wiseass, but went on more seriously, "Now that we know, though, we can protect ourselves so it never happens again."

22

All Aboard For Destiny

It was late in the day, but police departments don't keep normal business hours. Vincent went ahead and asked to see the chief. He knew he should have called first, but it wasn't far from the La Fonda, so it was a convenient stop.

"Workin' a little late, Mister Malone? Must be a paying client."

"Well, I hope so." Vincent smiled. Under different circumstances he might have taken offense at Stanton's tone, but he had gotten used to the policeman's ways. "Had a couple of questions about Miller, if you have a minute."

"Sure, come on back." Once settled into his office, the chief gave Vincent a serious look. "We screwed up again. You and Tucker must think we are a bunch of morons. There's no excuse for Miller escaping. How it happened is being investigated, and I'll take action to make sure the right people are held responsible."

"Don't punish anybody on our behalf. Stuff happens. The accident seems strangely convenient, but I'm sure you're looking at that. On the other hand, Miller may have been involved in planning it. Do you know if he had any visitors at the hospital?"

"You think Miller arranged his own escape?" The chief looked skeptical.

"I think it's possible. I don't have any evidence of it, but some things have come to light that make me suspicious."

"The accident was a minor fender-bender," the chief said. "The sort of thing that happens every day, given the amount of tourist traffic. Usually it's somebody gawking at some attraction, just not paying attention. Miller was handcuffed. They used zip ties—it's a budget thing—but they hadn't secured him in the van. I fault my guys for not following procedures. They were going a very short distance, and Miller seemed so passive. While they were stopped at an intersection, a car bumped them on the side. They both got out and were talking to the driver when Miller jumped out of the back and took off. They chased him, but my guards said he just vanished. When they got back, the other car and the driver were gone. The whole thing took a matter of a few minutes."

"Don't suppose they got information on the driver?"

"Nope. They described him as an older white guy, but that doesn't mean anything—fits half the tourists in Santa Fe. No name, nothing. They had just asked him for his driver's license when Miller took off."

"How about the car?"

"They knew from the tag that it was a rental. White four-door—they think it was a Chevy. Rentals are pretty common in this town, again because of tourism. If it was a setup, somebody did a good job."

"How about visitors for Miller?"

"None that we're aware of. The only people on that floor were hospital staff, mostly nurses and cleaning people. The way it's set up, our guard wasn't watching that room in particular—he was guarding the entrance to the floor. So, if someone got onto the floor, they could have talked to Miller, and we'd never know about it."

"How about a phone?"

"He was never properly processed at the jail. That's why he was still in civilian clothes. His phone and other items were being held in his room at the hospital. They were put into the van when he was transported, too. We expected he would either be correctly processed into the jail or moved somewhere else, based on the judge's decision. He grabbed that stuff when he escaped."

Vincent almost felt sorry for the chief. It seemed to be one mistake after another at the moment. "What's going on with the sheriff?"

"We're in some kind of truce, or maybe it's a stalemate. He called me and said he'd talked to his guard, who claims Miller attacked him when he put him in a temporary lockup. But Ortega's not demanding anything. We're investigating, but don't have a lot of evidence regarding what happened. Miller being gone makes it doubly hard to prove anything. We have cameras covering most of the jail, but the guard apparently knew there are several dead areas, and that's where he took Miller—whatever happened, that's where it took place." The chief didn't look well. "Do you know why the sheriff might have one of his goons beat up Miller?"

"The guy who was killed at the church, Benson, along with Miller and Ortega, are all connected by crimes that took place in Cibola County in the '80s. It's a long, complicated story, but I think that what's driving current events is millions in stolen Indian artifacts." Vincent wasn't sure what to believe in the big picture, but decided the chief should share in some of the information that he had. "As we've discussed before about Miller, he's the son of a man killed in an accident, or maybe a murder that looked like an accident, back in 1988, near San Mateo. Miller may be avenging his father." Vincent spoke for a while, giving the chief background on how current events might be linked to those in the past. The chief paid close attention, especially when it came to how events might relate to Ortega.

"Do you think Miller is still in Santa Fe?" Police chiefs are, by necessity, mostly concerned with matters directly affecting their jurisdiction.

"I do. My gut says the driver of the car in the accident where Miller escaped was helping him, following a plan, and that all these various players have come together here for a reason. This isn't over."

They agreed to keep in touch. Vincent left, walking back to his car. The night was beautiful, the air crisp and cool, and the lights on the plaza lit the scene like a painting, beautiful and mysterious. The sidewalks were crowded with the usual mixture of tourists and street people. Some were partying, while others were on guard against danger. It was an odd mixture of people attracted to the same place for entirely different reasons, living together while remaining apart. Vincent shuddered, and a feeling of dread passed over him. Time to get home and lock the doors.

As he drove he called cyber guy, leaving a message saying that he was looking for another phone number, this one on a Father Joseph, first name possibly Bill. He said he thought he lived in Telluride, Colorado. And if he could get a cell phone number, could he then locate it? Finally, he clicked off. It was long past time for his day to be over. He was tired and felt like he was running in circles.

"Something wrong?" Nancy was sitting at the small kitchen table, having a glass of wine and working on the following week's schedule.

"Oh, not really. Had a conversation with the chief. Filled him in on the details about Miller. I was walking back to my car and got spooked. Silly, really."

"No, it's not silly. How many times have you trusted your instincts and it saved your life? You've told me about it, and I believe that stuff. You know Miller's still out there, and who knows what else is going on, including the loony sheriff. You need to be careful right now."

"I know." Vincent gave Nancy a hug. "Thanks for understanding."

If they hadn't been so tired, there might have been lovemaking. Instead, Vincent got a Tecate and joined Nancy at the table.

"I can't get rid of the feeling that everything I think I know isn't quite true, or isn't the whole truth. That someone is playing me, and if I could just think clearly about this whole mess, I would see it. The number one suspect is Miller, of course. And yes, I'm pissed because he fooled me, but there's more to it than that. I'm beginning to think he's known all along what was going to happen. Not the details, maybe, but he had something in place—he's had a plan from the start. It may even have included killing Benson. But the real plan goes beyond that. It's more than revenge for his father's death—I think he wants the artifacts as compensation for everything he and his family have been put through. I originally saw Miller as a fairly simple man who'd been badly hurt by the death of his father. Now I think he's both manipulative and clever, and that he's not only out for revenge, but to get rich, too."

Nancy shivered. "It's like he's two completely different people."

"It seems like that, but it's not, because one of those characters is just an act. He's just one person—a single, very dangerous person."

Pat Zangari had become something different from Professor Zangari. Physically and emotionally, he was unrecognizable. He'd spent most of his life trying to atone for his past, and he'd come to hate Benson, who had convinced him that stealing a few unwanted relics wasn't going to hurt anyone. Then, of course, someone died. He had lied to the authorities after everything blew up, and for some reason he'd never been charged.

As soon as he realistically could, he'd left the university and Las Cruces. The law might not have punished him, but he would punish himself. He gave up his career, his savings and high income, and anything else that he felt was poisoned by Benson and by his own bad judgment.

All those years ago, he'd migrated to L.A., which had been like moving to a foreign country. He'd lived on the street for months, learning how to survive in the most hostile environment he'd ever seen. It was a proper punishment for what he had done. With the help of one of the people at the homeless shelter, he'd gotten a job as a ticket seller at the downtown bus station. He'd been able to rent a small apartment, and soon his life consisted entirely of work and home, with almost no interaction with anyone else. He tried to forget the mistakes he had made. He even tried to forget Malcolm Benson, but it didn't work. His hatred for the man grew. As he endured his self-imposed punishment, Benson became to him an evil that might just encompass the entire world. As the years passed, Zangari suffered illnesses associated with poor diet and his new fondness for cheap wine, and any resemblance to the respected professor disappeared. Most people in his new, dark world shunned him while he ranted about the evil that haunted the world—the evil Benson. They thought he was out of his mind.

Even with his increasingly strange demeanor, though, he was considered a good employee at the bus station. He wasn't friendly, but management didn't particularly value friendliness, and he was very efficient. Errors were common among the ticket sellers—but Zangari never made a mistake. He was the perfect bus station employee, disliked or ignored by the people he worked with as much as he was appreciated by those he worked for.

One cold, damp day—unusual weather for L.A.—a young man had come to Zangari's window. He asked where he wanted to go and, after staring back for a few moments, the man finally spoke.

"I want to know why you killed my dad."

It may have been a stroke, or maybe it was just the madness that had always lain, half-hidden, in Zangari's brain, but he'd started to twitch, and eventually fell to the floor. The staff called an ambulance. He was taken to the emergency room at Good Samaritan Hospital. There had been a major pile-up on the highway, and the emergency room was full, so Zangari found himself abandoned on a gurney, unattended. Soon he'd been able to sit up, and he'd left. He had suffered brain damage, but the hospital staff didn't even notice he was gone.

With a clarity he'd never felt before, he'd purchased a ticket at the very bus station where he worked—without anyone noticing—to Las Cruces, New Mexico. He was destined to stop the evil Benson. He didn't know how he would do it, but he would start there. He knew Alex Wallace had gone to jail for selling artifacts because he'd been the contact with the buyers, but after all these years, he'd probably gotten out. Would Alex go back to Las Cruces? Zangari thought it very likely. He had a house there, and most people return home after anything that's intensely stressful, like going to jail. Zangari would keep an eye on Alex, and maybe that would lead him to that devil Benson.

The bus ride was long, much of it passing in the dark. He felt like a warrior headed to the ultimate battle to save his kingdom. He was a hero, bringing retribution to those who'd done evil. He once again had a sense of purpose, the feeling that his life had meaning—something he'd lost long before. He checked his pockets and fingered the small pistol and bullets. He was on a mission for God, and would not fail.

Now his fate awaited.

23

Evil Web Two

After receiving the letter from Sam Miller, Father Joseph made a decision. He would wipe out everything related to Joseph and become William Hamilton, exclusively and permanently. That meant leaving Telluride, though he hated to do it—the place had become his home. But he had no choice. Joseph had to be buried. The first step was to deal with the artifacts. He rented a truck and trailer, and moved them to a public storage facility in Durango. It wasn't completely safe, but better than keeping them with him. Then came the hard part: he had to leave and never come back. He hesitated. He loved his home and his new persona. Maybe just a few more days.

After some weeks of delaying his departure, a sheriff's deputy came to his door.

"Mister Hamilton, good morning." The deputy seemed nervous.

Joseph began to perspire. "Deputy, what can I do for you?"

"Strange thing, sir. We had an inquiry from the Santa Fe, New Mexico, sheriff's office about a resident named Bill Joseph—actually *Father* Joseph. He used to be a priest. They gave us this address, and we checked our records, and this property is listed as owned by Joseph. Now, of course, we all know you've been living out here for years, so the sheriff thought we should check and see if there was something wrong, or if maybe you know this Joseph guy."

Think. Think. Why would that have happened? "Sure, Father Joseph. We bought the house together, but it was put in his name. He's here some, but he travels a lot. He's a retired priest, and he's been traveling in Europe for the last year. He and I go back to seminary—at one time, I was studying to be a priest, myself. The last time I talked to him, he said he wasn't going to renew his phone contract because of the cost, and he was going to spend some months in a retreat at a monastery in Germany. But I'm sure he'll be in touch soon. He's kind of a free spirit, doesn't have any family. Is there something wrong?"

"Not sure. They told us the church was trying to locate him, but didn't tell us why. Kind of strange to drop off the grid and not have a phone." The deputy smelled something amiss, but wasn't sure what he should do.

"Well he's an old priest. Most of those guys are kind of weird, anyway. And Father Joseph was a bit touched long before he got old." Joseph grinned and pointed toward his head.

"Yeah, I've got an uncle like that. Well, thanks, Mister Hamilton. You know you might want to have some paperwork, like a lease or something, showing you have a right to be on the property, just to be safe." The deputy still looked like something was bothering him.

"Good idea. As soon as I see Joseph, we'll get that done." He gave his most innocent smile, and the deputy left. But Joseph was sure he'd be back.

An inquiry from the Santa Fe sheriff's department could mean only one thing: Matias Ortega. Joseph had heard about Ortega's connections to the past from Benson, but he didn't think Ortega knew about his own connection to him. But then, why the inquiry? Could it be that the church really did want to get hold of him? Because that wouldn't be good, either. First things first—he had to leave immediately, and there was only one destination that made sense: Santa Fe. He had to make contact with Miller, and find out what he knew, and how he could be handled. He dug out a gun that he'd kept for years, since his troubled youth, that had the serial number filed off. He wasn't completely sure, but he thought it still worked.

There was a secret room in the San Miguel Chapel. If he could get there, he could hide and watch. The old church had several of these rooms which had mostly been sealed decades before because of structural risks. They had been used as private study rooms in the past, although their original purpose was rumored to have been more sinister. The one Joseph knew about was tiny, and well hidden, with a small, concealed doorway that allowed access from the outside. It also had shuttered openings which allowed anyone inside to see into the church and out to the church yard. Anyone looking for Father Joseph would go to that church, so he would go there and wait. He was sure the current priest, who was young and stupid, wouldn't know about the little room. Joseph only knew because the old priest who'd been there before him had told him—he'd never have found it on his own. If he needed to, he could sneak in and out during the night.

"Any news on Miller?" Tucker was annoyed that he didn't have a client. He was eager for some court action.

Vincent frowned at his phone. "Not really. Talked to the police chief, but he says no one visited with Miller at the hospital—not unless it was one of the hospital staff who work on that floor. But my guess is that someone did get in to see him, and they made a plan for his escape. The driver of the car that hit the police van was described as an old white guy. Lots of those around, but it would also fit a couple of our potential suspects."

"Okay pick one."

"Silly to guess. But we know that Zangari—he's one of Benson's partners in crime—has a mobile phone that was recently in Las Cruces. I left a message for him on that very phone line, but he hasn't called. Maybe he was the driver, maybe he's dead, maybe only his phone was in the state. Father Joseph fits that description, too, but I haven't found him yet. So, we've got two old white guys. Of course, it could have been a young white guy in a disguise."

"Nobody does disguises, except your buddy Sherlock. And, I guess, the 'Mission Impossible' agents. Is that your professional opinion? Disguises?" Tucker had been in a foul mood to start with, and it was getting worse.

"Look, Tucker, I'm not laying bets on anything. We don't

even know why any of these people would help Miller. Or whether they knew him. It could just as likely be some uncle from Kansas that we've never heard of. So, don't get bitchy, I was just thinking out loud."

"Yeah. Well. You're right. I know I'm on edge. Sorry. You know, that relative from Kansas thing actually makes sense. We've started seeing conspiracies everywhere, even when there might be a very simple answer."

Vincent paused for a few seconds, thinking. "The simplest, most logical answer is that a bunch of people think there's a big pile of money somewhere, and they're tripping over each other trying to find it and run off with it. That's the other thing we don't know, by the way. The story about those relics—is it true? Most of the people involved in this case, with the exception of Stella, have a screw loose. Poor old Benson is dead, so I shouldn't speak ill of him, but he was as nutty as they come. I still don't know what's truth and what's fiction."

Tucker spoke. "I agree, there's a lot we don't know. On another matter. I called you because Hill wants you to get started on some new cases. He went over three of them that the firm has going that need some investigative work. He asked me to contact you and get you going on them. Strange thing is, they're all relatively old cases—weeks old, at least. Suddenly, they need your undivided attention? See, there it is again: another damn conspiracy. But doesn't it seem weird? I told him you were occupied for the rest of this week cleaning up some details on the Miller file, and he said okay, but he wants you on these cases starting the first of next week."

"Yeah, the timing seems awfully convenient. But I did sign up to work, so having a few more jobs should be a good thing. I'm not even looking at the sheriff, so maybe this is really just based on the fact that we signed a deal to make things more formal. It wouldn't be the most unusual thing for him to pass me some work right after that, with no conspiracies at all."

"I hope so. I'm losing sleep watching our backs. And I'm old, damn it. I need my rest. Be here Monday morning and we'll get started on these new-old cases." He clicked off.

Despite what he'd said to Tucker, there was no way in hell this was a coincidence. Hill wanted him off the Miller matter. The obvious reason for that would be that he suspects Ortega is mixed up in it somehow. Vincent had been looking in other directions, but this fairly screamed at him to aim his binoculars back at his old nemesis, Ortega.

"Malone."

"Is this the world-famous detective, Vincent Malone?"

"Only if this is the king of bullshit, George Younger. What the fuck is goin' on in Durango?"

"Nothing good, my friend. Word is going around that they the local DA has decided to charge you with the murder of your old chum, Ken Simpson. When and how they plan to go for it, I don't know, but my sources for this are pretty good."

"Fuck!"

"Yep. I don't believe they have any real evidence, though, so

I'm not sure what brought this on. From what I hear—although this is reading between the lines some—they don't have a real case. They just want to put you out of action for a while. And it must be important, too, because this could really bite these guys in the ass later. Someone with real power is pushing for you to be locked up."

Younger was one of the toughest lawyers Vincent had ever met. If you were going to legal war, he was the first guy you wanted on your side.

"It seems to be a common problem, me upsetting the powers that be. I don't think the chief would arrest me, but if there was a legal excuse, then the sheriff here in Santa Fe would not only arrest me, he might just beat the shit out of me while he was doing it. Any connections up there to a guy named Matias Ortega?"

"Not a name I've heard. Of course, in my opinion, almost all rural sheriffs are more criminals than lawmen."

"Yeah, I've seen that pattern. I was thinking about calling you, by the way. I need a hand, if you have time. This is for a paying client, so you can bill me reasonable hours. Got a name and address for a guy who lives in Telluride that I need to talk to. There's a good chance he's here in Santa Fe right now, but I'd like to know for sure. If you could swing by this guy's place and see if he's there, that would be a big help. Be careful, though. This is connected to money and murder. And if he's not there, I'm also looking for some stuff he's packed away, probably in large crates. Indian artifacts, really old relics. That's where this is connected to money. Anything you can find out about the guy would be helpful. Not an open-ended budget, but not tight, either." Vincent gave George the address and Father Joseph's name.

"Catholic priest. A whole head full of bad memories there. Any chance it would be okay to punch this guy a couple of times?" Younger sounded like it would make his day.

"I'll leave that to your discretion. Any chance you might get some advanced warning on them filing charges?"

"Probably not. I have an inside connection, but she has to be very careful—she needs the job more than she needs me. Anything happens, I'll sure let you know."

"Thanks, George. Keep up the good work, Durango is a better place because you're there, even if the leading fucking citizens don't think so."

Home, sweet home. It was an unusual thought for Vincent, but it was the middle of the afternoon, Nancy was at work, there was a breeze through the kitchen window, and he had a Tecate. Why in the world did he ever leave this place?

He was home to think, and maybe try to put together a plan. There was a lot going on, and a wrong step could be very bad. He needed some quiet time to figure out his best course of action, apart from hiding in the bedroom until it all blew over. He decided not to add that option to his official list, at least for now.

There was an intensity in the air that he could feel. Something was going to come to a head, soon. The threats coming from Durango and Ortega worried him the most, but how should he deal with them? He made a note and labeled it *Number 1: asshole Ortega.*

Everything else could almost be summarized simply as Miller. *Number 2: Miller.* But of course, there were a whole host of subcategories under that rubric. Joseph, Zangari, the illegitimate son, and, of course, Ortega once again. And something else had been on his mind lately: Stella Stratton. The thought of her was nagging at him. Did he know all he needed to know?

She hadn't been that upset about Malcolm's death. Maybe that was just because of his age. Someone dies in their nineties; you don't go around wailing about the tragedy of it all. Mostly you say things like, "Well, he lived a good life," even if that wasn't true. He kept telling himself that was all it was, but it still bothered him. Then the money for Miller. Why was she paying for him? Oh, he knew the official explanation, that she wanted the real killer caught, but most people simply weren't that logical—they were governed largely by their feelings, and emotionally her actions just didn't sit comfortably. In a sense he'd talked her into it, but it had been almost too easy. She had plenty of money, true, but most people who had lots of cash didn't give it up very easily. He wrote on his paper *Number 3: Stella.*

After some more thought, he added *Number 4: Hill.* Maybe he was jumping at shadows, seeing conspiracies around every corner, but he had a fair bit of faith in his gut—and his gut was suspicious.

Making the list made him feel better. The beer helped, too. It wasn't an endless list, thank goodness. All the items were things he could identify and, probably, deal with. In a much better frame of mind, he decided to take a nap. The world could manage without him for a few hours, he thought groggily, then wondered if it was such a good idea—but he took the nap, anyway.

24

The Truth Will Set You Free

"Hey, how 'bout dinner? I brought takeout." Nancy stood at the foot of the bed with a bag of something that smelled delicious.

"You're home. It's dark. I guess I slept too long." Vincent wasn't happy with himself.

Nancy sat down beside him. "Maybe you needed it. Nothing wrong with that. Come into the kitchen. I brought home a new steak sandwich we just added to the menu at the Crown. The customers love it."

"It makes me feel old, napping all afternoon and into the night. My god, I'm an old man."

"Stop feeling sorry for yourself. Sure, you're getting older. Name somebody who isn't. It's okay to be tired. You've been going nonstop for days, so relax. I won't tell a soul." She gave him a kiss. "Now get up. I want you to try this sandwich while it's still hot." Nancy went into the kitchen. Vincent got up and freshened himself.

"What's got you so depressed you had to go to bed?" She was one smart, observant lady.

"I'm that easy to read?"

"Yep."

Vincent put on a pretend frown. "It's a couple of things, from Miller to Ortega. But the one that's surprised me is Stella. I was thinking about how all of these things are connected, and I was having trouble fitting some of Stella's actions into the picture. I know this is an off-the-wall question, but do you think she could have something to do with her own grandfather's death?"

Nancy stopped and gave Vincent a funny, ill-defined look that he couldn't read easily. "I thought it was odd that she was willing to pay for Miller's defense. I know she said it was to get to the truth, but that doesn't make it less odd. Also, and I didn't mention this because I thought it made me sound shallow, she didn't seem to grieve too much over her granddad."

"Bingo. That's exactly what I started to think about. But I couldn't get past those impressions to anything that might be a motive. There are obvious reasons: they weren't close, so she wasn't that sad, and paying Miller's fees would help lead to the truth. But the more I thought, the more everything seemed out of whack." Vincent was enjoying the delicious steak sandwich. He gave Nancy a thumbs up as he took several bites. "The other thing that popped into my head was that time when they both disappeared. I know she got a call from her grand-dad, but Miller seemed to vanish at the same moment. It could be unrelated, but I remember thinking at the time that it was another strange coincidence."

"For a fact, she's a bestselling author," Nancy added. "I've read four of her books, and she's great. But it was my under-standing that this conference was targeted at indie writers, and that's not Stella. She's with one of the top publishing houses in the industry."

"Did you ever talk to Cindy about Stella while she was staying at the Inn?"

"No. We've talked a couple of times while all this has been going on, and Cindy never said anything other than that she was really sorry that Stella had this happen to her. Why would Cindy know anything?"

"Not saying she would, just wondered. Think Cindy would be offended if I asked her some questions about Stella?"

"My goodness, Vincent. You know Cindy as well as I do, probably better. Ask her whatever you want. If she thinks it's out of line, she'll tell you so. When did you get so sensitive?"

Vincent didn't need a pretend frown, this one was real. "I guess because you two have become such great friends, I don't want to do anything that might make Cindy upset with you."

Nancy called Cindy and put her on speaker.

"Hey guys. What's going on? Not sure I've ever received a group call from you. Must be something about Jerry, right?" Cindy sounded upbeat, but maybe slightly worried.

"I don't want this to sound like gossip," Vincent answered. "You know a lot of what I do is run down possibilities and check them off my list. Been working on the defense for Sam Miller and looking into all of the possibilities of what happened in the murder of Malcolm Benson—that's Stella Stratton's granddad. One of the things that is causing me some issues is Stella's reaction to her granddad's death, and her willingness to cover Miller's legal fees. Like I said, this may sound like gossip, but I think there may be something I'm missing. I know people talk to you, and I'm sure you must have talked to Stella when she was staying there, so I thought—and Nancy reinforced the idea—that I should ask you if you got anything from Stella that might help me."

"Vincent, *this is Cindy*. Lighten up. And stop making gossip sound like a bad thing. I love gossip." Cindy giggled. "You just want to know if I think there was something going on with Stella that you should know. I didn't talk to her that much. I liked her, but she wasn't here all that long. On the first night, the ladies drank quite a bit. They got a little loud, so Stella went out to the gazebo, and I joined her. She seemed down. I don't know if you know this or not, but her dad committed suicide. She told me that she'd been thinking about him, and about how hard it had been on her mom and her. She didn't say much, but there was a hint that it had something to do with his job at a university, some controversy. That was all she said about herself—she mostly just talked about the Inn and her books. You know, she didn't fit into that group. The rest of the ladies all knew one another, and had gone to events like the conference together, but Stella wasn't someone they knew before this. They were all independent authors struggling to sell a few books, and Stella was a superstar, a bestselling author with a major publisher. They didn't really get why she was there."

"That really helps. I noticed she never talked about her dad, even though she mentioned her mother. I thought it was probably just a divorce. There's an amazing trail of misery that seems to have followed Malcolm Benson. Did she say anything about her granddad?"

"Not that I recall. Like I said, we just chatted that one night. You think she has something to do with his murder?"

"I don't really have a reason to think that, but her unusual behavior has me wondering if there are things she didn't tell me. Probably just some family secret she thought didn't matter. But it feels like Stella hasn't been completely truthful."

"Sometimes the truth can be painful." Cindy sounded sad, as if she were thinking of something specific, maybe in her own life.

"Thanks, Cindy. That really helps me. Say hi to Jerry."

"Vincent, you need to come out and see us more often. Jerry needs someone to talk to once in a while besides me. Plus, Mary still makes extra portions of her goodies just for you, and then when you don't show up, Jerry eats them. He doesn't need the extra weight."

They disconnected.

"I miss them." It was Vincent's turn to be melancholy.

"I know you do. They've been great friends. Why don't we ask them out to dinner tomorrow? That would be fun." Nancy gave Vincent another hug.

It was early, but Vincent called, anyway.

"Yeah." Obviously cyber guy had been asleep.

"Sorry to call so early. Do you want me to call back?"

"My god, Vincent, it's six a.m. Jeez, man, I am emphatically not a morning person. What do you want?"

He reminded himself he needed cyber guy, and to be polite. "Got an oddball request. Maybe not something you can do, but if anyone can, it's you."

"Okay, fine. I'm not mad. I'm awake. What do you want?"

"Sometime in the late '80s or early '90s, a man named Malcolm Benson was fired from New Mexico State University because he had an affair with one of his students. I think the student's last name was Smith, and she was pregnant. The university settled with the student so she would keep quiet. There was some kind of agreement, maybe even filed somewhere. The child's name is Jackson Smith, and he may or may not live in Florida. I need to know her name and where she is today. And, if possible, a phone number for Jackson Smith."

There was a long pause. Then uncontrollable laughter. It went on for quite a while, then segued into choking and coughing, as the man laughed too hard for his own good. A moment later, it sounded like he was crying. Vincent debated hanging up. Maybe the guy had suddenly gone crazy.

"Dude, I know you live in your own bubble, but sometimes you seem to live in a completely separate universe. Do you know how impossible that is? Smith? Do you know how many Smiths there are? A deal with a university that may or may not be filed? That might be stuffed in a file cabinet in the basement of the administration building with thirty years of cobwebs? I don't do breaking and entering." There was silence. At least he'd stopped crying. "Look, this is a waste of my time, but if you're willing to pay, even knowing that the chances of me getting something are very close to zero, then send my usual retainer, and I'll see what I can do."

Vincent said thanks and hung up. The guy could have just said to send money in the first place, without all the hysterics. He retrieved the newspaper and got a cup of coffee, found the sports section and checked for any news on the Rockies. He missed the Denver paper, with its local focus on hometown sports teams. He'd debated several times about a trip to Albuquerque to see the Rockies' AAA affiliate play, but so far, he hadn't gone.

"What do you think about me asking the Olivers to have dinner with us at the Crown? I know it's my place, not some fancy-fancy restaurant, but it sure would be convenient—at least for me." Nancy was wearing a very attractive robe over her very attractive body, Vincent noticed. Nancy noticed him noticing, and blushed. "Hey, what's with you ogling your soon-to-be spouse? Somethin' in that coffee?"

"Just noticing how lovely you are, even early in the morning."

Nancy showed her appreciation with a curtsy and kiss. She smiled as she went to get herself a coffee. "What's on your agenda today?" she asked, sitting down and taking the *Living* section of the paper.

"Got some calls to make. Need to keep shaking those trees. Might go by and see if the chief will talk to me. Nothing really important. Sort of feels like I'm waiting on the next shoe to drop. I fully expected the cops to recapture Miller. But now, after this much time, I'm thinking he's really well hidden or long gone. So, the whole case could just dry up. But something tells me there's still more to come."

"You didn't answer my question about dinner with the Olivers."

"Sure. I love the Crown. That's perfect for me, and I bet that suits them, too."

Nancy went into the bedroom to get ready, and Vincent heard her talking to Cindy about dinner. He returned to his sports section and was reading the basketball scores, something he didn't actually care about, when Nancy came back into the room dressed for work.

"Cindy said that sounded great about tonight. Something else she wanted me to tell you. She's not real sure, but she thought she saw Stella here in town, around the plaza, day before yesterday. She said it was just a glimpse of someone, but she sure thought it was Stella."

Vincent stopped reading the paper. "What would she be doing here?"

"How would I know? You're the detective."

She shared some of Vincent's wiseass ways, but she was lovely all the same.

25

It Happens All The Time

Zangari arrived in Las Cruces and immediately felt afraid. It had been a long time since he'd been back to the place where the evil had begun, and it frightened him. The bus station was downtown, but it was a small city, so everything was fairly close. Still, if he wanted to go all the way to campus, he would need a cab or a car. Even a little activity outside his normal routine made him dizzy. He found an empty bench inside the bus station to rest. He'd spent a lot of time in bus stations, so it was comforting. His memory had been all fogged up for the past few days, but now, as he sat, he thought about the young man who had spoken to him—who'd asked him why he had killed his dad. But he hadn't killed anyone. He had to be talking about the man who died in the mountains, the one who was killed by the motorcycle goons. Benson had said it didn't matter, that it had nothing to do with them. But it did.

He was going to find Benson. The man had to pay for all of the grief his sins had caused. But first he would find Alex Wallace. Alex was a gentle man whose mistake was getting mixed up with the scheming Benson. Patrick trusted Alex. He had his old address book from years ago. He'd clung to a few things like that—they helped him feel a little less adrift and disoriented in the chaos after his time with Benson. It contained the phone numbers for all his old friends all those years ago, from a time he'd still been somebody. Patrick smiled as he flipped through it—page after page of old friends.

He looked up Alex Wallace. More than thirty years had gone by, but he knew Alex would still be there. He was always so cheap—he'd be in that same small house forever. He pulled out his wallet and counted his money. Not much. He sat wondering what he should do, then decided to spend a little money to take a cab to Alex's house. He was sure Alex would let him stay there, and he could get something to eat. He felt something like relief at the prospect.

There were two cabs parked in front of the station. He showed the address to the first driver and asked how much. The guy looked at him like he was nuts. "Shit, man, that's not far. Say, fifteen, plus tip."

Without a word, Zangari walked to the next cab and went through the same drill. "Not far. How 'bout ten bucks, including tip?" Zangari smiled and got in. It was a short drive, but would have been a pretty long walk. As he watched the cab drive away, he wondered if he should have asked the driver to wait. He shrugged, went up the steps and rang the bell. A middle-aged woman opened the door.

"Can I help you?"

"Yes. I'm looking for my friend, Alex Wallace. This is his house, isn't it?" Zangari hadn't realized how tired he was, and he wobbled a bit on his feet.

"How do you know Alex?"

"We used to work at the university together. A long time ago."

Her expression softened. "Are you okay?"

"Oh, it's just been a long day. Or a long couple of days, really. Maybe if I could get a glass of water?"

"Sure. Do you mind sitting on the front porch? I'll be right back with water."

"No. I don't mind. Sitting is something I do real well." He gave her a smile. She smiled back.

She was back in just a few minutes with a glass of ice water. Patrick took a long drink. He smiled at her and took another.

"What is your name?"

"Patrick Zangari."

"Well, sure, I remember my dad talking about you when I was a kid. My goodness, where did you come from?"

"California."

"Did you come for the funeral?"

"No." He looked at her. "Whose funeral?"

"Alex's. Didn't you know?"

Zangari closed his eyes and passed out. When he awoke, he was on a couch inside the house. He tried to get up.

"You should just stay down. I don't think you're ready to get up." It was the woman from the porch.

"I'm really sorry. It's probably been a couple of days since I had something to eat. But I should go now. I'm so sorry about Alex. Are you related to him?"

"Yes. I'm his daughter, Doris. Look, just lie back down. I

have some chicken soup heating and crackers ready. You should eat and you'll feel better."

Zangari smiled and lay back down. "How did I get inside?"

"My neighbor helped me. I thought about calling an ambulance, but I decided if you were basically just hungry, I could fix that myself." She smiled. "Why are you here?"

"A man I didn't know asked me why I killed his father. It was so strange, but I knew who he meant—he was talking about a man who was killed in San Mateo. I wanted to talk to Alex and find out where Malcolm Benson was. I guess I was afraid."

Doris looked at Zangari with sympathy. "They're both dead. Alex died of a heart attack when Benson was still here, and Benson was shot in Santa Fe. The police don't know yet who did it."

There was a long pause as Patrick sorted through the unexpected information. "Maybe it's best. Malcolm wasn't a good man. But I'm sorry I wasn't able to see Alex again. He was a good friend."

Doris smiled.

Vincent's phone vibrated as he was getting into his car.

"Malone."

"Malone, this is Detective Sanchez. Any chance we could get together for a cup of coffee this morning?"

"Only if you're buying."

"Deal. Know where Kari's Coffee is?"

"Yep."

"Say about fifteen minutes?"

"I'll be there." He wondered about his last conversation with Sanchez, and his attempt to shame him into doing something that might help put the brakes on the out-of-control sheriff. Was this going to be a report on what he did, or just a friendly way of delivering the latest order from the sheriff telling Malone to get the hell out of Dodge?

Kari's was a small coffee shop, mostly catering to locals rather than tourists, on Johnson Street, not far from the Georgia O'Keeffe Museum. When you entered, the aroma of coffee and their special scones was almost beyond words. *This place is worth visiting just for the fragrances,* Vincent thought. He wasn't a coffee snob—for the most part, McDonald's coffee was just fine for him—but he had to admit that at this moment he really wanted some of that great-smelling coffee and one of those scones. He spotted Sanchez.

"Didn't figure you for a Kari's type." There was an insult buried somewhere in Vincent's words.

"Only when I have time and good company." Sanchez smiled, but Vincent went on alert.

What the hell was this? Sanchez being friendly? Maybe some of his deputies were going to jump Vincent and toss him into the infamous jail. He made himself smile. "Okay, what's going on?"

"Get your coffee. Just have a couple of things I wanted to go over with you."

Sanchez seemed open and relaxed, not at all normal for him. Vincent got a cup of coffee, but skipped the scone. The young woman at the register indicated that Sanchez— "that man sitting over there," she said, with a toss of her hair—had already paid. He took a seat.

"First," Sanchez began, "I quit the sheriff's department, as of yesterday. I've taken a job with Santa Fe Police. I'll be handling community outreach and major crimes investigations. There's lots we need to talk about related to that, and about how it might affect your dealings with the sheriff. But first, the chief asked me to give you an update on the Benson killing and the Miller escape."

Vincent was stunned. This wasn't at all what he'd been expecting.

"You quit? Not fired, but quit?"

Sanchez nodded. "First, the Benson matter. We got some forensics back. Benson wasn't even shot with the gun Miller was holding—it hadn't been fired at all. And there were no powder burns on Miller. So, if we still had Miller in custody, we'd probably be releasing him this morning." Sanchez paused and sipped his coffee. "Benson was killed by a small-caliber gun, with a direct hit to his heart. We believe he was shot at very close range, so most likely it was someone he knew, or at least trusted. He died instantly. We have some fibers and partial shoe imprints, both male and female. We've searched the church with a full team, and we found several rooms the resident priest didn't even know were there. Apparently, they haven't been used for years, except for one. A very small room with access to the outside had recently been occupied. We don't believe that someone could just stumble across these little hidey-holes, so whoever was there most likely had some kind of connection with the church. That has led us to think we need to question Father Joseph, except we haven't been able to locate him. He was in Telluride, living under an alias, but now he's disappeared. We're treating him as a suspect, and we'll be issuing an alert on him as a person of interest in the Benson murder. We're still doing research, but we believe it's possible that Joseph and Benson knew each other in the past. We know from his granddaughter, and from the current priest, that Benson had come to the church looking for Father Joseph. One more bit of news related to this. We've gotten calls in the last few days from Stella Stratton's mother and her publisher, both saying she seems to have disappeared, asking for our help locating her. We believed she had left Santa Fe and returned home, but it looks like that might not be right, although we have no leads on where she might be."

"What's with the information dump?" This was a gift horse, and Vincent was a cynic, so he was going to examine its dental work in minute detail.

"My previous employer thought you were scum and should be run out of town. My current employer thinks you're a community asset and, within reason, should be kept in the loop. I'm still not sure what I think." Sanchez looked genuinely confused.

Vincent had to laugh. "Well, welcome to the light side. You're going to be much happier." He was still trying to absorb what he'd just heard. This changed everything. "Will Miller be charged with his escape?"

"Not sure. The chief said he was going to talk to the DA. I'd think there's a deal we could work out if he'd just come forward and give himself up. I'm not here to negotiate that, it's just my opinion. The whole thing was a screw-up, and Miller has some pretty serious claims against the county and city, so most likely there's a way for this to be forgotten and everybody just walks away—including that meathead of a jail guard."

"Well, that might be best. Any idea whose gun Miller was holding?"

"None. It's old, might not even work. The serial number was partially removed. The biggest problem is the age, though. It goes back into a time when the records weren't very good. Even if we had a serial number, we're not sure we could trace it. I don't think we'll ever know who owned it."

"So, who killed Benson?"

"Hey, you're the big-time investigator. I should ask you."

"Ah, but I asked first."

"Easy answer: we don't know. Miller would still be a suspect, but how do you explain him killing with one gun, which we can't find, and then he's standing over the body with another gun by the time the police arrive? Not sure there's any scenario that fits that set of facts. So maybe he's still on the list, but at the bottom. Stella Stratton's disappearance might put her on the list, but we don't have any motive for her to want her grandfather dead, so that looks like a reach. Father Joseph is involved some way, but we have nothing at this point to link him to the crime itself. Of course, there's that ol' policeman's standby: it was a random killing by someone unknown, most likely a deranged homeless guy."

They both chuckled.

"Round up the usual suspects!" Vincent left Kari's without a scone, but with the feeling that it was something of a new day, and there was a fresh spring in his step. He pulled out his phone—and got Miller's voice mail, of course.

"Sam, this is Vincent. Look, there's a really good chance that if you turn yourself in to the police that all charges will be dropped, including anything to do with the escape. You need to contact me or Tucker. Don't do anything stupid, because this is your chance to get out of this mess. The gun you were holding didn't kill Benson. If you hadn't escaped, they'd be releasing you right now. Please give one of us a call and let's get a deal worked out."

He called Stella—more voice mail. "Stella, I don't know what is going on, but people are looking for you—your mother and publisher, for starters. They contacted the police here. Miller is in the clear. The gun he was holding was not the murder weapon. Please give me a call. If something's wrong, I can help."

He called Tucker—and surprise, surprise, got voice mail. Apparently, nobody answered their phones anymore. He filled the lawyer in on the details he'd learned from Sanchez, including the bombshell that Sanchez had quit the sheriff's department and now worked for SFPD.

Now he waited, an investigator's most frequently used—but least discussed—skill, and not one of Vincent's strong suits. In the past, he would spend the time getting drunk. Instead, he headed toward his favorite bar for an iced tea, smiling all the way.

26

It's True, Believe It Or Not

"Mister Malone, this is Stella. I'm sorry about all of this. I haven't been completely truthful, but I had nothing to do with my granddad's death. I don't know who did it, though I know it wasn't Sam. I have a lot to explain, I guess. I'm in Santa Fe. Call me back and let's talk."

Vincent had gone to the restroom and left his phone on the bar. Great—now someone had called and left *him* a voice mail. He listened, then called back immediately. *Please answer.*

"Yes."

"Stella? This is Vincent. We definitely need to talk. Where are you?"

"I'm with Sam. We're staying at the Hotel Chimayo de Santa Fe, just off of the plaza on Washington Street. Do you know where that is?"

"Sure. You know, that's like hiding in plain sight." With Sam? What was going on?

"Maybe it wasn't the best place to hide, but no one's found us." There was a hint of defiance in her voice.

"Can you meet now?" Vincent wanted answers. What the hell was this "we" and "us" stuff?

"Sure. There's a bar inside the hotel, in the front. We'll be there."

She clicked off. What the fuck? They were "hiding" in an upscale hotel just a block from the Santa Fe Police Department headquarters? How bizarre is that? Of course, it was the very last place anyone would look. Smart or stupid? Vincent wasn't sure. He left the Crown and decided it would be quicker just to walk the few blocks to the hotel.

He entered the hotel bar and spotted Stella and Sam, sipping beer, looking for all the world like tourists. Perfect camouflage in a town full of them.

"I'm glad you're both okay. I had all kinds of wild theories about what might have happened to you." Vincent's greeting seemed to reassure them he was on their side, whatever side that was.

Stella looked at Sam and they seemed to come to some conclusion.

"I'm going to tell you my story first," she began. "I lied to you about me leaving Santa Fe. That's not what happened. I was sad, very angry, and didn't want to see or talk to my mother. I sort of faked my departure, and instead checked into this hotel. No plan. Just wanted to be alone for a while. Probably could have just told everybody to leave me alone, but instead I hid from everyone. Then Sam escaped, right down the street. He had his cell phone in the bag from the police van. He called me and asked if I would help him—he had no idea I was hiding out. I couldn't decide what to do. I know I should have hung up and called the police, or called you or something, but

I didn't. I said I'd help. Probably broke the law in some way, but what I was thinking was just that he needed help. I'd thought about him and his father and my granddad a lot—about who was really to blame and who just made some mistakes. I was sure he hadn't killed my granddad. If he had, he wouldn't have just stood there with that gun. Something else happened. So, I made the decision. I asked him where he was, and it turned out he was almost directly in front of the hotel. I gave him my room number and he came up."

Stella straightened and took a sip of her beer, all to gather her thoughts. Vincent waited. She continued, "It was awkward at first. We hadn't exactly been enemies, but we'd been pretty close to it. He said he called me because he didn't have anyone else and I had offered to pay his legal fees, so he thought I must believe him. From there he began telling me his whole story. The horrific consequences to his family and how it all became an obsession. The more I listened, the more convinced I was that my wonderfully eccentric granddad had done some really evil things. I wished I could believe that those things had happened for other reasons, but it became clear that Malcolm was partially, if not totally, at fault. I listened to all of the work Sam had done, hiding and observing, selling his mom's house to have money to pursue his quest. Somewhere in our conversation, it also became clear to me that he thought the money should be his, that those relics were his by right because of the suffering he and his family had gone through. We disagreed about that, but I knew I was going to help him, anyway."

"Stella," Vincent interrupted, "I don't want to break into

your story, but there's something that's really been bothering me. Your dad committed suicide because of what happened at the university. Why didn't you hold your granddad responsible for that?"

"Suicide? My dad? No, that's not right. My mom and dad are divorced, and he lives in Ohio. Why did you think he committed suicide?"

"The first night you were at the Blue Door Inn you told Cindy Oliver that your dad had committed suicide."

"No, I never said that. Well, who the hell knows what I might have said? I got pretty drunk that night. But I wouldn't have said that. I think I said something about it was like a suicide in my family when my parents got divorced, and that had happened because of his being fired from the university. But the firing had nothing to do with my granddad, it was because of changes they were making in their master's degree programs. My dad was just the odd man out. He had a great recommendation and got a job at a small college in Columbus. My mother didn't want to live in Columbus—she wanted to go back to Chicago, her hometown. They fought and fought, and eventually divorced. Cindy just misunderstood what I said when I was drunk. My granddad was a big pain in the butt to my family, but I loved the old goat."

"This may come off as super rude, but you didn't seem all that upset when he was killed."

"Sounds like you think *I* might have shot him. We all grieve differently. But mostly, it was just that I knew he only had a few weeks to live. He told me what his doctors had said in Florida. I'm sure all this traveling around and reaching into the past had something to do with his health, but you can't feel too bad for a man in his nineties who was weeks away from dying. I was upset it happened that way, but I was glad it was over for him."

"Did you have anything to do with Sam's escape?"

"No, she did not." Sam jumped in. "I told you they'd think that," he said to Stella, then turned back to Vincent. "Nobody helped me. As far as I know, that car running into the van was nothing more than an accident. I sure didn't arrange anything. When it happened, I just made an impulsive decision to run. Over the years, I've become pretty good at adapting to whatever environment I needed to. Years of investigating my dad's death had given me lots of experience at hiding. But as soon as I hit the street, I knew that in this situation I was going to need help. I shouldn't say this in front of Stella, but I was also attracted to her. I know she's gorgeous and I'm skinny and bald, but even bald men can dream. I needed help and I wanted to see her, so I called. I didn't know that she was supposed to have left Santa Fe. As far as I knew, she was still here—and she really was, as it turned out."

"Do you know where the artifacts are?"

"No. Strange, isn't it? I've spent years learning the story of my father's death in amazing detail, but I've never been able to find the treasure. When I started, this was a righteous quest to uncover the truth, but the last few years have really been just a treasure hunt. Stella's right. I was rationalizing, deciding that the money belonged to me. It's not money, they're cultural artifacts, and they don't belong to anyone except the Indians. Stella's helped me see that I was wrong."

"You must have made some guesses as to where it is."

"Oh, sure. It was clear to me pretty early that Benson didn't have it. I'd watched him on a couple of occasions in Florida, and he wasn't living in luxury. Based on some bar gossip, it seemed evident without various women helping him, he would have starved to death years ago. Alex didn't seem likely, either. He went to jail, and I think Benson promised he'd get some money when he got out. I got to know one of the BIA agents who worked Alex's case, and he told me—after many drinks—that was what they thought. If that was true, then at one time Benson knew where the loot was, but he had either forgotten or it had been moved. My best guess as to who has the treasure would be one of three guys: Father Joseph, Patrick Zangari, or Matias Ortega."

"Do you know where Zangari and Joseph are now?"

"Nope. I made contact with both of them recently. I sent a letter to Father Joseph in Telluride. I'd discovered the connection with the church, that Benson had given them some of the artifacts. He actually bragged to the local Las Cruces paper about what he called his 'donation to the church.' Since the priest had left town, I thought he might have needed to rent a trailer. It cost me some big bucks and a large bar tab for the rental clerk, but I got a copy of the record of his rental, which listed a destination in Telluride. After some more snooping, I found out he was using a new name."

Vincent was impressed by the results Miller had gotten.

"What about Zangari? No one knew where he was, as far as I can tell."

"Just luck, mostly. I called and talked to a lot of people at NMSU over the years. Actually got to know one lady a little, though this was all over the phone. I told her I was doing research for a book about the archeology digs in New Mexico, and she seemed to buy it. Anyway, while I was talking to her, gathering information about Benson, she casually mentions that Zangari must be in Los Angeles because they received a job reference request some time ago from the Union Station Greyhound bus personnel office. Just dumb luck that she mentioned it to me. I didn't do anything about it just then. But not long ago, after I talked to you, I decided I should try and contact Zangari. The only contact information I had was that bus station reference, so I flew to LA from Albuquerque and went to the station. He was there, selling tickets. I wouldn't have known him if I hadn't been looking for him. I'd seen pictures in the paper, but he looked like a completely different person. Very creepy-looking. But there were name plates for all the ticket sellers, so I could tell it was him. I walked up to him and asked why he'd killed my dad. Stupid thing to do, but that's what I did. He fainted or had a stroke or something, and I ran out of there and got on the next flight back to Albuquerque. When I got to Santa Fe, my money was getting low, so I decided to hide on the street. I'd lived on the street before. I saw you once around then, and took off. I was feeling down at that moment, and I really didn't want to be interrogated." He paused, looking sad. "I thought the things I did would drive them both here, Joseph and Zangari. I believed the artifacts were hidden somewhere around Santa Fe, and that stirring the pot would bring them here and lead me to it, but I haven't seen or heard from either of them."

"What happened that night when Benson was killed?"

"I know you probably won't believe this, but what I told you and Mister Tucker was the truth—as far as it went. I never saw whoever did it. I saw the body, and when I walked up to look closer, I picked up the gun—by reflex, I guess. Then, in a matter of seconds, the cops were there. I still have no idea who called me and told me to go to the church. My first guess was Joseph, but I had no idea who it was."

"I haven't asked, but I'm assuming you're okay with the idea of working out a deal with the authorities to end this latest little problem."

Vincent didn't want to inadvertently end up giving the guy legal advice—since he no longer practiced law, that would be a big no-no—but Miller really needed to jump on this. Fighting the system has a long history of being more trouble than its worth, and at the moment he had the system right where he wanted it—ready to negotiate.

"Yeah, of course. I just want to leave and not have to look over my shoulder for cops all my life."

"The police are ready to make a deal, and I'm sure the DA will go along with it. To be clear, this isn't them being all kind-hearted. It's because of the beating. You can sue their asses off, if you want. But that would take years, and a lawsuit is never, ever a sure thing, no matter how good things look at the outset. If you're ready, we should contact Tucker and get this done. The police will still want you to make a statement about any involvement you had with Benson. They have some good detectives, and they know about some of the past problems. My guess is that they know about the missing artifacts, so they could ask you some pretty detailed questions."

"I'm ready."

Vincent called Tucker, got his voice mail, and left a message regarding the deal the SFPD was proposing, which would clear Miller of any charges and bring no new charges for his escape.

"You guys aren't going to run, are you?" Vincent thought he knew pretty much the whole story now, except for the two biggest questions of all. Who killed Benson? And where were the millions in stolen artifacts? He didn't want Sam or Stella to be linked to either of those issues, mostly because he liked them, and would end up hating them if they tricked him again.

It was Stella who spoke up. "We'll stay in Santa Fe and clean this up the best we can. We don't want to lie anymore." She gave an odd look to her maybe boyfriend that suggested she was reminding him that he had to toe the line.

"Good. I'm sure I'll hear from Tucker in just a little bit. Let's plan on meeting with Chief Stanton in the morning at his office. It's just down the street about a block, in case you haven't seen it. Let's make it nine o'clock. Any changes, and I'll call you."

They said their goodbyes, and Vincent left. As he was walking through the Plaza, his phone rang.

"When do you need me there?"

"Hello, Tucker. I suggested to our wayward friends that we meet at the chief's office at nine in the morning. I think this can be resolved pretty quickly. Mostly, I think the chief will want a statement regarding everything Sam knows about the Benson killing, which also shouldn't take long. I thought you should be there to make sure this is all on the legal up-and-up."

"Of course, I need to be there. But if Miller's genuinely innocent, then who did it?"

"Not real sure. We still have good suspects, but of course, as of tomorrow, I guess we don't have a client anymore."

"Is Ortega still on the list?" Tucker's interest seemed unusual.

"Yeah, I'd keep him on until it's cleared up. I don't think he did it. I think it was only the artifacts that he was after, but who knows? We know he has a temper, so under the right circumstances, something could have triggered violence from him."

"I talked to Hill. He wants us to stay with the investigation and see if we can clear Ortega of any involvement."

Vincent chuckled. "Well, that's an interesting turn of events. Does that mean Hill thinks he's innocent or guilty?"

"I don't think he knows. But you're already knee-deep in this, so he wants you to finish. See ya in the morning." Tucker clicked off.

Vincent decided to head home. His plan was to sit on the back porch with a Tecate and think about life while he waited for Nancy. It was a good plan.

This whole thing with Benson makes me wonder about my own life. Benson was obviously a fun guy to be around, and a lot of people liked him, but he spread grief like it was fertilizer. Am I that guy? My drinking days were pretty bad, but did I really hurt people? Probably only my mom and dad, my brother, a couple of aunts and uncles. Plus, numerous girlfriends, and of course, the ex-wife. That's probably all. Damn, I was more like Benson than I would ever admit to anyone else. Could I still be doing it without even knowing it?

27

Alice, Don't Go Down That Hole

Vincent took his coffee outside. It was a cold morning with snow flurries—not comfortable, but it fit his mood. Santa Fe is a high-altitude city, and its winters come early. He'd spent much of his life in Denver, and wasn't a fan of snow, but for this morning it was fine. He knew he'd enjoy living in the boring climate of L.A., with temperatures in the seventies every day. But seasonal changes seemed to make life more noticeable. The trees changed, the birds were different, people changed, and the world seemed more alive.

"Some reason you're sitting in the cold and snow?" Nancy had stuck her head out the back door.

"I'm being stimulated."

"Not sure I want to know what that means. Come in, I'll fix you some toast."

As Vincent got up his phone vibrated. "Malone."

Younger launched into things without preamble. "Looks like your Father Joseph also goes by the name, William Hamilton. In Telluride he's known as a reclusive author, although no one seems to know what he writes. Got a little inside dope on Joseph-Hamilton via a nice little bribe—which will be included in my bill, by the way, as a 'miscellaneous disbursement'—and apparently someone official was looking for Joseph. But when a sheriff's deputy showed up to check on the house, Hamilton said Joseph was on some kind of sabbatical and was incommunicado. The deputy filed a report saying it was bullshit, in official cop language. Right after that, Joseph-Hamilton vanished, but not before he made a run to Durango with some kind of cargo, which I've been able to track—that's another 'miscellaneous disbursement,' FYI—to a self-storage facility not far from my office. The manager there identified Joseph from an internet photo of him in front of the Santa Fe church. The manager was willing to gossip for beer money, but he drew the line at opening the unit and letting me see what was inside. My guess is that was only off limits because I hesitated to up my bid."

"Great work. I'm pretty sure I know what's in there, but we'll keep the higher offer in reserve. Was he renting the house in Telluride?"

"Nope. That part was easy—it's right there in the public record. Bill Joseph is the owner. No mortgage, so at one time the good father had a wad of cash. It's a nice place. I wouldn't think he would just walk away from that unless he was being chased."

"You're a good man. Stay in touch."

Vincent clicked off. It felt more and more like Father Joseph was the killer. He had the artifacts, and wanted to hang onto to them, which gave him a motive. It seemed like he'd had opportunity, too. Benson had said in his note that it was Father

Joseph who called and wanted to meet. If you took the note at face value, then Father Joseph could have simply waited for Benson and then shot him. Vincent knew the good Father had been in Santa Fe. Maybe he still was.

He brushed some snow off and went into the cozy kitchen. The toast was on the table, but Nancy had returned to the bathroom to get ready for work. Vincent called out to her. "Sorry about that. That was Younger I was talking to. Looks like Father Joseph has been living a double life. Most likely killed Benson, too."

Nancy stuck her head into the room. "The priest killed Benson?"

"Everything is pointing that way."

"My goodness, how sad it that?" In many ways Nancy was a romantic, and often disappointed in the world.

Vincent rode with Nancy to her parking spot near the Crown. From there, he set off on foot for the police station. He saw Tucker standing out front. "Everything okay?"

"Don't know. They haven't shown up yet. No problem, right?"

"None that I'm aware of. Probably just running a little late."

Sam and Stella appeared. "Sorry, guys," Sam said. "We overslept a little. We're ready."

Tucker and Vincent breathed a sigh of relief. They'd both had clients who'd promised one thing and then did another. Chief Stanton greeted them in the small lobby of the police department building and showed them back into a large conference room. After a round of introductions, he began.

"First, Mister Miller, I want to apologize again for your experience at the jail. That should never have happened, and we've taken steps to ensure that it never happens again. I think everyone involved has had some things occur that they are not proud of. So probably best if we could put them behind us. Your treatment after you were arrested was inexcusable, but your escape was a crime. I know it seems odd that you could commit a crime by escaping when you weren't guilty, but as Mister Tucker can tell you, fair or not, it was a crime. We screwed up and you screwed up, though I'll readily admit that ours was worse. What seems like the best way to handle this is to agree that we all had some fault, and then wipe the slate clean. I've discussed this with the DA and the city attorney, and they've agreed." He pulled out a document. "The city attorney has drafted this release of liability agreement. I wanted to get this to Mister Tucker before this meeting, but the city attorney was only able to get it to me just now, so you're getting it as soon as I am. What's being proposed is that we will give you a commitment in writing that we won't pursue any criminal charges related to the escape, while you sign this liability release related to the matter in the jail. I know Mister Tucker will need time to read this over so he can give you his advice, so, unless you have questions, I'll step out and let you discuss it."

Stanton stood to leave, but Sam stopped him. "I do have a question, actually," Sam said, looking directly at the chief. "I'm okay with the proposal being offered, unless there is something in the agreement that doesn't match up with what you've said.

But I'm not okay with that goon who beat me up still being a cop. I thought that bastard was going to kill me, and didn't show even the slightest bit of emotion while he was doing it. He should have never been hired to be a cop, and he sure as hell shouldn't be one any longer. What happens to him?"

Sam had gotten a little heated, but Stanton stayed calm, sitting back down. "Mister Miller, you're right. It's not in the agreement, but I assure you, he's been fired. We've got an odd system here, where we've got both a police department and a sheriff's department, and the sheriff has agreed to fire his deputy. I will personally do everything I can to make sure that he's never hired in law enforcement anywhere else. My first choice was to charge the man with attempted murder, but if I'd done that, then we were going to have a fight on our hands with the sheriff, and maybe even the DA. To make this deal work, I agreed that he'd just be fired. If that isn't enough for you, I understand. But at that point, the deal that's on the table will be pulled."

Miller looked at the chief. "It'll have to be enough, then. It's a fair deal. I appreciate what you said. It makes me feel a little better."

Sam stood up and shook the chief's hand, and the chief left. Tucker read the agreement, taking time with the details, but it wasn't very extensive, so it didn't take long. "There needs to be a few changes. Mostly legal stuff, but still—give me just a little bit. And by the way, I highly recommend that you sign this, it's a good agreement."

He got up and left the room, and they sat in silence for

a few minutes, just waiting. Finally, Sam spoke up. "Mister Malone, do you know where Father Joseph is?"

Vincent hesitated. "I don't. He's not in Telluride, which is where he was living before. There some chance he's in Santa Fe."

"You know; he is the one who has the artifacts."

"Yeah, he probably does. You know, there's a chance those artifacts are cursed. Might not be a good thing to have them." Vincent looked serious.

"Maybe. But that sure is a lot of money."

Tucker came back in. "The chief is going to initial the changes we made, and he and you will sign. As I said before, this is a good agreement—you should sign." Tucker went over the agreement with Sam and Stella, and Sam said he was ready. He and the chief signed, and the chief gave Sam a copy, with one for Tucker as well. Outside, Sam and Stella said their goodbyes and left.

"Think he'll let it go?" Tucker watched them walk away. "The money, I mean."

"Not sure. He's spent a lot of years looking for revenge and that money. Might be hard to just drop it."

"Yeah. He's got a good thing going with Stella, though. Be real stupid to lose that over some baubles." Tucker sounded like he was speaking from experience. Being lonely was the ultimate curse.

Vincent headed back toward the Crown, making a stop at the Plaza Cantina. He got a Tecate and went upstairs to the outside balcony seating. From here, he could watch as the tourists gathered around the vendors hawking various wares on the sidewalk below. It was a strange tradition to sell your crafts on the street—strange but familiar, and therefore comforting. He was thinking about what Tucker had said. He knew he wanted to get married to Nancy—he'd do it today, if she'd agree—but he also knew she was hesitating, and that troubled him. His phone vibrated.

"Malone."

"Couldn't find anything on the woman. If the university made a legal agreement, it doesn't seem to have been filed in any public record. That type of agreement, from way back then, would probably never even be transferred to electronic files, which is all I can access. So, dead end with the university. Since we only have a last name, and it's the most common last name there is in the whole damned Anglo world, I have nothing on her. But I worked my butt off trying." Cyber guy stopped like he was expecting applause. Vincent remained silent. "But, and it's a big but, Jackson is an unusual first name, even with Smith as a last name. Did extensive searches. Nothing in Florida, but found a guy in Georgia. I sure can't guarantee this is the Jackson Smith you're looking for, but I found *a* Jackson Smith. And he looks to be about the right age, so this is the best I can do."

"Hey, that's great. Good job. You really are amazing." He hoped that heaping on praise when the guy was clearly looking for it might reduce his bill, though it probably wouldn't work. "Any chance you found contact info?"

"Yep. Got a cell phone number." Cyber guy gave him the number.

"Thanks. You're the best."

He clicked off. Now what? *Probably some poor guy with the same name who's going to think I'm nuts, but so what? It's better than nothing.* Vincent paused and thought about what he wanted to say. *Hey, are you the evil son who killed his long-lost father? Nah, I need a different approach.* He sipped his beer and watched the tourists. Some of them seemed to be watching him right back. Strange feeling, like he was at the zoo. He ignored the thought and called the number.

"Hello," came a man's voice.

"This is not a crank call. Please hear me out. You don't know me—my name's Vincent Malone. I'm a private investigator in Santa Fe, New Mexico. I'm *not* a cop and I'm not working for the cops. I'm trying to find the Jackson Smith whose father was Malcolm Benson. Are you that person?"

The guy didn't disconnect, but he didn't say anything for a moment either. "I know who you are. My father told me about you. I know I'm in trouble, but I didn't kill him. Honestly, I wouldn't have minded killing him, but I wasn't the one who did it. Can you help me?" He sounded tired and afraid.

"Where are you?"

"Santa Fe."

"Where in Santa Fe?"

"Homeless shelter. Not sure of the address. It's run by a guy with a long white beard. He's been real nice to me."

"I know where that is. The guy with the beard. I call him Santa Claus to tease him, but his name's Butch Collins. Don't go anywhere, and if you need help, ask Butch. I'll be there soon, maybe thirty minutes."

Had Jackson killed Benson? It was possible, no matter what he'd said on the phone. Should he call the chief? But Jackson had asked for help. Vincent figured he could at least talk to him before he went sic'ing the cops on him. Even so, he checked to make sure he had his gun when he left the bar. He found it in his pocket, right where it should be. Better safe than sorry.

28

Old Man Dream

In The Recent Past—Florida City, Florida

Malcolm had agreed to meet, though he'd carefully picked a very public place; the Florida Keys Outlet Marketplace in the food court. He was going to meet a son he didn't know, who might wish him harm—and justifiably so. He'd been living in an old, rundown house in a very poor part of Florida City, waiting to die. The son was a complication he hadn't sought or wanted. Mary Smith, the boy's mother, was nothing but a distant memory. He wouldn't know her if she was standing right in front of him. The fact was, most of his life was becoming a blur, disappearing slowly—evaporating from his memory, it seemed to him. He was dying. It wouldn't be long, and then, thankfully, it would be over.

He took a bus to the shopping center. He'd been here before, a long time ago, just to be around people, but that was something he hadn't done in years. He got some terrible, very expensive coffee, and waited. The boy had said he was tall, with long hair, and on the skinny side. Jackson Smith. Why in the hell had she named him Jackson? Probably something to do with Stonewall Jackson. He remembered that Mary was from

266

the South, but by now he'd long forgotten exactly where. The boy said he was coming from Atlanta, which was probably where his mother lived. Why would you name a kid after some asshole general? His own mother had given him the god-awful name Malcolm. His mother had told him it was an old Scottish family name. *Well, fine, but is that any reason to saddle me with it?* He'd always hated it. He wanted to be Jack, or Bill, or something else normal.

"Mister Benson?" Standing next to his table was a young man—Jackson Smith, obviously. Tall and skinny.

"You must be Jackson. Have a seat."

Jackson sat down, noticeably nervous. "I've waited a long time to meet you. I hope it was okay I called you. My mother said you were a lot older than her and that you might not want to even meet with me. I'm glad you agreed to see me."

Malcolm was surprised: the kid was nice. Polite and respectful. *He might not want to kill me, after all.*

"Well, yeah. I'm a wee bit past my prime. Lived a long, eventful life, but now I'm at the end. Don't really know why you wanted to see me. I've got no money, and most of the people who know me have asked *not* to see me, rather than the other way around. Of course, you weren't around when I was a real asshole, so I guess you're the only relative, except maybe my granddaughter, who doesn't hate me."

Jackson just stared. "Well, there are some reasons I could hate you, but I don't. My mom has been honest with me, and even said that she was more responsible for what happened than you were. She's been a great mom, and always said good things about you."

Always said good things about me? That caught him by surprise, and he actually began to cry. He hated being an old man, not being able to control his emotions. But he didn't have a choice, so he cried. Jackson got up and hugged his dad, which made Malcolm cry more.

Jackson bought them some sandwiches and iced tea. His dad didn't look well, and he was obviously worried about him.

"You're a good person, Jackson. I wonder how you would have been if you had grown up around me." Malcolm chuckled and smiled at his son. "Probably wouldn't be half as nice."

They talked at length, with an easy, real connection. Jackson asked if he should call Malcolm "dad," or something else. They decided that "Dad" was a little too weird, given that they'd only just met, but his granddaughter had always called him "Papa," so they settled on that.

"I don't want you to be sad," Malcolm said. "I'm going to tell you something, but I'm not looking for sympathy. I'm telling you this because you need to know, so you can understand other things I tell you, okay?"

"I guess. Not sure what you're going to say, Papa, so I'm not sure how I can agree."

"You just agree. You know you trust me, so just say yes."

"Okay, yes."

Malcolm smiled and patted his son's shoulder. He really liked this kid—go figure. "So, don't interrupt, let me finish what I have to say, and then we can talk. Some months ago I was diagnosed with cancer. The big C. At first, they didn't know how long I had—might have been years. Well, like a lot of shit in my life, it didn't go that way. The cancer spread. It's in my brain now. The last time I saw that asshole doctor, he said I probably just had days to live. That was three weeks ago—that's how much that bastard knew. But it's close, I can tell. No reason to be sad. I lived a long time. There was one thing I wanted to do before I died, but until now I'd decided it wasn't going to be possible. I want to see my granddaughter, and I want to clean up some of the mess from my ugly past. If you help me, then I can actually do that. Will you help me with my last wish?"

"Of course. I mean, as long it doesn't involve hurting anyone."

"Well, shit, there goes the best part of my plan." He laughed, which led to a fit of coughing. Once the convulsions had slowed enough that he could swallow, a few sips of tea helped calm his throat. "Hell, no, this doesn't have anything to do with hurting anyone. Maybe scarin' 'em just a little, but it's for a good cause."

Malcolm told Jackson his plan, which began with them renting a car and driving to Las Cruces, New Mexico. He wanted to drive because he wanted to see some of the country, and anyway, he hated airplanes. He could still drive, but not for a long trip like this. Malcolm said he still had some credit cards that worked, so they could charge the trip on the cards. He winked at Jackson, telling him that by the time the bills showed up he'd be dead, anyway. Jackson did not think it was funny, but Malcolm did—more laughing, more coughing.

"Something you should know. There's one hooligan who's threatened me. If you can believe this, the guy is the sheriff in Santa Fe, but he's actually nothing but a thug and a bully. If I was younger, I'd beat the shit out of him. But I'm not, and he could be dangerous. You need to think about that before you agree to go. And if you want to go with me, we're only doing it if we bring a gun with us. We can buy one here—right here in this mall, I mean. Even an old coot like me can buy a gun. Have to wait a few days, but that's about it. I don't plan on shooting anyone, and I don't want you to, either, but we're not going into this guy's back yard without some protection."

He could see that Jackson wasn't at all sure about this part. "Is he threatening you?"

"He wants my Santa Fe treasure," Malcolm said simply, as if it made sense.

"I don't know what that means, Papa." Jackson liked saying "Papa," even though he was quickly deciding Papa was whacko.

Malcolm told him the story, starting with the digs in New Mexico where he'd met Jackson's mother. He told him about giving the artifacts to the Catholic priest, and the incident when the surveyor was killed by the hoodlums he'd hired to provide security for the digs. He told him everything he could remember, good and bad. It felt like a confession, the story of a good life gone bad.

"I want to go to Las Cruces to see Alex," he said, "because he's in trouble. But then I want to go to Santa Fe. I want to find the priest, get the artifacts, and give them back to the Indians. Ever since I took those artifacts I've been cursed, and I don't want to die under a curse. I don't have much time, Jackson—we need to get started. Are you ready?"

Jackson got his Papa another glass of tea and told him to rest a minute. Could any of this be true? It all sounded bizarre, but he knew the part about his mother was true—she'd told him the same story herself. But, stolen Native American artifacts worth millions? That seemed more like an old man losing his mind. Still, did it really matter? Malcolm wanted to go on one last adventure before he died. The fact that it was probably nonsense wasn't really relevant. He would go on this crazy road trip with his dying dad—how could he possibly say no?

"Are you sure you'll be able to ride in a car that long? Are you in any pain?"

"Nosy, aren't you? I don't remember your mom being nosy. Maybe it's a generational thing. Sure, I can ride in a car. How hard is that? Might have to take a few more bathroom breaks, but I'm sure we can cope with that. I have some medicine for the pain. What I don't have is a couple of damned weeks to stand here arguing with you. So, are you in or out?"

Jackson could see that growing up with his dad would have meant living in a completely different world, and one that probably wouldn't have suited him at all as a kid. But as an adult, he could enjoy his father's take-charge ways. "Sure. Let's get started." Malcolm surprised him with a hug.

The first order of business was getting a gun. They went to a sporting goods store, and in less time than it would have taken to buy a tennis racket, Malcolm owned a gun. It was the cheapest handgun they had, but Malcolm said it was fine. They got bullets and their receipt, and were told they could pick up the gun in three days. They agreed that it might be best if Jackson was in charge of it. They definitely didn't want Malcolm, with his failing memory, to forget it in some gas-station restroom along the way.

Next, they needed a car. Jackson had arrived in his car to see Malcolm, but it was on its last legs. No way would it make it to Las Cruces. Renting a car presented more hurdles than buying a gun. Malcolm's driver's license had expired about eight years before—no license, no car. The manager at the rental place had seemed sympathetic, though. They'd lied a little bit, claiming Malcolm was going back to his hometown one last time before he died. It was a good story. The manager said he'd rent the vehicle to Jackson, even though he didn't have a credit card, as long as Benson had one. It was bending the rules, but for a good cause.

"Should you call Alex and let him know you're going to be there?" Jackson asked.

"Probably not. We don't know for sure how long it'll take us, and he'd just worry. I think it's best if we just show up."

During the three-day wait, Jackson learned more about Malcolm's health, and became increasingly concerned about the trip and what it might do to him. He thought about calling his mother and asking her advice, but that seemed like it would turn into the beginning of a very unusual family argument. He decided he either had to trust Malcolm to know what he could and couldn't do, or just not go. They got a call: the gun was ready.

After packing the car, they stopped and picked up the gun on their way to Jacksonville. It was a simple route—get on Interstate 95, and don't get off. The drive took them up the coast of Florida, where the scenery was magnificent and the weather glorious. They eventually arrived in Jacksonville, stopping more often than Jackson would have liked. It was going to be a long trip. They decided Motel 6 was the best choice for sleeping, pretty much solely because Malcolm liked their commercials.

Leaving Jacksonville, the route was simple once again: get on Interstate 10, head west, and sooner or later you'll arrive in Las Cruces, New Mexico. It would take several days, but it wasn't rocket science.

They talked a lot along the way. And Malcolm slept a lot. He had a few spells, but mostly he was upbeat. They would never be a real father and son, the kind who'd had a life together, but in some ways what they had was better. They'd become friends.

"Wake up, Papa. Twenty-five miles to Las Cruces."

"Well it's about fuckin' time. Find a place to stop, I need to take a leak."

29

My Last Wish

Vincent spotted Butch as soon as he entered the homeless shelter. "Hey, Butch. How's it goin'?"

"Not bad, Vincent. How 'bout you? You and Nancy set a date yet?"

"No. I think she's dragging her feet. 'Course, if I was thinkin' about marrying me, I'd hesitate, too."

"Well I bet it's not you, personally. It's because of what you do. She was always cautious. She suffered a lot when her husband died. I thought at one point that she might actually not make it. That's a lot grief to live through, and then put yourself right back out there, possibly to have to go through it all again one day. I think if you were a store clerk, the wedding bells would have already rung. Just give her time. She wouldn't work at it this hard if she didn't want to be with you. You're one fortunate son of a gun, Malone."

"Yeah, I know it, Butch. I'm looking for a guy who called me, know where he is?"

"He's in the back, resting—seems exhausted. I gave him some food and had him lie down for a bit. Seems like a good kid."

Vincent went into the back, where there was a single person—a man on a cot. Must be him.

"Jackson?"

"Yeah. You Malone?"

"I am. Vincent Malone." They shook hands.

"Wow, you're a big guy." Jackson nodded his head like something suddenly made sense. "Malcolm trusted you. Said if I needed help to call you. It's funny, you called just when I was trying to decide whether or not to call. I've sort of been hiding out, but in the open, here with the homeless folks. But I can't do this much longer. Street people must really be tough."

"No question, it's a hard life. You said you're hiding. Does that mean you're hiding from the police?"

"I guess. I know this will sound goofy, but I think I was just hiding in general because I didn't know what I should do. I could see the police thinking I shot Malcolm, but I didn't. I wanted to tell them what happened—still do—but I was afraid someone might shoot me before I could tell my story."

Vincent gestured for Jackson to sit back down on the cot and pulled up a chair.

"Why don't you tell me your story, and then we can decide on how to contact the police?"

"Where should I start?"

"I know you met with your dad in Miami. Maybe start with that."

Jackson Smith told Vincent about how he'd made contact with his dad and met with him in Florida City, a suburb of Miami. He covered every detail he could think of: Malcolm asking to be taken to Las Cruces, the danger of this guy Orte-ga, the priest who had the artifacts. He talked about renting the car and buying the gun, about their many days in the car, and about their eventual arrival in Las Cruces.

"Malcolm wanted to contact his granddaughter. He knew she was in Santa Fe because he followed her on the internet. He was really sharp most of the time, for a man his age. I told him, I didn't think it was a good idea, but he seemed to think she could be in some danger if Ortega found out she was in Santa Fe. Anyway, he ignored my advice and called her, and she came down that night. After she arrived, there was some kind of argument between Alex and Malcolm, and Alex died of a heart attack. After they were questioned by the police, they left for Santa Fe. Malcolm stayed in touch with me the whole time, calling me on my cell, but without being obvious about it, because he didn't want to tell Stella about me. He decided we should return the car to the rental company. It was in my name, so he called and left a voice mail for me, saying where he was leaving it and where I should turn it in. I wasn't sure why we were returning it, but I did what he said. Then they went to Santa Fe, which left me in Las Cruces without a car. He'd given me some cash, so I took a bus to Santa Fe, figuring he'd find some way for us to meet up once I arrived."

"Why wouldn't he want Stella to know about you?"

"I'm not sure. I think it was probably just that he didn't want us comparing notes. I'm pretty sure my dad didn't always tell the truth, and maybe he couldn't keep his lies straight. The other possibility I thought of was that he might not trust her.

While we were driving from Florida, he told me that he hadn't talked to her in a long time."

"So, what happened next?" Vincent wanted to keep the story moving.

"Well, for one thing, he met you. He liked you, and he'd decided to tell you everything he knew, and ask for your help. He really just wanted everything cleaned up as best it could be. He called me right after he got the call from Joseph. He said Joseph had been hiding at the church when he and Stella were there and had followed them, which was how he knew Malcom was at the Hilton. I didn't want him to go, but he said it was time. I wasn't real sure what that meant, but I think he was saying it was his time to die. He asked me to meet him at the church and told me how to find it. He said he would take a cab to get there, that he'd seen several of them outside the hotel. I got there long before he did, and just waited. I saw him get out of a cab, and almost immediately some guy approached him. I swear, it looked like this guy walked straight out of the wall of the church. There must have been an opening or something, but I didn't see one. They were standing in the yard in front of the church. They talked for quite a while, but I wasn't close enough to hear what they were saying. Then the other man—I know now it was Joseph, but I didn't know that then—pulled out a gun. I could see they were arguing. I had started in that direction when I clearly saw Joseph pull the trigger—but nothing happened. Malcolm pulled out the gun we bought in Florida and aimed at the priest. I yelled out to them and they both jumped, surprised. I think my dad had forgotten I was there. The priest took off running. I yelled at him to stop, but he just kept going."

"No one else saw this?"

"I don't know. There wasn't anyone around that I saw. There were some homeless people camped out down the block, but they were pretty far off. When I got to Malcolm, I could see that something was wrong. He'd lost all color and seemed to be in pain. I told him I was going to call an ambulance, but he said no. He was still holding the gun. He said he was sorry things hadn't worked and that I should go home, that I should be sure to be nice to my mom. He gave me a weak smile and then he put the gun to his chest and pulled the trigger. I yelled. I couldn't believe what he'd done. I still don't understand it, but maybe it was the pain from the cancer—maybe he just couldn't take it anymore. What I did next was completely stupid. The priest's gun was on the ground, where he'd dropped it, I picked up my dad's gun, then kneeled down and said goodbye. I took our gun away, but I left the priest's gun there. Maybe the police would identify him from the gun and he would be a suspect. I had seen him try to kill my dad, so in the heat of the moment it made sense to me to do that. I just ran. I've been on the street since then, trying to decide what I should do."

Vincent thought for a moment. "Have you ever talked to Sam Miller?"

"No. That name doesn't mean anything to me."

"What do you think your dad was saying to Father Joseph?"

"Oh, I'm sure it was that he wanted the artifacts back, be-cause he was going to return them. Based on what I saw; the priest must think he owns the artifacts, after all these years."

"You broke the law when you took the gun, and again when you didn't come forward with information about the death of Malcolm Benson. That's obstruction of justice and withholding evidence—there might even be a few other charges a creative DA could add. Most likely, though, if the police and the DA know the truth, they won't prosecute you. The problem is that there's a chance they'll think your whole story is bullshit, and that you killed your dad, in which case you could be charged with murder."

"I'm in a pile of shit, right?" Jackson lowered his head into his hands.

"Yes. But the good news is that you have the truth on your side. That may sound like Bible-school talk or something, but it's a practical truth as well, because there should be forensic evidence to support everything you have said. However, without an eyewitness backing your story; you could be convicted on circumstantial evidence. My advice is turn yourself in, which will help make it believable that you're innocent, and then hire the toughest criminal lawyer I know."

"There's one other thing I want to try to get right. My dad wrote out a statement saying that the priest is the person he gave the artifacts to so many years ago. It would be so great if his last wish of returning the artifacts to their rightful owners could happen."

"I think I can help you with that. Do you have the statement he wrote?"

Jackson reached into his coat and gave several loose pages

to Vincent.

"My dad said he trusted you because you weren't a bullshitter. I hope he was right."

"He was."

Tucker, Vincent, and Jackson Smith walked into the Santa Fe Police Department and asked to see the chief. The chief came out looking a little confused.

"What's going on guys?"

Vincent pulled out the plastic bag holding the gun that killed Malcolm.

"This is the gun that killed Malcolm Benson. He shot himself. This is his son, who witnessed his suicide. He panicked, took the gun, and ran. He's turning himself in."

Tucker spoke up next. "I'm representing Mister Smith, and I'll want to be present during any questioning."

For a few moments, the chief just stood there. Then he waved to one of his officers, who searched Smith and handcuffed him.

"Take him to the interrogation room. Mister Smith, we'll have some questions for you in just a little while." The officer took Smith into the back.

"Want to join me in my office?" It wasn't so much an offer as a request. Tucker and Vincent followed the chief. "So, what's this all about?"

Vincent gave the chief a short version of what had happened, including the encounter with Father Joseph. He explained about Benson's cancer, and that he'd been near death and in increasing pain. He said it looked like Malcolm had stashed the artifacts on church property long ago and later, when it looked like he wasn't coming back, the priest had taken them. He tossed in the connection with Ortega from the past, and his theory that Ortega was looking for the artifacts along with everyone else. Then, to round out the picture, he explained who Jackson Smith was, and how he was trying to help his new-found father make his final wish come true by finding the artifacts and returning them to their rightful owners.

"Am I supposed to just let him go now that you've explained everything?" The chief's expression was not quite a smile.

"I believe his story, but I don't expect you to take it at face value. I'm guessing that there's evidence out there that will back up at least part of it. Of course, he's the only witness we know of to how his father died, so what you make of his account is in your good and capable hands." Vincent smiled. He might as well have said "here, this is your hot potato, and meanwhile, we'll defend him to the hilt," but being that direct might have been taken as a challenge.

"I'll talk to him and to the DA, and we'll decide what the charges might or might not be. I'll tell you right now that we've withheld some of the forensics because we did not want all the information in the media. The coroner told us that Benson was within hours of dying, and that he must have been in unbearable pain. Plus, since the cancer had spread to his brain, he might not have been thinking clearly. Your other client, Sam

Miller, was at the scene very soon after this happened. Did he see anything?"

"He told us the same as he told you. He didn't see anyone."

"That sure is a lot of traffic in an open space, and nobody saw anyone else, plus there was a gunshot."

"It could happen." *Couldn't it?* "Benson pushed the gun against his chest when he pulled the trigger--that would have muffled the sound, so unless someone was close by it would not have been loud." Vincent was getting tired of these questions circling back to be answered from a new perspective. But he believed Jackson. It fit with everything he knew about Benson. He was done, everyone could see that, and he wanted to get the artifacts back and decided to go to Santa Fe to do it. The priest objected, and Benson was defeated. He wasn't going to live to fight another day, so he just gave up, and to hell with anyone it messed up. He died the way he lived—wrapped in his own bubble, oblivious to his effect on others.

"We'll take Smith's statement now. Are you both going to join us?"

"I will. Mister Malone has some other matters to attend to, unless we need his guidance, in which case we'll call him back." Tucker was speaking in a more stilted way than usual—probably his police station voice.

"Well, Mister Malone, don't get into any trouble taking care of your other matters." The chief got up and left the room.

"Not very appreciative of us solving all his crimes, is he?" Tucker muttered.

"Just being selfish. He wants to solve them himself. How

do you think this is going to work out?" Vincent knew the law as well as Tucker, but this particular case was almost all grey area.

"It'll be up to the DA. I'm sure he'll listen to the chief, but he'll make up his own mind. It'll be a legal question wrapped in a political mess, with a little topping of pros versus cons—they have to wonder about the downside if they pursue this and lose. Someone will make a judgment call and hope it's the right one. One thing I'll guarantee is that they won't ask us. Actually, I'll guarantee you two things—the other one is that if they decide to go to court, I'll have that jury bawling like little babies."

30

Beginnings and Endings

Bright sun was streaming through the small kitchen. The brief cold spell was over, and the sun was treating Santa Fe to a spring-like, warm day of hope. Vincent sat at the table, staring off into space.

"You look like you're thinking some big thoughts." Nancy came in ready for work, grabbing a second cup of coffee.

"Yeah, maybe I was." He smiled at his lovely roommate. "I've spent most of my life just getting to the next day. For a big chunk of that time, I'm not sure I thought too much about anything meaningful beyond just surviving. Now, I seem to think a lot about why I do things. Or even what I should do—what's my purpose? It's strange for me. Is this just an old-age thing, or what?"

Nancy chuckled and gave him a hug. "It's me."

"What does that mean? Are you bad for me?" He was smiling.

"What I mean is, it's us. We've both lived just for ourselves for a long time. Now there's someone else to think about, to worry about. My goal for years was to survive the day, but now I worry about you, about whether we'll make it, about what'll happen in the future, about whether we'll get sick, about how I would survive without you. Our relationship is driving our brains crazy, but in a good way."

"So, love is all about going nuts?"

"A little. We need to take the next step. And it's my fault. I've been dragging my feet. We need to get married, make that lifetime commitment. Are you ready?"

"Call Cindy and put the wedding train in motion." Vincent stood and gave Nancy a hug. "You're everything that matters to me."

The drive to Durango was glorious. The mountains seemed to be alive with color, which was a real contrast to his last trip there. He'd borrowed the Inn's van to accommodate the cargo he expected to carry. It wasn't much fun to drive, like his own beloved Mustang, but the road was mostly vacant, and Vincent was in a great mood. He'd left Santa Fe before dawn and expected to be in Durango by midmorning, where Younger would meet him at the Lone Spur Café for a late breakfast. His stomach growled just thinking about it.

The scenery was wonderful, but the trip was uneventful. He reached Durango and headed to the restaurant. Vincent was aware that he was at some risk entering Colorado, and especially coming to Durango, given the unresolved issue of him being a suspect in the Simpson murder. But this trip was vitally important to a number of people, so he was willing to take the chance.

Younger had installed some special equipment at the Telluride cabin of Father Joseph to keep track of his activities. Within hours of getting a message from Younger, Vincent was on the road. Younger, meanwhile, had sent someone to keep an eye on the good father and make sure he didn't go anywhere. Vincent wanted to have a chat with the priest, but did not want to alert the man in advance, since he'd probably just take off again.

The moment Vincent entered the Lone Spur Café, intoxicating aromas almost knocked him down. He saw Younger chatting with a group of men sitting in a booth, and waved.

"Hey, you made good time," the lawyer said as they grabbed a vacant booth. "Nothing has changed at this end."

"Good, because I really need something to eat. Had no idea I was on the verge of starving until I walked in here." The waitress showed up right on cue and took their orders. Vincent smiled in anticipation. "Anything new with my little local problem?"

"Nothing I've heard. My contact in the DA's office said I was a slob and kicked me out of her tidy little apartment. I think we may still see each other, but for the moment, she's not talking to me." Younger shrugged. *Que será, será.* "My sense is that someone's pushing to get you charged for the murder, even though there's absolutely no evidence—but that someone seems to have backed off, for some reason."

"That points to Ortega. Any reason you know of that he'd have influence in Durango?"

"Not that I'm aware of, other than just cops supporting cops. But this seems like more than just taking a cop's word over a citizen's. It's very personal, and maybe political, too. Which leads us to the Maxwell Franks Law Firm and its thug of a leader, Franks Junior. What his problem is with you, I'm not sure. Why he would push and then back off, I'm also not sure. One obvious possibility is that he killed Ken Simpson, or some of his goons did, and just to keep things tidy, he needs someone to take the fall. Presto! —he thinks of his good friend, Vincent Malone."

"That sure seems like a lot of trouble to just clean up something that might not cause much concern amongst the local police, anyway. A dead hoodlum usually doesn't get the local leaders all that agitated."

"Yep, good point."

The food arrived, and all further discussion was postponed.

"So, what are the risks with Hamilton-Joseph today?" Younger leaned back, looking full.

"I think we should assume he's willing to kill to protect himself," Vincent said. "Once he's aware of who we are, he'll feel trapped, so he'll be dangerous. We know he tried to kill Benson, and only failed because the gun jammed. Once you cross that line, you're more likely to kill again."

"I've got one of my motorcycle buddies watching the property now. He'll keep us informed if Joseph leaves, or if someone else shows up. And he can lend a hand if things get ugly."

"Good. Guess we should head out." Vincent paid the check.

"Yep, the distance as the crow flies is about fifty miles, but we're headed into the mountains. The drive to Telluride is two or three hours, but his cabin is this side of the city, so a little less than an hour and half to the cabin."

Vincent had been impressed with the mountains north of Santa Fe, but the territory he entered now made them seem tame. The van did its best, but several times Vincent thought it might be faster to walk. They eventually turned onto the pitted dirt road that led to Joseph's remote cabin. With no more reason to be stealthy, Vincent parked near the front door.

Leaving Younger standing behind his open van door, Vincent approached the cabin door. It opened, and he recognized Bill Joseph. He didn't see a weapon, but his hand closed around the gun in his own pocket, just in case.

"Father Joseph, my name is Vincent Malone. Like to talk to you about the missing artifacts."

The man gave Vincent a dirty look. "What are you, some kind of cop?"

"I'm a private investigator working for the estate of Malcolm Benson. You remember—the man you tried to kill."

That ratcheted up the tension, and earned him an even dirtier look. "Why should I talk to you? You're just some private cop. You've got no right to be here."

Vincent needed to get Joseph's attention before the guy did something stupid. "Benson left a signed statement naming you as the person who had hidden the stolen artifacts in your church many years ago. We have documentary proof that you sold off a portion of those artifacts on the black market and used the proceeds to buy this very nice cabin. We have a witness, Benson's son, who saw you try to kill Benson, but your old gun jammed, and he's given us a sworn statement to that effect. We also know where the artifacts are stored in Durango. We have video of you placing them in the storage. In other words, we have sufficient evidence to lock you up for something very close to the rest of your life."

As Vincent talked, the color drained from Joseph's face. He looked unsteady and leaned against the door frame. "What do you want?"

"We want justice. Justice for the people harmed by Benson and you. Justice for the people who died and the lives that were ruined because you and Benson were greedy and small. We want peace for Benson, who died thinking he'd been cursed because of the stolen artifacts. We want justice, that's all."

Joseph seemed to almost literally become smaller. "Tell me what you want me to do."

"Let's go inside, and I'll explain it to you." Vincent helped Joseph into the cabin, and Younger joined them. They sat at a large, rustic table, and Vincent explained the deal. No action would be taken against Joseph if he signed an agreement that gave Vincent the right to take the artifacts from the Durango storage and return them to the New Mexico Pueblo, from whom they were stolen in the first place. The agreement would also contain a statement, saying that Joseph had hidden the artifacts for years in the church in Santa Fe, and had sold some to purchase his cabin.

"Why should I trust you? What if you take the artifacts and then just give the cops all the evidence, anyway?" Joseph was regaining some of his strength.

But this wasn't a negotiation. "You have no choice. I have no desire to put you in jail, and I don't care about this cabin. You can live here, sell it, whatever you want. I want to return the artifacts to the Indians. I want it to be over. If you don't trust me, you go to jail. So, it's like I said—you have no choice."

Joseph grabbed the pen and signed the agreement.

"I need the key to the storage." Vincent wasn't sure if he hated Joseph or felt sorry for him, but he sure was ready to be done with him.

The drive back to Durango seemed shorter, and there was little conversation. There were no issues at the storage facility. Younger helped Vincent load the two crates into the van.

"Some of that stuff you told Joseph was a lie." Younger was smiling as Vincent prepared to leave.

"Enough of it was true. I just didn't want him weighing risks versus rewards. Sometimes you just have to help people do the right thing. We're a good team—you stay in touch."

They shook hands, and Vincent headed to Santa Fe. It was night as he drove through the mountains, and they had a different feeling than when he'd been on his way to Durango. Like he was being followed, or like there were ghosts in the van. He was very glad when he reached Santa Fe and home.

The meeting with the leaders of the Pueblo would be at the site of Jake's old gas station. Vincent had worked with Sam Miller and Tank Cooper, Pete's Bar owner, to organize the handoff of the artifacts. Sam and Stella would be there, too.

"I think this is our first road trip."

Vincent smiled at Nancy. They were in the van with the crates in the back. He appreciated Jerry letting him borrow the van again. The crates had been in storage in Santa Fe while arrangements had been made with all of the parties.

"Do you think the artifacts were cursed?" Nancy wasn't entirely comfortable with the crates in the back.

"Not sure I believe in that kind of black magic. It's just old things handed down by someone's dead relatives. I've got a box with some of my own stuff like that."

Nancy perked up. "You have what?"

"Well don't you? You've probably got multiple boxes. Stuff from your parents, your husband?"

"Yeah, sure. But I didn't know you did." Nancy sensed sadness.

"It's not much. But we all do that. We hang on to things that remind us of something, or of someone—both good and bad, I guess. Those crates contain family items belonging to the Indians. They're memories of something lost."

They rode in silence for a while. Once they got close, they could see quite a few cars and a crowd of people. Vincent pulled the van up in front of the old store. Sam and Stella came up to the van.

"We've been talking to the tribal leaders," Sam said. "This is a really great thing that you've made happen. I really don't know that I would have returned these things—all I saw was money, and some kind of payback for my family. I never thought about the family that these things belonged to in the first place. Thanks, Mister Malone, for helping me be a better person."

"Well, the person who's most responsible for what's happening here is Malcolm Benson. He created this mess, and the consequences that followed, but in the end, he was the one who made sure that these tribal treasures were returned."

Stella came up and gave Vincent a hug.

Soon a spiritual leader came forward from the Pueblo group. He chatted with Vincent and they shook hands. Then the man spoke to everyone there.

"Today is a great day for our Pueblo. Some of our most sacred history is being returned to the place where it belongs. We know that some people think we do not appreciate these treasures. That's never been true—what we've been is powerless to stop the people who wanted to take them from us. Today we want to say a special thanks to Vincent Malone," the leader nodded in Vincent's direction, "and to Sam Miller." The leader paused. "Sam Miller has been on a quest to find out about his father's death, which happened not far from this spot. Quite a few bad things happened in this situation, all because a few selfish people wanted to steal valuables from people who weren't able to protect their own property. But maybe we can help provide some peace for some who've been involved. Sam's father, Vic, was killed by people who thought they were doing something good, when in fact they were doing something bad. Vic Miller was just doing his job. And another man, Jake

Sullivan, died in this very spot shortly after Vic Miller was killed. Jake managed to buy Vic Miller some time, though in the end he couldn't save his life. We don't know for sure what happened to Jake, but if he was killed by a man, that man will live a cursed life. Let's hope the return of these relics will let the rest of us live a life of peace and joy."

Finally, the leader said something in a language that few people there understood, but that gave a shiver to everyone, nonetheless.

"You know, we never had that dinner with the Olivers." Nancy was sitting in the sun at the kitchen table, smiling.

"What happened?"

"You didn't show up."

"Wow, how rude was that?"

"Yup, it would have been way rude, but I called them and canceled, because I knew you weren't going to show up when you had all that other junk going on."

"You must be psychic or something." Vincent smiled, enjoying their banter.

"Yeah, that's me—I'm definitely 'or something.' I've asked them for dinner tonight. Does that fit your plans?"

"My plans are to be wherever you are for as long as you'll have me."

"You know you're full of it, don't you?"

"Yeah, I know."

Epilogue

Stella Stratton

The budding relationship with Sam Miller didn't last. Stella took a long vacation, and told everyone to leave her alone, including Sam, and especially her mother. She thought a lot about her family and how her granddad had caused so much harm, mostly just by being so self-absorbed. She didn't think he was a bad man—he just lacked empathy. She wrote, and then strong-armed her publisher into releasing, a nonfiction book that explored the fundamental weaknesses that resulted from our schools and other civic institutions developing people's job skills while neglecting their character. It was a flop. Because of the way she had forced her publisher to bring out the book—threatening to drop them if they refused—they instead dropped her. She never wrote a book again, but she reconciled with her dad, and moved to Columbus, Ohio. Her dad helped her get a job in the college library, and she seems to be at peace.

Sam Miller

When an obsession ends, it can leave a big hole. Sam had fallen madly in love with Stella, and her rejection, combined with the end of his quest for justice and money, left him feeling lost. He knew he was good at investigating things, though, and he liked to snoop. Plus, he was impressed with Vincent Malone, who seemed to have his entire life under control. So, he decided to become a private investigator. In a decision that would only have made sense in pulp fiction, he decided he would go to New York City to start his new career. Things didn't go as planned. He enrolled in a school taught by idiots, and once it was obvious that they'd scammed him, he demanded his money back, only to be attacked by the instructors. After some weeks in hospital, he went back to Oklahoma City and got a job as an assistant manager of a Whataburger, based on a great recommendation from the franchise owner in Grants, New Mexico. He often wondered what his life would have been like if he'd kept the artifacts. He really didn't believe in the curse.

Patrick Zangari

Under the care of Doris Wallace, Patrick's health improved dramatically. He was soon well enough to travel back to L.A., but was reluctant to leave. Doris said she was fine with him staying with her if he wanted to—and he did. There were even rumors that they were involved in a romance, though they both dismissed the idea as ridiculous gossip. Doris was younger than Patrick, but neither was really sure of their ages, so it didn't matter all that much. Patrick was even smiling lately.

Father Bill Joseph / William Hamilton

Joseph felt cheated out of the artifacts—some kind of convoluted logic had actually persuaded him that the relics rightfully belonged to him. Joseph never faced justice for his actions and therefore it was never known for sure who made the calls that created the gathering at the church where Benson died; but, of course, Joseph had made the calls and he also called the cops after he hid and saw Benson kill himself. His original plan of killing Benson and Miller had not worked; but if Miller was framed for Benson's death he was still rid of the threats to him. He lived to a ripe old age, but the few people who interacted with him said he never smiled and seldom talked. There seemed to be a curse on his very existence. There were rumors about him dressing as a priest. It seemed odd behavior for an historian, but mountain people are tolerant folks.

Jackson Smith

The experience of meeting his father was important to Jackson. He often talked about his conversations with Papa to his mom and, between the two of them, they developed a very unrealistic picture of Malcolm as a genius who had done a lot of good for the Indians, and who'd been honored by the university as a result. It made them feel better, and Malcolm had never cared much about stretching the truth.

The Ladies

Dorothy Evans

Gave up writing and went into politics. She was a natural-born bulldog, and soon had more enemies than friends, but seemed to revel in the conflict.

Lucy Martin

Continued to write romance novels. She contacted the Inn

a couple of times, asking about Vincent and whether he had married yet. She kept saying that she was coming back and that she wanted Vincent to pick her up, but she never did.

Elsa Chambers
Never said much of anything that we are aware of, but she became a well-known author—who refuses all interviews.

Marsha Adams
Stopped writing, saying it hurt her wrists. There was a rumor that she'd taken up sky-diving, but that seems absurd.

Honoring the Characters Who Didn't Make It

Malcolm Benson
Few people would have described him as a good person, but during his life many people wanted to be part of his circle. There was an energy around him that attracted people. He lived a long life, causing both pain and joy, not always in equal parts. The curse, if it ever existed, was lifted due in large part to his actions, so maybe he could now rest in peace.

Alex Wallace
Did mostly the right thing in a long life. In a moment of ethical ambiguity, he picked the wrong friend, and it ruined his life—but he still liked the guy, right to the end.

Vic Miller

A good, hard-working man, who just wanted to do his job and go home. His modest ambitions all centered on his family. He's now honored by his son, and by the people to whom he never meant any harm, the Pueblo Indians. The leaders of the Pueblo community petitioned officials to have a section of the highway where Miller died renamed the Vic Miller Memorial Highway.

Jake Sullivan

He wasn't murdered. He fell from his porch when he tripped on a loose board. Failing eyesight is a serious thing. The Indians placed a plaque where he had died, saying he was a true friend and a man of great courage.

Ken Simpson

He was evil and not much good for anything while alive, and the complications resulting from the unsolved death of Ken Simpson are just beginning for Vincent Malone.

Almost everyone else will return in the next
Vincent Malone novel: Durango Two-Step. Visit
TedClifton.com for details.

About the Author

Ted Clifton has written mystery novels which feature the settings of New Mexico and Oklahoma, places where Ted spent considerable time. One of his books, *The Bootlegger's Legacy*, won the IBPA Benjamin Franklin award and the CIPA EVVY award. Today Ted and his wife reside in Denver, Colorado, after many years living in the New Mexico desert.

Keep in touch

Once a month, I send my readers a newsletter with a little of everything in it: southwest US culture, be it art, recipes, or local sights; my thoughts on writing and reading; book recommendations; updates on my current writing project; and from time-to-time a short story.

To sign up, visit **TedClifton.com** and either wait for the pop-up window, or scroll to the bottom of the page. Everybody who signs up receives a mystery gift, with my compliments.

You can also learn more about me and my latest books by visiting **TedClifton.com** or emailing me at **ask@tedclifton.com**.

Books by Ted Clifton

The Bootlegger's Legacy

(Prequel to the Pacheco & Chino mystery series.)

When an old-time bootlegger dies and leaves his son Mike a cryptic letter hinting at millions in hidden cash, Mike and his friend Joe embark on a journey that takes them through three states and 50 years of history. What they find goes beyond money and transforms them both.

This is an action-packed adventure story that partially takes place in the early 1950s. It all starts with a key, embossed with the letters CB, and a cryptic reference to Deep Deuce, a neighborhood once filled with hot jazz and gangs of bootleggers. Out of those threads is woven a tapestry of history, romance, drama, and mystery; connecting two generations and two families in the adventure of a lifetime.

Winner of the IBPA Benjamin Frankling Digital Awards (2016 Silver Honoree).

> *"The Bootlegger's Legacy takes the reader on a wild ride through Oklahoma's bootlegging history. It makes for a wonderful escape into a fascinating, dangerous, and strange*

world filled with characters your mother warned you about. Most readers will only ever interact with these types in make believe, but while the ride lasts it's a rollicking good time."

—Self-Publishing Review, 4 Stars

"Although the mystery elements in this novel are certainly engaging enough to keep readers turning pages, it's Clifton's superb character development that makes this story a transformative journey of self-discovery. The noteworthy narrative also includes vivid backdrops, brisk pacing, and a meticulously researched, historically accurate account of the Prohibition era in Oklahoma and Texas. A tale with an authentic, immersive setting, inhabited by well-developed, endearing characters."

—Kirkus Reviews

Dog Gone Lies

(Pacheco & Chino Mysteries Book 1)

Sheriff Ray Pacheco returns from his introduction in The Bootlegger's Legacy to start a new chapter as a private investigator, along with his partners: Tyee Chino, often-drunk Apache fishing guide, and Big Jack, bait shop owner and philosopher.

The trio are pulled into a mystery immediately when an abandoned show dog appears at Ray's cabin and the dog's owner is reported missing. Ray and his team pursue leads that bring them into confrontations with the local sheriff, the mayor, and the FBI, while in the meantime two bodies are found—neither of which is the missing woman.

Sky High Stakes
(Pacheco & Chino Mysteries Book 2)
Tired of spending his days fishing, Ray Pacheco takes on his second assignment with his partner Tyee Chino when the state Attorney General asks them to find out just what the hell is going on in Ruidoso, New Mexico. With the town's sheriff in the hospital with a mysterious illness, acting sheriff Martin Marino is running rough-shod over everyone around him.

What seems like a simple assignment becomes more complicated when Marino is found dead, shot at close range while sitting in his patrol car on Main Street. The suspects include most of the town, from Dick Franklin, manager of Ruidoso Downs racetrack, to bar owner Tito Annoya, to members of the local law enforcement.

At the same time, Ray has an uneasy feeling that the AG is withholding critical details about what exactly is going on in Ruidoso—and why the state was so slow to respond.

It all comes to a surprising conclusion with the involvement of a Spanish princess, a drug lord gone mad, and a few other lowlifes . . . and leaves Ray wondering if maybe fishing wasn't so boring after all.

Murder So Wrong
(Muckraker Mystery #1, with Stanley Nelson)
After his first day as a political reporter in 1960s Oklahoma, Tommy Jacks finds himself investigating the murder of a competing reporter at the state capitol. The mystery becomes

a story of intrigue, love and tragedy, involving a would-be mentor, a gorgeous lover, a jailed father, an adopted mom, and shocking violence.

Murder So Strange
(Muckraker Mystery #2, with Stanley Nelson)

In an exclusive residential neighborhood, a U.S. Senator's wife has died. Tommy Jacks and his fellow journalists don't believe the police chief's story blaming it on natural causes. It has the smell of a crime. So begins a new journey set in the 1960s involving numerous dead bodies, high-tension political intrigue, police corruption, the drug underworld and unsavory hidden pasts. Tommy has a lot to write about in his My View political column.

Only in his second year as a political columnist, he finds new romance and emotional healing among a chaotic mixture of characters, from his new mother and his recently out-of-jail father to his acerbic journalistic mentor and antagonist and a foul-mouthed lawyer of questionable ethics, all wrapped inside the saga of two competing daily newspapers still at war.

Lurking in the shadows is the powerful and corrupt police chief, who seems to think it might be best if Mister Jacks, even so young, was dead.

Murder So Strange continues the 1960s saga of Tommy Jacks: Muckraker.

Murder So Final
(Muckraker Mystery #3, with Stanley Nelson)

Tommy Jacks, reporter, encounters new love and old threats while covering one of the most brutal U.S. Senate races in history. With a massive oil fire threatening the city of Tulsa, three candidates face off: a ruthless oil baron, an idealist college professor, and a reverend running under the God Party. When the race suddenly turns deadly, the winner may be the last man standing.

The final book in the Muckraker trilogy, *Murder So Final* brings to a close the stories of Louongo, Albright, Robbie Gilmore, Tracy and Ray Jacks, and Tommy himself.

And More...

To keep up-to-date on all of Ted's newest books, visit www.tedclifton.com.